Some Love

Some Pain

Sometime

Also by
J. California Cooper

A Piece of Mine

Homemade Love

Some Soul to Keep

Family

The Matter Is Life

In Search of Satisfaction

Some Love,
Some Pain,
Sometime

J. California Cooper

Doubleday

New York   London   Toronto   Sydney   Auckland

PUBLISHED BY DOUBLEDAY
a division of Bantam Doubleday Dell Publishing Group, Inc.
1540 Broadway, New York, New York 10036

DOUBLEDAY and the portrayal of an anchor with a dolphin are
trademarks of Doubleday, a division of Bantam Doubleday Dell
Publishing Group, Inc.

BOOK DESIGN BY TERRY KARYDES

Library of Congress Cataloging-in-Publication Data
Cooper, J. California.
Some love, some pain, sometime / J. California Cooper
    p.   cm.
1. United States—Social life and customs—20th century—Fiction.
2. Man-woman relationships—United States—Fiction.   I. Title.
PS3553.05874S55   1995
813′ .54—dc20
94-45833   CIP

ISBN: 0-385-46787-7

First Edition
October 1995

10 9 8 7 6 5 4 3 2 1

Acknowledgments

I am indebted to my editor, Arabella Meyer, for her understanding, consideration and wise counsel. She helped me in many ways; I learned. My appreciation and gratitude to her and all those who worked with her on my book.

I thank my daughter for her understanding ways and her helpful heart.

I am grateful for the support of Mrs. Geraldine Payne of Marshall, Texas, Ms. Rebecca Carroll of New York and Ms. Ruth Beckford, author, of Oakland, CA. You both were wonderfully smart.

I thank all of the readers of my books. You are, everyone, magnificent to me. I really thank you from the bottom of my heart.

Dedicated with Love to

Joseph C. and Maxine MIMI Cooper, my parents
Paris A. Williams, my chile
John E. Walker and William Scott,
best brothers-in-law
My wonderful spirit-sister Willita T. Reagan
and husband, John

Special and Extraordinary Others
Adam Clayton Powell Jr.   Thurgood Marshall
Carl Sandburg, poet   Louis L'Amour, author
Lena Horne   Tina Turner   Wadie Amar
Gloria K. Duggan   John Brown   Nat Turner,
abolitionist   Dr. Carla Harris   Sweet Alice Harris
Gloria Toolsie   Charlesetta McMillan
Mother Clara Hale   Karen Boates
Green Chimneys, Children's Service
Earth Island Institute   Mary Alice Bomar
Piney Woods, African-American School
Emma Rogers and Candace

My Chickens
Mr. McAdoo, Mr. Doo, Ms. Bertha, Ms. Mamie,
Ms. Chick, Ms. Shirley, Ms. Chanel, Betty Boo,
Mr. Roos, Little Ms. Mimi

Especially
To all those who love and fight for the very young,
the very old, trees, animals, water and all living
things we are losing from the earth.

I Love You
For all the wonderful things you do to fight the
mindless, the heartless and the careless.

It is rather obvious why I chose this title. I believe
it is what life is much of the time. When I think
of great lovers in history, there was always some
pain involved. Maybe not for everyone, but
most likely.

    I, also, think Love is beautiful and feels good. I
think what some people do with it, who do not
know what they are doing, is what makes it painful
. . . sometimes.

Listen to this poem:

Love entered in my heart one day
A sad, unwelcome guest.
But when it begged that it might stay
I let it stay and rest.

It broke my nights with sorrowing
It filled my heart with fears
And, when my soul was prone to sing,
It filled my eyes with tears.

But . . . now that it has gone its way,
I miss the dear ole pain.
And, sometimes, in the night I pray
That Love might come again.

So maybe it is not Love that hurts, maybe it's
the person we love. It can even be a lack of Love.
Because Love itself is beautiful.

    I named this book what I think about Life;
Some Love, Some Pain, Sometime.

Contents

Femme Fatale

See, there's one thing I have learned (and I didn't have to get to be no one hundred years old to learn it either), I know that if you want to find yourself some happiness, you have to get up and go out and work hard for it. Them people that sit and wait just might wait forever! You got to get out there and do something to help yourself. And I knew I had a long way to go cause where I was sittin there just wasn't nothin!

I was born way back up there in some woods you probably ain't never heard of. My mother and daddy loved each other so you know they loved me. My daddy's name was Roscoe Lee. I was a girl, but that's what they named me.

They added a Mae so it was "Roscoe Mae Lee." I loved my daddy, but I ain't never even liked that name.

My daddy was a loggin man, a big built man. My mother was built big too. Strong, but still feminine, my gramma say. My mother helped my daddy do some of that loggin work. We had lots of land and all kinds of trees on it. How my mama got to be so husky, I don't know, cause my gramma is a little bitty thing. Well, with them both bein so husky, you know I am too. But I am very feminine too. Yes, indeed.

I was spoiled, chile, spoiled. Anything I wanted, I got. Within reason. Mostly food. Cakes, pies, candy, cookies, cobblers, ice cream. They just packed all kinds of fat cells in me. But I am big-boned so I carry it well. Yes indeed.

They dressed me pretty enough for a child livin in the woods. Always clean and fresh. Remember how some people say, "She sure is going to be a heart breaker!" I was real small, but I remember them sayin that about me. A heart breaker! Now, I didn't really know what that was, but they seem to think it was a good thing to be. Their eyes flashed when they said it, and Mama and Daddy always grinned. Gramma lived with us and she would shake her head, but she smiled when they said it too.

Our house was kind of a big log cabin, naturally, with all them logs outside. With some of the money my parents made, they built a attachment to our house, another log cabin, and opened a little grocery store. I guess they got tired of going all the way into town to do their shopping. It wasn't real big, just stocked staples and things these country people out round here use a lot.

That's another thing, out here there wasn't hardly nobody to play with cept on Sundays when church was going on. And you weren't supposed to be playin then. If their parents come to the store, they wasn't there long enough to get into a game or nothing. It's just too far for a child to walk through all these woods less it would be a emergency or something.

Anyway, we were all happy . . . Gramma says. Then one day Daddy fell from a tree into the river with the branches on top of him. My mother rushed to him and tried to move that huge branch while trying to swim in the muddy riverbed. She finally had hold of him and was strugglin to get him loose, but my daddy had broke his neck and that branch was just carrying my daddy on down the river. Mama couldn't pull him loose and she wouldn't let go of him. Then, it was too late to let go. See? She went down with him. Down that ole river to death. It wasn't just the branches, Gramma say. Mama WOULDN'T let go of him.

I hope you never have to feel how much that hurt. Only me and Gramma was left. Us . . . and all that painful hurt. The empty kind of pain that makes a home in your heart. Such big people as mine took up a lot of room in the house. Loud laughter, or arguing in all that space of all them woods. But the most empty place was my heart. No big strong arms to hold me, or throw and catch me like my daddy did. No big strong arms to hold me with all that love and tenderness my mama wrapped around me whenever I cried or even when I just went close to her. It was like I was dropped in a well and couldn't stop fallin in all that empty darkness. Thank God I had my gramma and she had me.

Gramma took over all the business and kept on runnin the store. She had to, cause I was in school. When it was time for me to get to the main road for the bus to school, I had to walk a long, long, silent, empty road all by myself. Gramma standin there at the door. I cried, but she gave me a good, long stick and told me, "Get on down that road like you got some sense. You got to do what's for you to do. Stop wastin time. I'm too old and you too old (I was seven) for me to have to walk you down that road. (She'd kiss me.) That ain't the worse road, nor the longest road you gonna have to travel in your life! Now, go on and get started on this one. You goin where they might make you ready for the rest of your roads. I needs help my own self!"

But, sometimes, when I got off the bus comin home from school, she would be standin there, waiting for me. We would hold hands or hug round the waist all the way home. I would tell her things from school. Try to make her laugh. She would tell me things from the few people who came to the store, tryin to make me laugh. A little time would pass and we was alright. We still missed Mama and Daddy, but we made peace with it. It was us loving each other. Oh, you got to have some love, see? Yes, indeed.

Now, that was fine, just what we both needed for a long, long time. I have no complaints about my gramma. Love from your family is some of the best love. But time passed and I was growin into my teens.

We had us a little TV. Gramma didn't spend much money, ever. Whole lot of my good time stuff was gone with my mother and daddy gone, but Gramma did buy us a TV. We was so far out from any electric rays that we couldn't get but one channel and it was kinda hazy fuzzy. But sometimes I could see some things clear. I saw pretty women, handsome men and love stories. I looooved the

love stories. One of the programs talked about this Femme
Fatale and that's when I realized that one of them Femme
Fatales was in me. Couldn't nobody else see her, but I knew
she was there. I felt her deep down inside me. See? Yes,
indeedy!

I was in high school then. Everybody liked me, boys
and girls, but no boy liked me "Special." Well, I was so big
and strong and healthy. Big head, big arms, big legs and
breasts. Round and feminine it seemed to me. I was pretty,
to me. I was everybody's friend because I was fun. Laughed
a lot. Sometime to keep from cryin, but they didn't know
that.

My gramma had kept my hair braided all my life,
sometimes only takin it loose and combing and braiding it
once a week. Old as I was, she still did it because she liked
to and I let her because I loved her. I had long, long hair all
the way down my back. But them boys didn't care nothin
bout my hair or nothin else I had, because I was always left
alone when people paired off at school parties and such.
See?

Physical shapes have always been in style, ain't no gettin around it! Forever. Boys liked me but they wanted
something better. Something to make other boys jealous,
which I guess I couldn't do. So when it came to love, it
wasn't so much prejudice as it was preference. See? They
could not see the Femme Fatale that was in me.

Still, I would look down and round myself and know
for sure a Femme Fatale was in there, just couldn't nobody
else see her. That hurt. Well, one or two boys did see something, but they wasn't what I liked, cause . . . boys come
in styles too! The track star, the football star, boys in the

school band, that kind. They had their style. Cute, tall, short, husky and all. Yes, indeed.

I might as well tell it all. There was one boy named Wyndel. He seemed to like me a lot. He was a nice, fat, young man weighed about 200 pounds. Now, some men can weigh that and fit the fashion style. If it be in their shoulders, chest and leg muscles. Wyndel's was mostly in his waist, thighs and arms and such like that. It makes a different shape like that sometimes, see?

Well, we graduated from school. Wyndel went on to mechanics school cause he loved cars. Plus it pays good money. I just settled in at home to help Gramma cause she was getting even older and all that and she had been taking care of me all my life. The business was very good because people knew from all the years we had been there that they could count on us. They ordered and we bought, we ordered what they wanted and they bought. So things were workin out all right. I worked in the store most of the time at that time.

I could mostly do what I wanted to do, but there wasn't anything to do out there where I was. Didn't have to keep any special store hours cause we had a bell people could ring if they wanted something. You might think being in a store would bring some men I could meet and like, sometimes. But let me tell you. Out here?! These women get a man and he don't ever get out of their sight! Married or not, see? And they hold on to them men for their dear life. They snatch up them men so fast in high school, ain't none left, no how . . . and they never let them go! You can practicly see their fingerprints on his clothes and skin. If she die first and he's left behind, likely somebody, her best friend, maybe, is already at the house and got her hooks into him the minute the wife takes her last breath! So workin out here in this store didn't help me in the love business, no way.

I know we all sisters and all that, but we just got some different kind of sisters out here, I guess. They sisters, but they are women first! Single women, honey! Black ones and white ones and any other ones! Personally, I don't think men ought to have that big a priority in anybody's life cause we just as important as they are. Because I am a woman to me, whether I have a man or not! But you can stand back and have a attitude if you want to, just you are going to have to wait a little longer for the man who wants you to come along and find you! Specially out here where I am! Yes, indeed!

Anyway, I don't know if you evvvvver been lonely. Chile, chile, chile, that is one of the most hurtin things. Hurts all over your mind and slowly takes over your body til you are only one big empty hurt, all day, and for sure all night.

Now I know they got this thing where you can make love to yourself!! But I don't like that. I don't want to be my own thrill . . . see? I want a man to be my thrill. I feel the same about other women's married husbands. I don't want one of them. I want my OWN man. That's how I lived then and now.

I got so nothing seemed to matter to me at all except that there wasn't never no arm around me, no lips on mine. Nobody close to me. Chile, I was lonely. And gettin older. I'm tellin you I liked to died sometime. You hear me? I don't rightly know who said it, but the night is just right, just made for makin love. That moon shining down on two people sure is different when it is shining down on only one.

Well, to tell the whole thing, I got so lonely I even started liking Wyndel and sent him a message. When he came, I didn't do it too quick, but, finally, I asked him, "Wyndel? Have you got a woman?"

Wyndel grinned. His little fat chin adding a lip to his cute smile. "Girl, what you talkin about?"

"I'm talkin about have you got a woman? A lover?"

He laughed a minute then he took a deep sigh and said, "I ain't interested in no girl, Roscoe. I just work on my cars."

I took a quick breath. "Well, I ain't talkin bout girls. I'm talkin bout men and women, feelings and stuff. Don't you ever think of having a woman of your own?"

He took a screwdriver from his pocket. Said, "Welll, sure I think . . . about it. But don't nobody seem to want me. So I don't worry bout it."

"Stop lyin, Wyndel."

Wyndel sat down and put his head in his hands, resting his dimpled elbows on his knees, and grinned again. I struck out again, on this new road. Said, "Well, I do, Wyndel. I . . . like you, as a man."

He looked up at me. "Well, can I have a picture of you, Roscoe?"

I looked down at him. "Wyndel, I'm offerin you my heart."

He was the one who blushed first, then I blushed and that was how we started. We made a date that was to be a special date and that made it a special night, I thought. I dreamed of that night, even with Wyndel. I was going to make love for the first time!

The night arrived, Wyndel came over, smilin and grinnin. Nothing in his hands. No flowers, no candy. Now ain't nothing wrong with a fat lover, nothin! They're better than some skinny ones . . . I heard. But Wyndel came over in his regular clothes. He was bathed and clean, but you got to do more than that when it's a special night, see? Was a button off his regular shirt. Shaggy ends to his clean everyday pants. He wore sandals with socks! Ugh! Toes hangin over the sole. Nothin special did he do for this special date, but come over. You know, men come like that in all sizes. He was not prepared, nor dressed, for a Femme Fatale.

The Femme Fatale was bathed, perfumed, nails manicured and polished (I learned that from TV), powder sweet-puffed, hair done by Gramma and hanging down my back touchin on my butt, face made up so pretty. DONE! You hear me?!

But Wyndel not making it a special time was only my first disappointment. Him not knowin what he was going about doing and making it seem like a struggle in a wrestlin match was my second disappointment. Never gettin it done was my third.

After the struggle, Wyndel saying, "This stuff ain't so good as it's sposed to be, is it?" was my final hurt for the night.

I started thinking about registering at the college up here in town, it's a good, big one. Gramma said I could go, money would not be a problem cause all we did was save it. But, finally, I did not want to leave her alone. She was my gramma and I loved her. We had a bond.

So, I decided Wyndel and I could still be friends. Go to shows over in town, to music concerts once in a while, things like that, you know. Well, we did those things for about a year. A year filled with lonesome days and then lonesome nights and I'm a year older, too. Then . . . we tried makin that love stuff again.

This time it was special for him. He dressed special and took me to dinner at a special place in town. Took me to a special hotel, out of town, out of the woods. Like a honeymoon. It worked out. Not the best to fit a dream, but with possibilities, see? He had been asking questions of older men and I think he must have bought a piece or two. Anyway, when we were through, he ordered room service, "A light repast," he said. "Oh, and some wine, if you please." Chile! And after we had the repast, we did it again! So it must have been alright.

Not too long after that, Wyndel wanted to get married. So I knew there was a Femme Fatale in me!! I didn't know if I wanted to marry Wyndel or not, cause forever is forever! But I also knew I was not gonna sleep myself around cause I was not a floozy. I got better sense. Gramma often said, "You better not let everybody know what's up under your clothes. Your future husband might not like it and it'll go bad for you if you love him and he finds out." So, I had sense.

Anyway, the next time, when Wyndel said, as he was layin beside me, arm around my waist, "I am a fool for beauty," I loved him. I said yes to the marriage. He gave me a nice engagement ring cause he worked and made good money as a mechanic. So now, I was engaged.

I started my hope chest for real. I even dreamed about

my home with Wyndel. Sleeping with him every night, being with him every day. Waiting for him to come home to me. Loneliness is something, chile. It can make so many things look like love . . . to you, if your need is that great. Wyndel was happy too, I know it.

Then things got all messed up. First, Wyndel started with asthma, coughin and sneezing so much. Then, my Jesus, the doctor said he had heart trouble. He had to slow down. Wyndel was so scared. So was I. I thought I loved Wyndel and I did love him. What's the difference? It hurts me to say, but . . . before the marriage, Wyndel died. And I mourned . . . truly.

After that things were kinda going along alright cept Gramma was slowin way down and I had to take her to the doctor pretty regular. Soon she was bedridden. That made her mad, but I was scared and almost got sick myself thinking of losing my gramma. She was all my family.

When I was in her room one night, tryin to make her eat, teasing her to make her laugh, to get well, she told me to "Stop and hush a minute." She told me to get a little shovel from where she kept it and lift up the floorboard in the closet and dig out the little metal box with the huge lock on it. She told me where to find and keep the key (it was a very good plan so I'm not gonna tell you). I did all that. We opened the box and Gramma and me counted out 17,000 cash dollars. Mama and Daddy's and her life savings. She fondled it, patted it, kissed it and straightened it out. She was almost well again as she talked to me.

"Now . . . Roscoe baby, this here is all you gonna have when I'm gone." She held her sweet little hand up to stop me from puffin up and crying out to her. "It ain't no whole lot." She rubbed the bills again, smoothing them out for the thousandth time, I know. "But it's more than some people has or see in a lifetime of hard . . . hard work. I . . . I always meant to do somethin with it for . . . myself too. But . . . you . . . go. Go travel somewhere with your . . . See somethin. Have a fine dress from somewhere sides the Sears catalogue. I . . . I opened a charge account from J. C. Penney!" Her eyes beamed up at me, proud. She poked into the metal box. "See? Here it is! Ain't it pretty?! Now you use it . . . someday." (Oh, Gramma, my heart cried.) She lay back on her pillow, her little hand holding the card was trembling, but she kept talking. "I wanted a long bus ride, maybe. See some place sides a tree, though, Lord knows, they some of the most beautiful work He ever done." She sighed, a sick sigh.

"Now . . . it's your turn. You go on down them roads in your life I always told you about. This here money will pay the toll on some of them roads you didn't know would cost you too much." She seemed exhausted, but she had more to say.

"Oh, Gramma, I don't want money. I want you! See? Gramma, everybody is going from me."

Gramma dropped her hand onto my knee. "But I want you to have it. It's your mama and daddy's money too. It's already yours. I just want you to be me, for awhile, and me to be you, for awhile, as you get out and find some happiness for yourself. You deserve it. You been a good chile, all your life. You stayed right here with me like I wanted you, needed you, to do, and I didn't have to ask you. Not once. Chile, you could'a been gone."

She rubbed the money for the last time, then lifted the

bundles and dropped them in my lap. I put them in the box neatly and closed it. She handed me the key, the key to her little life, with a small weak smile. I locked the box and placed it back under the floorboards into the ground just like she had always kept it. And I cried, and I cried, and I cried.

Not too long after that I put Gramma in the ground, right beside my mother and father. Excuse me if I don't want to talk about it. The pain is too deep. Goes too far. I grieved. I grieved. All the people who came for the funeral went home and . . . I grieved.

The garden Gramma had worked and was so proud of, her flowers, her food, her lawn, her window boxes, were all dying. Either watered too much or not enough. Everywhere I looked I saw her, but she was not there. Evenings, I dragged in from the store. I was there all day now just to keep from coming in a empty house. No little body in no little rockin chair lookin at the TV. Not bent over the store counter, not sewing at her table lookin out the window smiling at me as I made my way up the road to her and home. No wrinkled, calloused hand patting me on my head or back. I would look at her little high-top shoes that used to click all over the house and store . . . and cry. No more Gramma. No nothing. I was alone. See?

I wanted her back. I only really knew her, my family. I was so lonely, so lonely and so empty. But I still felt the blood in my veins, the bones in my body. Watched my mind think. Felt my heart beating. I was still alive. I wanted to live.

I took them shoes of hers she ALWAYS wore into town and had them bronzed. Told them shoes they were

Gramma going with me to see SOMETHING. I gave everything in the store away to the people I liked and trusted and some I didn't trust so everyone knew the store was empty and wasn't no use to breakin in it. Packed my things and Gramma's shoes in a suitcase and hit the road that would lead to the road that would lead to my life.

I was twenty-three years old, a Femme Fatale single woman and it didn't look like my happiness was comin to me. So I was gonna go out and get it! See? Yes, indeedy. I wanted a husband and some children. I wanted to come back up to my peaceful woods and life, a good life, near those who brought me here. Lord, what modern man would want to come live up here and run a grocery store and make love to me? My mind told me to get on out there and see.

I needed me a big city with lots of men, single men, cause I couldn't use no other woman's man. If a woman's got two men, one, the unmarried one, is mine to choose. If she got one and she married to him, then he's hers under God, and I wouldn't mess with that. See?

The little college town, about seventy miles up the main road, had grown into a good-size city now. I covered everything up from the dust, locked the doors up tight, put a sign on the store door, said, "BE BACK SOON" and I hit that road like my gramma told me, with her shoes packed in my bag, in my own car. Now!

When I got to the city I pulled into one of the visitor places they have. I had been to the city before, but I never did stay in no hotel and I had a plan for this trip. I asked the information lady for the middle best hotel with weekly rates and the best way to find a decent apartment in a safe place. I got the information and a map. Started, chile!

That evening I was relaxing in my hotel room, had dinner sent up. Chile. By the next week I had found two apartments I liked. I sat in my car and watched the neighborhood to see what was happenin and how many men went in and out and around. Talked to the landlady managers and asked, honey, asked about the tenants. Mostly married or mostly single? I chose the one with two single men livin in it. Even if I didn't like them, I knew they would have some friends visiting sometime. See? And the landlady, Ms. Mimi, was real nice and helpful with information that would make my move easier.

Now . . . I don't know how I knew to do all this, so it had to be that Femme Fatale running my business. See? I moved in and bought a few things to make my apartment a warm, cozy, female place. Glittering drapes with plenty glamour gold threads running through it. Colorful flower curtains for the little kitchen. Incense holder and incense, naturally. A shiny satinese glamour bedspread. Bath towels with gold flecks in em.

I liked flowers, but I thought the real ones were a little expensive and you would have to get new ones all the time and I wanted flowers everywhere, all the time. (You know, I was used to just going outside and picking mine.) Anyway, I got some plastic ones. They were strange-looking flowers, but they had a lotta color, so I got em and put them everywhere. These were all for the Femme Fatale part of me.

Of course, I got some pots and pans and pretty dishes cause it's truly bout one of the best ways to a man's heart. I don't care bout what all these women say about a slave in the kitchen. Good food is a great and wonderful thing, chile, and I like to eat good myself. I'd take care of that slave part later anyway.

I was seeing those two men all the time. We just spoke and I smiled.

Then, I started looking for a job, cause I was not going to spend all my daddy, mama and Gramma's money. I had to think of "just in case" I didn't find the man I wanted. I wasn't just looking for one who wanted me. No Lord! This is my life too! See?

I got a job at the college filing student records and finding the lost ones. Paid enough to keep me from spending my other money, less I wanted something special.

All that done, I went to the beauty parlor. Chile, you know they wanted to cut my hair?! My hair!! No, lord, not my glory! I told her to clip the ends and cut me a few bangs. I'll wear it braided in a crown on my Femme Fatale head and wear it hanging down my back when things get special. I want to spread it out on a pillow! See?

Then I got those false eyelashes you glue on. Long ones. And I got those false fingernails that look so long and pretty. They were gonna pluck my eyebrows, but I looked at theirs and decided to let mine stay natural. They painted my toenails too, and I asked for a few gold specks on them. A few ladies laughed, but I didn't care. Hell, these are my toe nails. And a Femme Fatale can do whatever she wants to!

My teeth were already good and my eyes were clear, when I could keep them false lashes from fallin in em. Then I decided to change my name. I kept my daddy's name, "Roscoe," but I added "Darlin" and made it legal. "Darlin" is a sweet-talkin name!

Now! I was ready! don't you know?!

I had been watching the two men who had apartments on my floor. One, I found out from Ms. Mimi, was named Roland, between thirty and thirty-five years old, and he was a postal clerk. He was kinda thin for my taste. His hips seemed to be pressed forward from his body, you know how some people are built? And he stood back on his legs. He was always carrying some books or some groceries. He seemed to be neat and clean and quiet. Never heard no noise from his side. He must have done all his carryin on away from home cause I only saw one woman visit him once or twice. She was neat and clean, too, but I could tell she wasn't no Femme Fatale. He lived in #4.

I was between them at #5.

Now, #6 was a big husky man name of Hudson. All muscle, chile. He was some kind of physical education assistant teacher at some high school. He wore colored undershorts and jogging suits and things. He ran early every morning and after he came in from his job. He had a nice Afro cut and was very clean. His skin always looked moist and shining, healthy. He smiled a lot. And had all kinds of different women come to his place a lot, so I knew nobody was really takin his heart. Wasn't no Femme Fatales there either. Just was all up to me. See?

Well, I didn't pay too much attention to #4, Roland, after I got to seeing #6, Hudson, cause Hudson was it! With them big ole musclly arms and legs, small waist and high-set behind, #4 Roland just didn't stand a chance with his pale, slim self. No, indeed. Oh, he had a behind, but he pushed it forward so it didn't stick out none. He wasn't ugly, but he wasn't Hudson either.

I started comin home from work, cookin good food and leavin the door to the hall open. I put a little fan in my little kitchen so the smells would get out the door. I got a lot of food cooked that way and I didn't want to eat it all or waste it. (Some more of Gramma's teachings.) So finally I just put some water on with salt, pepper, garlic and onion and boiled it. It really smells good, you just don't eat it. Chile, that stuff smelled good and went all over the halls.

Every night, after I heard the first one get home, I shut my door and put on some good blues or jazz, kinda low, only high enough for them to just hear if they didn't have no music on and I knew they hadn't had time to turn their music on yet.

I bought the best perfume, sweet, but light, to wear when I left for work every morning. Even sprayed a little whiff in the hall near my door. I made sure I was up and out before they were so they could smell ME as they left for work. If ole runner Hudson was gettin up and out before me, I sprayed a quick whiff in the hall before he left out the house.

I was movin right along, but I stayed out of too much sight til I could catch the way of city clothes and things. Then, after a bit, in the evenings if I went out with a girlfriend, or even a man friend I had made at work, I wore the best, most sexiest smell the saleslady said was in the world! Even puffed a bit of that in the hall. I DARED one of their women friends to smell better than me, because I am a Femme Fatale, see?

But I didn't make too many man friends at work. Everything in due time. I wanted to see how these two worked out, especially Hudson, before I got someone who might turn out to be in the way. Sides, I didn't plan to make love to everybody in the city. Anyway, I was asking God for His help so I knew I was going to try to do it His way much as possible.

I started joggin bout four weeks after I moved in. Every time rent was due it was time to add a new move. Had two white joggin suits. Wasn't no way you could miss me, see? Wore one, washed one. I got tired of all that runnin, but it did me some good anyway.

At night I would close my eyes, dreaming of Hudson and his big bright smile. He had beautiful teeth. Everything about the man was beautiful and healthy. He even drove a nice little sports car, convertible. Roland had a settled-in Audi.

On the second month I started sittin out on the porch. Ms. Mimi had chairs out there. The first one to stop and sit a spell was Roland. I said to myself, "You might as well head on out if you sittin there for me, honey!" But we talked a little bit about the daily news and all them good smells coming from my kitchen. (smile) Roland was interestin, but he was not Hudson.

Hudson was really givin me those big grins. He had done even started stopping by my open door, sniffin, and hollerin in, "Sure smells good in there, Darlin!" I would have something kinda pretty on this big, brown frame of mine and I would step out to him, smilin. Food and me smelling good! I'd say, "You must have dinner with me one day." But I wasn't gonna let him eat my paycheck up til I knew we had a chance! I said, "I'll invite you over one evenin when the ladies aren't knockin your door down." I smiled up at him.

He smiled back down. "I'll see that they don't come to my door if you just tell me when."

I smiled a little smaller smile, and flicked my false eyelashes at him, saying, "I'll let you know," as I closed my door.

Now, Roland, sometimes he would holler under my closed door, "Say, Darlin (I love my new name), you got to give me some of that food, or the recipe, cause you be drivin me crazy with all that good cookin you doin in there!"

I'd open my door so he could see I looked good even as a slave in the kitchen, and get a smell of the other me besides the cook and I would smile at him, cause you got to practice, you know. I would say, "You need to stop teasin me." I would wave "good-by" as I bat my lashes and shut the door.

Bout one week before the rent was due again, I been there about seven weeks then, I invited Hudson to dinner. I put on my best hostess gown, low neck, my best low, sweet music, polished my imitation flowers, fluffed my pillows (bed and sofa) and all the rest. Chile, the dinner was good! Baked, then smothered the turkey wings, herb rice (he likes health) and black-eyed peas, baked yams, hot biscuits, Jell-O mold salad and ice tea, buttermilk or lemonade. That man liked to killed himself he ate so much! I know why he runs . . . he better!

Two nights later he said he wanted to take me to dinner. I dressed as good as I could (and I could). He made his number one mistake. He took me somewhere nice you could take a pay-back date. It wasn't special. I thought I could fix that later if I ended up with him, so I kinda enjoyed the evenin. When we got back home he invited me to see his apartment. I went.

He had a nice apartment. Bachelor type, barbells, weights, all that man stuff. I liked the smell and looks of mannish things even though I ain't never been around any, really. Well, when he reached out to kiss me . . . I let him. Hell, this is what I been workin on and for. Ain't it?! When he wanted to go a little further, I let him. I knew this Femme Fatale was working on him, you see?

Now, I have only known one man in a bed and that was Wyndel, so I did not really know what all to expect. But I knew from all these people I see walkin round on this earth, there must be something mighty special about doin whatever it takes to get them here.

Well, he flexed his big muscles and did all kinds of exercise in the bed. You could sure tell he was athletic. But the one muscle that would have made a difference was the one he didn't know what to do with it. See? All that body and, far as I could tell, it was only good for show and running and eatin. I'm not talkin about "how much" of it either. I wanted to tell him, "Listen, it ain't no lance. Don't throw it! We ain't in the Olympics. We in bed tryin to make love. Win a heart. Not a medal."

Chile, when it was over, he laid back and grinned at me, proud of his flexing muscle self. I smiled like a real Femme Fatale, got up, slowly gathered my clothes and slowly sashayed out of his place, right down the hall to my place without a stitch on. I was so disgusted with myself, I didn't care bout bein naked. I had made a mistake! I did want a man, a husband, but I wanted to stay with him, married for the rest of my life. The lovin has got to, ought to, please, be good. It ain't everything, but it's well mixed in the foundation of love and marriage. It's part of the foundation. My gramma had talked to me about love!

Now, I had had two men and I couldn't be through lookin. I don't want a lot of men in my body. I want to be one man's Femme Fatale and I hadn't found him . . . yet.

I bathed, went to bed and said my prayers. "God, why do I have to be done this way? I ain't done nothing to hurt nobody. All I want is a husband, what You said You created man and woman for." I said some more, but that ain't your business. You know, I thought I heard a answer in my head? Said, "God didn't pick that man, you did."

I was sluggish the next day. Was late to work. Came home, shut my door, didn't put nothin on my stove. To hell with a man. I did that about three days. Didn't want to see nobody.

The fourth day, I was sittin on the couch eating a half dozen glazed donuts when the knock came on the door. Knock! Knock! My mouth was full, but I flung out, "Yea?"

It was #4, Roland. His voice was actually concerned. "Ms. Darlin? Are you alright?"

"Yea! . . . No!" Donut spit flyin. I didn't get up to open the door, but still he talked. "I thought if you were sick or something, I'd bring you some of my dinner. It might not be as good as your cooking, but at least you would eat." I looked at my donut then, at the door for a minute.

"Can you hear me?"

"Yes, yes," I said. "I hear you." I thought I needed some

tender care from someone, so why not let him be kind. "Yes, please. I would appreciate that."

"Okay," he said, "be back in about an hour." Then he was gone.

He brought some really tasty chicken and rice soup, homemade. Crackers, a side dish of asparagus, a chilled apple, sliced, with cheese, a tall glass of water with ice and a slice of lemon in it. Fit for a queen . . . or a ailing Femme Fatale. He left me to eat alone, which I was glad I could chew in peace, cause you know eatin in bed can be messy if you ain't used to it. The next day my soul felt a lot better and I was up and out on time and my life felt better to me.

But I made some steps in my life over the next few weeks that I don't like to think about. Anyway, I made more friends at work and some of em I went out with and, yea, one I brought home and slept with. Only one, but this bed stuff was adding up and I had only wanted ONE man in my memories. None of them had the slightest possibility of being the one. And it wasn't just sex was the reason. They didn't seem to want nothing. Or know nothing about love . . . And family. I curbed all that desperation when I saw where I was headin. I could go on back home and be lonely without bein miserable.

I figured I could use a new TV at home in the country, so I bought myself a TV, but the deliveryman left it downstairs at Ms. Mimi's place. As she was telling me it was there, Hudson was coming down the stairs going to start his running. I asked him to take the TV upstairs for me before he left. Listen to this.

He said, as he passed me by, "Can't do it right now. I'll be back in a few hours, I think, and I'll bring it up for you then. If you can get somebody else to do it, let em, cause I'm not really sure when I'll get back." Voice over his shoulder, and he was gone. Never did stop. He must be mad cause I never let him in again. I frowned, a little hurt that he didn't think enough of me to even do this little thing. Ms. Mimi gave a funny little smile and said, "This is the 'ME' generation. If it ain't for them it ain't important. Leave it here, Roland will be here in a little while, he'll be glad to bring it right up for you. Now, Roland, I like."

I wasn't much interested, still smarting from Hudson's attitude. I said, "Yea . . . he is nice."

Ms. Mimi spoke as she walked me toward the stairs. "You know what he is doing?"

"No, mam. I don't know much about anybody round here, evidently."

She smiled. "He is trying to get his daughter. His ex-wife gave his baby away without tellin him. She was pregnant when they broke up, but she didn't tell him that either. He wants to raise his own child."

I turned to her. "Sure is gonna be hard for him to get a new wife. He got a ready-made family. A child!"

Ms. Mimi looked over her glasses at me, said, "A child is only something more to love. You get a chance to raise a child, love it, teach it right and do it with a man you KNOW is going to treat any children you give him right because he ain't runnin from his child! He is facing his responsibility. Fightin for it! It's taking most every dime he works for. Some people would give anything for a child."

"Well," I started up the stairs, "you're right. But it's still gonna be hard for him to find a woman who wants some other woman's child."

She wasn't through. "Ms. Darlin, I know you know how hard it is to find anything good that you want to spend your life with. Or even have dinner with, one night. Ms. Darlin, I was thinking you had some sense. I know what you doin. I been married three times. Only one of em had everything I wanted the way I wanted it and he died. I loved the other two, too. They weren't bad. Well, the first one was cause I didn't know what I was doin yet. But the next time I did know what I was doin. I wanted someone kind who thought of someone besides himself. And honest. Like that ole Hudson. He ain't got nothin to do later on, he just don't know who he's going to run into on them trails he runs on and he wants to be free."

I know I could'a gotten annoyed at her talking to me like that, but she was talkin to me like family talks to you. I had missed it and I needed it.

"Wait, wait a minute, Ms. Darlin. I want to show you somethin you need to know for what you are tryin to do." I noticed she was still a shapely woman as she ran back into her apartment. I knew men had liked her, a lot. I knew this was her house and she was independent. She sure must have some sense. I took a deep breath and waited just like she asked me to.

The woman came back out with a Bible! in her hands! Now, me and Gramma used to go to church every Sunday, and you know I believed in God. I said my prayers. But I was not ready for nobody to preach to me! I didn't need that!

My manners came through for me, though, and I stood there to listen, having decided I would start steppin away as soon as she came to the end of the first scripture. She opened the book and, with a well-manicured fingernail, pointed to a place, then read it to me. "The final age of this world is to be a time of troubles. Men (that means women too, she said) will love nothing but money and self." (She had my full attention.) "They will be arrogant, boastful and abusive; with no respect for parents, no gratitude, no piety, no natural affection. They will be implacable in their hatreds, scandalmongers, intemperate and fierce, strangers to all goodness, traitors, adventurers, swollen with self-importance. They will be men who will put pleasure in the place of God, men who preserve the outward form of religion, but are a standing denial of its reality. KEEP CLEAR OF MEN LIKE THESE." I looked to see where that was. Second Timothy, 3:1–5. Well, I declare! It almost got everybody I had been meeting!

"That's just about everybody livin in this city, Ms. Mimi!"

She closed the book. Said, "That's who you are out there with and that is what you have to choose from or not. This is the 'ME' generation. If you ain't had sense enough to see that yet, just wait, they will knock it in your head. Now, here comes Roland. Watch him take this upstairs for you."

I laughingly said to her, "Ms. Mimi, I am not lookin for a husband and I certainly am not tryin to get Roland."

She looked over her glasses at me again. "Ms. Darlin, I am a woman and if I don't ever know nothin else, I know you, dear." She turned toward Roland who was coming in the door. "Evenin, Roland. Listen, your neighbor has a TV down here and wants to get it upstairs to her apartment. I know you're tired, done worked all day, but . . ."

He touched his cap to me, said to her, "Sure, where is it?" And that was that.

Ms. Mimi followed us upstairs, arms raised to try to catch Roland if he stumbled. We went into my apartment, Roland put the TV where I said I wanted it, then he left saying, "I have promised old Ms. Thompson a ride to an appointment she got, so I got to go. If you don't like it there, I'll move it later when I get back." Then he was gone. But Ms. Mimi wasn't.

Ms. Mimi walked around my apartment, just looking at things. She said, "Girl, it ought to hurt your eyes livin in this place the way you got it fixed!"

I said, "What? Why?"

She said, "Everything in here is shining, glitterin, or blasts out at you. Why you need all this gold glitter thread in everything you got? You like that? And look at all these plastic flowers, dusty. They ain't successful in fooling nobody that they are real. Why you need all that imitation stuff? Who are you? What kind of woman are you?" She didn't sound mad or mean, just sounded bewildered. "I noticed you when you got them false fingernails, and . . . and them eyelashes. What you need them for? Grow your own. Natural is beautiful when it's clean and done well."

I sat down on the couch, hard, ready to cry. "Ms. Mimi, I am a Femme Fatale and this is how a Femme Fatale lives! I think . . . thought everything was beautiful!"

She sat beside me, "Well . . . it is, if each piece was off by itself somewhere, but not . . . not all together." She looked around the room again. "You been givin men the wrong impression of you. This stuff ain't you. You are not really false and gaudy. And a real Femme Fatale is not false and gaudy either. She has charm, she is clean, she is restful and her home is pleasant and peaceful. A man can be rested and content around her. He can relax and be himself, think and hear himself think. She has manners, she is courteous, she is thoughtful and kind. She has style . . . and class. Not the kind that you see dressed up on a bar stool, but the kind that when you see her you know she is a lady of value, inside and out. That is what make her so fatale and irresistible. She is hard to beat when it comes to making things to satisfaction and happiness. Contentment."

I sniffled, my ears so wide open, hearing everything she was saying, because that is what I want to be. A real Femme Fatale.

She spoke again. "I see you love flowers. So do I. You know, you can get one real bouquet a week and for the rest of this stuff, get you some silk flowers instead. Soft, quiet colors. Put them all around. Show you got some taste and style. They're beautiful, and restful to the eye. This is more to the taste of a whore. She needs all these bright, blinding things so that a person never really looks at her. You don't need these things." Ms. Mimi stood up to go. "Unless you really like them. If you like them, keep them." She smiled at me. "Well, I got to go now and tend to my own business. Come on down sometimes and I will show you what I mean about style."

You know I was goin!

But, first, I sat there in my little "whore" rooms and I cried like a baby. Maybe I wasn't so smart and maybe I was foolin myself about bein a Femme Fatale. I really hadn't done anything anybody else could not do . . . give my stuff away. I mean my body. I was disgusted with myself and I felt defeated. I was alone, lonely and felt like givin up. Giving up what? I didn't know, but I felt empty inside again. I just sat there and cried and cried . . . and cried. All my hopes runnin down my face from my eyes. I finally got up from the couch about three o'clock in the morning and fell across my bed. Tired. A failure. I hurt, chile.

When I went to work in the morning, I tried to get out the house quietly so I wouldn't have to see anyone, specially Ms. Mimi, but Ms. Mimi opened her door as I passed. She had to be waitin for me. Lord knows, I wasn't ready for her.

She smiled a serious smile and looked searchingly in my eyes, which I kept cast down. She said, "Miss Thing, Miss Darlin, I thought you might be feelin bad cause I talked about all you been doin to help yourself. Don't be. I am very proud of you for all the things you did for yourself. You were seekin and that is what a smart Femme Fatale does. She just changes when she is runnin up the wrong road. (Made me think of Gramma.) You love yourself and that's the first thing. You're goin to find what you need. What you want. You're made of good stuff, girl. You've got what it takes to take what you want when you find it. Don't feel bad, feel ready. Cause that's what you are gettin . . . is ready!"

I smiled, then I hugged her. She hugged back, tight. I left that house feeling better and by time I got to my car . . . I felt good.

In the next couple of weeks, after I saw inside Ms. Mimi's apartment with all its muted, soft, earth tones, her feminine white bedspread and her understated sculpture and art, I knew what she meant. It was like being in a rich, quiet, beautiful, warm and cozy cave that held promise and could lead to anything. I changed my "decor" and my inner Femme Fatale was satisfied and comfortable. Yes, indeedy.

I still went out with fellows, but, now, they had to bring me home and leave because I was lookin for something special and I was lucky enough to know what kind of special I was lookin for.

For some reason I had been watchin Roland. He was quiet, but he was busy. He smiled a lot. And once I saw him with his shirt off and he might have been slim, but he had some nice arms and shoulders. Muscles. Not big and bulky, but solid and showed strength. Finally, I asked him if he would like to collect on his dinner. He said, "Sure would." And I made plans to cook it.

He came, he ate, we listened to music (the Femme Fatale kind, slow, funky and good) and we even danced. Then we talked and talked about life and our dreams and how we were. He told me all about his little girl. I was glad to hear he was about to win his case. He left, with only a kiss to my cheek. Friendly. For some reason I appreciated that.

We began to do that pretty often during the next couple of weeks. When I shopped I began to pick up the things he liked to eat and I was very pleased to find out he was doing the same thing for me.

One day when I didn't feel good, he brought me my dinner in bed again. A beautiful tray. A small bottle of wine, a rosebud in a small vase, a nice piece of fish broiled with parsley and butter and some little small boiled potatoes.

I didn't look too good, because I didn't feel too good.

Had a old nightgown on, you know what I mean. But the
care he had gone through with my meal made me feel
much better. I knew he was coming back for his dishes in a
little while, so after I ate, I ran through the shower and put
makeup stuff on and a pretty nightgown.

When he came back and got his dishes, he noticed the
change and smiled at me. Said, "Darlin, I think a massage
would be just the thing to bring back my friend to feelin
good again. And it will help you sleep real good."

I mewed, purred, "You think so? I would love one . . .
I guess."

"You got some lotion?" I showed him, pointing. "Okay,
let's put it on to heat." I thought to myself, "This man
knows what he is doing. Has he had all that much practice?" But I smiled and slid down into the bed.

When he was getting started, I tried to turn over on my
stomach, but he stopped me. I tried to keep my gown on,
but he got it off. Gently, but he got it off. Now, I am not a
weak woman, but I just ain't had too many experiences like
that. He just said, "Bashful? I'll take care of that," and
pulled all the shades down and turned off all the lights
except one little one across the room.

Welllll, he started at my toes, honey, and slowly,
S L O O W L Y, worked up to the top of my head, then
told me to turn over. I didn't want to, but I did. Slowly, like
a Femme Fatale. He had done already seen all my private
business. Not all, but almost. He started at my toes again.
Chile, honey, chile.

Now, maybe you wouldn't have done it, but by the time
he got to my shoulders, I just didn't give the least care at all
what he saw. He had pulled my legs apart when he did my

legs, one by one. I forgot to be ashamed. At the end, he pulled me to him and took me in his arms. Somehow his shirt had come off while I was facing the mattress.

In a weak voice I said, "But I'm a sick woman." My last thought was, "You gonna go through all the men in the building?" Then I had to stop thinking because he was talkin to me. Listen,

"I know you're thinkin you don't really know me. But I know you. I been watchin you. Carefully. You don't have no men runnin in and out of your apartment. I like that. You're clean. I like that. You're smart. You work for yourself. I like that. You've got beautiful hair and a fine, big, healthy, beautiful body. I love that. I know you lookin for something. (His pants came off.) And I am too. (He got in the bed and took me in his arms again.) So, I think maybe we ought to look together. I want to make love to you. (The rest ain't none of your business.)

Now, I have to tell you . . . that man was sweet, sweet, sweet. And gentle with me like a newborn baby. And he might be swayback and have no behind much, but that's the only kind I want from now on. You hear me? He ain't missin nothin he needs. I broke off three or four of my false fingernails throwin my hands out gainst the wall behind the bed and I don't know where my false eyelashes went. He was not the wild one, I was.

I hollered, chile, I hollered. I was singin. I know #6 heard me and I started to feel shamed, but I couldn't stop hollerin and moanin, so I, in my mind, I just said to #6, "Jog on that."

When Roland left me the next morning he took my mind with him. Sure did. Yes, indeedy! I tried to be ashamed of how I gave myself to that man so fully, but I just kept stretchin and feeling my body and smiling. See?

Well, he just brought my Femme Fatale out! I spent a little more money on nightgowns and pretty little things to wear around the apartment. Kept some real flowers every weekend. Bought some real down love music, Ray Charles, Bobby Blubland, Anita Baker, Gladys Knight, Patti La-Belle. Love music filled my rooms and Love filled my heart.

He cooked for me, I cooked for him. He served me like I was a queen, which to me, I was. I served him like he was a king. Which to me, he was. When we made love, I massaged him, after, til he slept. He massaged me some-times, before. I didn't let him get up after either. I had fluffy, scented, warm towels to rub over his body, after, and something nice and silky, his pajamas I made him buy. He put on the bottom, I put on the tops.

He liked books. I read to him . . . love stories. Some-times he read to me, poetry and stuff, and we talked, we talked. He liked to keep up with the news, so I read a few things out the news every day, so I could talk with him about it. I know there are magazines that say it's dumb to do these things, not liberated at all. But remember, they are talking to single, lonely, unhappy women. With what I was doing, I was learning things myself. I began to read more books. Was more aware of things around me and in the news. You got to learn things and grow. See?

We went for long walks. Sometimes I said I was busy and didn't see him, but I had to get a rest from all this Femme Fatale, chile. I wondered what Ms. Mimi was thinkin, but I hadn't heard from her, so I knew she didn't think I was makin a fool of myself.

Well, I can't tell you everything, but three weeks more of Roland being with me every night and I decided we need to have a little talk. I told him the truth as I see it.

I said, "Listen, you coming in bout every night takin my lovin. Some of your clothes are in my closet and even my drawers. We eatin and sleepin together. Now what does all that mean? To you?" I let him know by that "to you" that I had ideas of my own.

He smiled. "It means we are very close."

I nodded. "Close to what?"

"To each other, Darlin."

"What do that mean?"

He smiled down at his hands. "What do you want it to mean?"

I smiled at my neatly manicured hands, my own natural nails. Said, "That's what I am tryin to get you to tell me. See?"

He was quiet for a minute. I was too.

He finally said, "Wellllll."

I asked, "Do you mean it when you say you love me or you just feelin good at that moment?"

He wasn't smilin now. "Welll, I mean it . . . at that moment."

I didn't smile either, but my voice was soft and low, my Femme Fatale voice, honey. "All we are goin to have between us are moments?"

He said, "Well, Darlin, I hope not. I don't know what to say."

Still softly, I said, "Welllll, I do. My gramma told me . . . If somebody love you, they want to be WITH you. They want to marry you. See?"

Well, he frowned and gave me, yeah, a strange look. He took a deep sigh, but didn't say nothing. So . . . I gave him his word back. "Well?"

He musta been ready, "Darlin, I don't know how you expect me to make a decision on somethin as important as marriage in this little time I've known you. It's . . . nice . . . what we have, but . . . marriage? How can you expect to talk about that so soon?"

Well, I had already thought, so I was ready. I ain't dumb and I am a Femme Fatale and I had my gramma's words in my head backing me up. See? I hated to say it, because I loved him now. I knew he was a good man in many ways and I . . . I just loved him, that's all. His sweetness, goodness, kindness and, yes, his lovin started it all.

I took a deep breath and said, "Well, #4, I expect marriage just like you must expect us to go on doing what we've been doin. But, you see, I don't have but so much loving to give in life, and if you ain't sure what you gonna do with my love, or even if it's worth enough for you to want to keep it, then I can't give you any more of it. I will save it for somebody who's gonna love my kind'a love. The staying and keepin kind."

He reached for me and I let him hold me. He said, "Darlin, let's don't go so fast. We got plenty time. You know I . . . think a lot of you. Think the world of you. But marriage is an important step. I've never been married. Wasn't married to my daughter's mother. Cause when I do marry, I plan to stay. Make it work. Won't be no divorce."

I saw Roland didn't tell all his business to Ms. Mimi. I said to myself, "Marriage ain't no more important than my body and I ain't gonna use up all my lovin before I find the true man I'm going to marry." I leaned back from him, gave him my sweetest Femme Fatale smile and said, "Well, sweetheart, let's say good night. I have some thinkin I want to do." I let my Femme Fatale shoulder show out of my robe and my Femme Fatale leg kept appearin as I helped him up and walked him to the door. Touched him a light Femme Fatale touch on his cheek as I turned my cheek to him for his kiss good night. He left hesitantly as he went through the door. I smiled my sweet, open Femme Fatale smile as I closed that door.

Then I sat down amid my love toned rooms and cried like a fool. Why did I have to do that? Would I lose him? Was I going to end up alone . . . with my little money? I cried, chile. But I knew I was right and if I didn't think enough of myself, nobody else would have to.

Then I went and gathered all his things in my apartment and at 4 A.M. I placed them neatly in front of his door. I had folded his things with love and tears, but I had to do it. Don't care how good it is to you, if it ain't good for you, let it go.

I got dressed for work and went and sat somewhere drinking coffee and thinkin, til 7 A.M. when I was due at work. That evenin I got in from work before he did. I didn't answer my phone or my door.

The next few weeks I never answered my door once I got in. I knew his schedule, that's when I went out to movies, out to dinner, even jogged again, alone. Cried sometimes, thinkin I'd have to go home to the country, alone, forever. Cause I don't want nobody but him. Him and his daughter. Five daughters, I don't care!

But, Femme Fatales are strong. So I fought against runnin over there and breakin down his door. I just told my body, "You just shut your mouth! It's my brain's turn!" Femme Fatales don't beg! See?

Bout a week later I decided I would answer the door the next time he knocked. I dressed for him and sat and waited. Bout three nights runnin. No knock came.

I got ready to die. (You really can feel that way.) Wanted to kick myself for not keepin what I did have. And for not being something that would have let him know I was the woman for him. I played all them same blue love songs over and over, only this time, they were so sad. Ole Femme Fatale was gone.

Couple days later I was sittin on my couch, crammin some glazed donuts I had bought on the way home from work. Just'a eatin and feeling sorry for myself. Crumbs everywhere. A knock came on the door and, thinkin it was Ms. Mimi, I moaned, "Come in." But it was Roland. And he was mad.

He walked in, put his finger in my face that was full of donuts and said, "You are drivin me crazy and you ain't feelin shit!"

I swallowed and jumped up to cut off the record playin somethin sayin, "Please, please, PLEASE." Said to him, "Have a seat, sweetheart?" Just as calm as I wanted to be. Ole Femme had done come back.

He sat down, got up, walked in a circle, then sat again. Said, "What is all this shit you doin, Darlin?"

I was smiling all inside myself. "Sweetheart, I've never hardly heard you curse before. What is the problem anyway?"

He reached for me, I let him touch me a minute then I moved away to find a different record. He reached again. "C'mere, woman. You know what you are doin to me!"

I looked serious and concerned and I wasn't acting. "I thought I gave you what you said you wanted . . . your freedom, time . . ."

He pulled me to him again. Beautiful, warm things exploded in my body, in my heart. He said, "Okay, okay, I been free. Thank you. Now." He held me away from him, looked into the slightly smiling, inquiring face of a Femme Fatale. I didn't say anything. Hell, we were playing hearts and it was his turn to play.

Finally he spoke. "I can't stop thinkin of you. Rememberin all those wonderful days and nights and the sweet things you do to make a man feel necessary and at home. (I felt wonderful, chile.) No matter who I am with (you ever feel good and bad at the same time?) I think of you. No one is as soft, as thoughtful, as smart, as sweet and loving as you are. When a woman touches me . . . now . . . I don't like it because it is not as soft, gentle as your touch. If a woman cooks for me, she just put it on a plate. It's not planned, colorful, balanced and beautifully served like yours. After we make love? (I nodded, slowly.) You massage me, hold me, love me. They sometimes throw you a towel, or tell you where the towels are. (They? How many is they?) They don't speak softly at the right time. They curse. I couldn't, wouldn't bring my child around them. They want to go out allllll the time. They don't know how to stay home sometime and play and read and talk or just take a walk. Baby, nobody seems to be like you. They couldn't make me forget you. Baby, you are, you are so much woman."

I started to smile at him and wrap my arms around him, but he wasn't through.

He frowned, said, "But you know, all my friends say all that changes after you get married. It all goes away."

I thought I should agree, because that is exactly what happens in a whole lot of marriages otherwise the divorce rate wouldn't be so high and I wanted a good marriage. I didn't want any divorce either. So, I said, "Roland, you are as good to me as you say I am to you. We BOTH do for each other. You don't lay back and order me to do things for you like you are the master and I am the slave. We both love making the other person happy too. That is what makes things different for marriages that work. Maybe your friends didn't put enough into their marriages to get anything out."

He just looked at me, pulling me close to him. Then he whispered in my ear, "We'll just have to make a plan so we can keep what we've got . . . til death do us part."

I asked, whispering, "Is that a proposal?"

He whispered back, "That's a proposal."

I laughed seductively (I didn't know I had donut sugar around my mouth). "I'll take it, I'll take it." THEN I let him kiss me and he licked all the donut sugar off as we laughed together.

Well, that was two years ago. Yes, we got married and we left our city jobs and moved back here to the country in these hills. I packed Gramma's travelin shoes up and brought her back with me, of course. There's her bronzed shoes over there by the fireplace. We got his daughter, our daughter. He made the store larger. Built all he needed himself, chile. He raises chickens and eggs for sale and breeds dogs because he always wanted to. See?

On Monday, Wednesday, Friday and Saturday, I am a wife and do all the things that keep my house runnin smooth and clean. I pamper him every day. I have no set rules for him because I like the rules he sets for himself.

Tuesday, Thursday and Sunday, I bathe, pamper myself, go to the beauty shop if I want to, whatever. He cooks. I lounge around in lounging clothes. I take care of my own nails and things now. (I kept breakin the other kind off.) I am a Femme Fatale every day, but especially on those days. See?

We are good parents. We are expecting another child in about four months. I am happy. I think he is. I think our child is.

But . . . on any day, I can be a Femme Fatale if I feel like it. Roland put a bell out here by the window so I can ring for him when I need him. So, see? I'm just gonna lean out the window and ring this bell. He closes up and comes right on in.

Look, here he come now.

See?

Do-It-Yourself Rainbows

You know, a human being can be a strange thing. Sometime they don't know which way to go. Heart saying one thing, brain saying something else. They always hoping. But if you can get that mind and that heart working together, you really got you something. It got to be right though. Brain got to have some sense. Sure is hard to get, sometime, when you get older, cause it's the evenin time of your life. It's usually when you get older cause Life takes Time, and the Livin ain't always easy.

Alberta Marie was born here in this city to a mama who just had too many kids for any one to get as much attention as they needed and the mama still get all the attention she needed for herself. Alberta, I rather call her

Berta, was fairly good at getting food off the table and
stealin clothes from her older sisters so she would have
something to wear to school. Her sisters probably stole
them from somebody else. They use to beat her up about
them clothes, but that just all seemed like part of life to
Berta.

Berta was kinda shy in school. Shamed I guess. Cause
one day them sisters came to the school and took them
clothes right off a Berta and left her standing in the school
yard in a raggedy under slip. I guess that's what survival is
all about, but I wouldn't a done my sister, or nobody else,
like that.

Well, the mama died. Some seriosiss of the liver from
alcohol. She just took her last drink tryin to forget all her
problems, and fell over dead. Problems all gone. Course,
them problems landed on all them left behind.

Didn't no relatives step forward. Didn't none of em
have a steady step. The younger kids was farmed out to
them foster homes. The older kids just took off on their
own cause they already knew how to do that anyway.

Sometimes a foster home can be worser than a whole
lot of things. A kid goes to one when they ain't big enough
or experienced enough to know how to live as things come
up, and they learn the hard way. It's pitiful what a child has
to go through to get to be grown. That goes for some of
them rich ones too. But poor ones? . . . Can't look out for
themself? Lord have mercy on all of em.

Anyway, Berta was in four or five of them foster homes
til she was about fifteen, sixteen years old. The last one was
in my community. The home was run by a woman, Ms.

Esther, who was a nice enough woman, just didn't have her own man and was always lookin out for one.

A man bout thirty-five, Spencer, lived right next door to me, asked could he court Berta. Now, Ms. Esther needed the money from them foster home people, cause she was raisin a group of her own kids on it. But Ms. Esther forgot about that and resented Berta for bein young and gettin a man that Ms. Esther thought should be after her own self.

Ms. Esther started slammin Berta around and callin her sluts and tramps and even a whore. Bad ugly ones. Bad ugly words. So Spencer asked, no, he told, Berta to come live with him and be his wife and like a child, she did. Her head hangin down and her feet draggin.

Later she told me, "I didn't know how to call them people and tell them to find me a new home and I didn't have a nickel for the call noway. And I was scared of what the next home might be like. They put me in a house with a woman cause I had been had trouble with the men before already. I had done some little dreamin about my future, what I wanted, what life could be like. But I didn't never have no real big dream or plan cause I didn't know how to do nothin to make no big dream come true. I dreamed of havin my own family. I wanted a . . . happy . . . home. I wanted kids, even then, so I could treat them better than I was treated. Love em. I knew there had to be more to life than what I was livin. Being hungry. Dirty. No clothes that wasn't secondhand. Housework all the time. Takin care kids I didn't even know and they didn't know me. We tryin to love each other, but don't know how cause we ain't never seen it bein done. Sure, we dreamed about the end of the rainbow. I KNEW there was somethin better. But I didn't know how to go about gettin to it. Everything was out of my reach. Spencer put marriage in my reach. A little house in my reach. A home. So . . . I went with Spencer. I was scared. That's all. Scared. So I went."

Now all this happenin in my own community right up under my face, and you might say I had to see these things. And I saw when Berta went to live with Spencer, he didn't rush as fast to get down to the marriage license bureau as he did to get to the bed. I thought Berta might be makin a mistake, but I couldn't help her, I didn't have nothing and my husband said "no."

I knew Berta was gonna be getting the short end of the stick, both ways. Spencer was a nice enough man, I guess, a good man, but there had to be some reason that he didn't have a wife. For one thing, he was a little man. Had a little car, a little job and a little apartment. Seem like everything he had was nice, but it was always little.

I know it wasn't none of my business, but she was a child, bout five years younger than me. I noticed everybody else who was payin any attention, which was Ms. Esther, was not hopin for happiness to be in Berta's future. So I went over to see Spencer and asked him when the weddin was goin to be.

He say, "Well, I reckon it will be by and by."

I said, "Well, you know Berta is very young and I think it is against the law for you to be in there with her if you are not married."

He say, "Well, the law ain't got no business tendin to my business."

I said, "Well, yes, they have business tendin to Berta's business, since she is so young and all. Somebody got to."

He say, "What you tryin to say?"

I said, "I am sayin I hope to hear bout your weddin soon. Fore you have trouble bout that young girl."

He say, "Any day now, little Ms. Busy, any day now. Soon."

I said, "Congratulations then." And went on home.

After they got married, Berta dropped out of school and went to work to help her husband. He treated her alright. Didn't beat her none. In about three years they bought a house. A little one. Still livin near me and my husband.

Now, this is a city, but in cities they still have some little towns inside the city. Poor towns. They call em ghettos and it be just like they done moved the country out here to the city cause the people who live out here are country and they brought it with em.

Anyway Spencer put a fence round that house and mowed his lawn in the front and planted a garden in the back. He always have a turkey or a chicken or a duck in the back, he be fattenin up for the next holiday. If they would'a had love, it could have been a little heaven. I thought, but I didn't know what they had really, cause Berta was shy bout talkin bout her husband.

That was their life. Eat, work, fool around the house, eat, work, fool around the yard. Stay home. First thing they listen to was the radio in the evenings, then when TV came out they finally got one. A little one. They ate, worked, fooled round the house and yard, looked at TV and go on to bed. He didn't take Berta out and that fence was to keep other people way from her, I think.

Now Berta was not a bad-lookin woman, so I guess he thought he better keep her at home. Safe from all other men. She did whatever he told her to cause she could see she had a little home, a little car and a few little clothes what she could call her own. Wasn't no foster there.

Berta didn't love Spencer like no lover. Later she told me, she loved him because he was good to her like nobody else ever was. The FUNdamentals without the fun, but what you gonna do? So she followed her brain and she didn't do no hopin. Just took life as it looked like it was. It was a necessary life, but it was livin down under the rainbow.

She did that for thirty years. Then . . . he died.

Berta cried a little for him. He hadn't been a bad husband. He was in his sixties when he died and she was forty-six. That can be a big difference for a lot of things, but he had been settled and secure. A first for her. Now, he was gone and she was alone.

She'd walk through the little empty house, sadly, and cry some more, cause it was lonely. In time, she began to walk through that little house, sayin, "It's mine. I got a little house, paid for. A little car, furniture and all that, paid for. It's all mine. I guess I am secure." But she was still lonely and she didn't know for what, cause she really didn't miss Spencer, she was just used to another person bein in the house.

Spencer hadn't left her no big insurance or nothin. She did a few jobs of day work a couple days a week and she had his small Social Security check. She had almost always, in the last few years, been able to save her money cause they didn't have no bills. She was alright if she didn't move to the left or the right too far or too fast. You know.

She kept the yard and house up, cause she had been doin it alone for years. She just took to lookin even more thoughtful and starin off into space.

Then, one day she just brought all kinds of things out that house and sat em on the sidewalk. Put a sign out that said, "See something you want, take it. I'm throwin it all away." Now the house was almost empty. She cleaned it up and sat around lookin out in space again.

Soon after that, I visited her like I do, now and again. She was sittin up in her livin room with tears in her eyes. Just sittin.

I ask her, "What's the matter, Berta? You missin Spencer that much? Still?"

She answered and sounded like she was mad a little. "No, I ain't missin Spencer, rest his soul. I'm missin life."

I did understand and I didn't understand. "Life?"

She said, "Life." She looked up at me, tears gone now. "I want to be happy in life sometime. Thrilled. Like . . . that song say; Flyin over the rainbow like a bluebird. There ain't never been no rainbows in my life."

I didn't say nothin, cause I knew what she was talkin about and I didn't feel like lyin to make nobody feel better.

She went on, "Spencer was alright. But in the beginnin it was like he was my father. In the end, it was like I was his mother. I didn't hate him, but I didn't love him. He just was a home for me. We ain't made love for years and when he was crawlin up on top of me, it still wasn't nothin cept somethin for him. I ain't never felt nothin in no sex. I know it's somethin to feel, cause love is too popular in this world. And I ain't had none of it. I ain't never had no climax in life and I am forty-six years old and pretty soon I am goin to die. I ain't done nothin but wash, cook, clean, rub and look at TV and read a little."

"Oh, Berta," I started.

"And I hate that name 'Berta,' cause it sounds like a piece of wood! Everything I got is cause somebody else gave it to me. I ain't never picked my life and nothin in it, for myself."

"Oh, Berta, I mean . . ."

"Well, I'm goin to change all that. I'm gonna get me a life of my own. With some love in it! And somebody who's a man, my age. I'm gonna get me a climax. If I have to build my own rainbow, I will."

I nodded my head. "You mean a climax to life like some point in it?"

She nodded her head. "That too! But what I mean is a orgasm. A orgasm." She looked directly at me like she was darin me to disagree or argue with her. "You may think that's nothin, but you been happy with your husband and you all was the same age and you picked him and he picked you. You ain't never looked like you was in misery to me, less it was about money. You ain't never complained bout no lovin. You got your own rainbow."

I smiled, "Well, I . . ."

She said, "Well, I am too."

Over the next few weeks, Berta was buyin things and redoin her house on the inside. I offered her my help, but she said, "No, I'm gonna do this all by myself." And she did.

When it was finished, I went to see it. She had kept the twin beds in the bedroom, but everything else was changed. It was furnished nice, but it was somethin about it like the Arabian Nights lady. And she had incense burnin. Flowin drapes, soft material couch, low tables and such. Soft colors. That little house didn't know what to do with itself!

I told her, "It looks good. Like a woman's house. You really workin on it."

She switched her little behind on by me. "And I ain't through."

When I left her house I was in wonder, but I smiled cause I blive people should build their life like they want to. I passed Ms. Winch, a widow and Berta's closest neighbor, who came out to the gate as I passed.

Ms. Winch smiled and beckoned to me. "Girl, what does her house look like? I seen all that stuff they was bringin in there. That ain't no real spensive stuff, but it ain't cheap either! She spendin that man's money like it was water. You better tell her somethin! His dyin done made a fool of that woman!"

Now, I don't worry bout what people think, less it's my husband. I just told Ms. Winch, "That man's money is her money too. She is a young woman. She ain't old as me and I ain't old as you. So if she don't do some livin now, when she gonna do it?"

Ms. Winch said, "Well, you a fool too," and went on back in her house her husband left her that was still just like the day he died and left it a long time ago.

Now, I thought about what Ms. Winch said. I realized that I had always thought when a woman got to be round forty, forty-five years old, her life was over, in a way of speakin. She was sposed to be lonely if her husband died and she was that age. But I wasn't so sure that was true. Who has to be alone just cause somebody left or died?

Now, I don't know was it a magazine or the TV gave her the idea, cause she had always done her own hair. But Berta commence to goin to the hairdresser and had her hair cut and styled. Then she started shoppin and dressin different. When I visited her one day, on her beautiful new dresser she had a rack of face creams and such, to get rid of wrinkles and such. She even had some on her face!

Well, I smiled to myself and was glad for her. Hell, be happy doin what you want to do.

Then, one day she jumped out that little car of hers and I looked in her face to say "hello" and Berta had her face made up. And was lookin good! She was gettin a new look! She looked so proud of herself and I was proud for her. Berta looked ten years younger! Well, her life had been slow, so her face wasn't raged with time noway.

I followed her in her house. I liked goin in there, it made me feel . . . different somehow. Like a lady, a woman. And I know I always been one anyway, but this was a different woman. I started to say, "Berta? Girl, you look good!"

She smiled, a happy smile, and said, "My name ain't

Berta no more. I got another name. My middle name is
Marie and I'm addin a 'La' to it, so now my name is
LaMarie." We laughed together and I said, "All right,
LaMarie!"

She poured some Dubonnet wine in some pretty little
glasses, handed me one and said, "This ain't nothin bad,
they use it in church sometime."

We sipped a minute. I don't know why, but I felt like a
modern lady.

She spoke first. "You know . . . some of the men from
my church done come here to see me. They were nice.
Maybe I could'a liked one of em, but they just all remind
me of Spencer. I don't intend to make love with Spencer
again, in no way. The only one who didn't remind me of
Spencer, I really did like, but he didn't come back no more.
That hurt. I have not tried sex with anybody, so it can't be
sex. But he didn't even come back to try to get some. That
means there is somethin I didn't have that somebody else
has. Well, I got to wonderin what it was."

I took another sip of wine. "Well, there ain't nothin
wrong with you, Ber . . . LaMarie."

She waved her hand at me. "I am makin myself over."

I had to put my two cents in. "My aunt says if you are
too easy to get, they don't want you no more."

She poured two more little drinks. "Your aunt got good
sense. And that can hurt more, cause you done gave em
some and they don't want no more. Lord, ain't people got a
lot of ways to be hurt?" She sipped some more. Her eyes
were bright and I just knew she had somethin she wanted
to say.

She did. "Listen, girl, do you know that 'On the streets' you don't need to look for no man? That they come lookin for you?"

I sat my glass down after I emptied it. "On the streets? What you talkin about? They ain't lookin for you, they lookin for anybody for twenty or thirty minutes! Them are strangers! You don't want no stranger!"

She sat her glass down. "No, I don't. But I been down there in the French Quarter, watchin them women. They don't look too sad."

I butted in. "They don't get paid for lookin sad."

She leaned forward in her fancy chair. "Yes, they look sad, but they don't look lonely."

I poured my own little glass of wine, I needed it. "They some of the loneliest people on earth. Even their own man don't really want em."

She shook her head. "They get plenty sex."

I said, "Ummm hummm, too much sex. You ain't talkin bout bein no prostitute at your age. At any age. Are you?"

She sat back, shakin her new-done head. "I just figure if the men go there to see women, they must not have a woman of their own at home. Now . . . one of them men got to be a good man, bout my age, just lost for a while. I might be the one who catches him. I ain't dyin of old age yet, and I figure if I am clean and good. A Christian woman . . . they'll think of that! Then, I will have the love of my life, maybe. And he must like sex, or he wouldn't be there! I ain't never in my life felt a twinge down there. Not even a tweak! I don't think I'm no sex maniac, but I know one thing. I meeeean to see what that stuff is all about and I'm gonna feel somethin (she pointed) down there fore I die! Now!"

It was my turn. I said, "Them men don't go down there for no love. For no good! They go down there for nookey."

"Well, I got some. I ain't gonna do it with everybody, Retha! I'm gonna be lookin for the ONE I might want to maybe marry."

I shook my head. "Well, if that don't beat all. Goin to the gutter to find a husband! I done heard of everything now! I done heard of all kinds of ways to get a husband, but I ain't never heard of this way! This is dangerous. You could lose your life out there, stead of finding some love. People don't care bout killin you out there in them streets. Give me another glass, I'll buy you some more today."

LaMarie got up to pour the wine. "Well, what am I gonna do? I'm not young. And I'm not old. But, I am lonely . . . and this is the way I see to do it."

I went home later, thinkin to myself, "She is a fool. But she won't be out there long. She gonna see ain't nothin out there worth havin. It's diseases out there that eat up penicillin, belch and go on bout their dirty death business." I got home to my safe home and locked the door.

Anyway, she went. In the evenins. She would leave her car home, take the bus, get off in the middle of all that stuff and just walk. She always wore a neat dress, a cute hat, white gloves and neat little shoes. She look like she was goin to church. LaMarie, LaMarie.

Next time we talked, she told me, "No, I ain't done it yet. Can't. It's some of all kind of people down there. I just tell the men I already got a date and I'm waitin for him. I have a drink at a bar now and then, but I'm careful cause I don't want none of them knockout things put in my drink. Mostly I just sit at the bus stop. Lookin.'"

I sighed. "Thank God for you not doin it yet."

She said, "Some of them young women laugh at me. And some of em get mad and tell me don't stand on their corner. I just tell them I pay tax for that corner and I'll stand there if I want to. But, mostly, I sit at the bus stop. It's so much to see! It's life, but it's a dead life. Them people ain't happy! Them men beat them women! One of them men ask me who my man was, I said 'Jesus.' He said, 'Do He know you out here sellin His soul?' I said, 'I ain't sold nothin yet.' Everybody laughed and said I was crazy. But I think they're crazy. One woman had been down there all day, tryin to get money to pay her rent, she said, cause she got kids at home. She made $5.00 each time for four times, then some of them other people took her money from her. She was cryin on my shoulder and I felt sorry for her and gave her $20 out of my own Social Security money. I'm glad I could help her, poor thing."

It was so sad, it was funny. I said, "You was her trick. She just used you. She lied and took your money!"

LaMarie looked at me a long minute. Said, "I hope not. But, if she did, anyway I did the right thing."

I began to pray for LaMarie. She had a good heart. And she needed God's help.

LaMarie didn't go out there every evening and when she did she was home before ten o'clock at night. Sometimes she just stayed home, looked at TV, fooled around her house or soaked her feet. She hadn't never took one of them men home yet, she was still lookin.

After awhile, she'd go again. Her style was changin and her clothes was gettin a little bit shorter and flashy. But she still wore the little white gloves and her little secretary-lookin hat. I started worryin again. Ms. Winch caught me one day walkin past her house, said, "Berta LaMarie must have a evenin job in some night club somewhere, don't she? She always goin off somewhere in the evenins and she dressin up all the time like a courtin woman. I know somethin is goin on."

I just said, "Well, tell me one day when I have time," and kept walkin.

I worried. I really worried. But I found out later, I needn't to have. Cause LaMarie was bein watched by somebody else.

LaMarie was always tellin me about her favorite bus stop where she felt safe. She told me about the older man, called C.C., worked in a storefront sold cigarettes, candy, gum, soda water, small bottles of wine, peanuts, you know, stuff like that. She said he was bout fifty-two years old, somewhere in there.

He told me later, in truth he had been watchin her since the first day she was out there in them streets at that bus stop.

C.C. ask the men goin in and out of the shop, "Who is that woman and who put that ole lady out on the street?" All them men laughed and said they didn't know her, but she wasn't no trouble cause she didn't take no dates. She just walk around and sit around and smile like a fool.

One of them men said, "I blive she got some money of

her own. If she keep foolin round out here, I'm goin to relieve her of it. I'm watchin her. I always say 'Hello' to her. One of these days, when I got time, I'm gonna sit down on that bench and tell her the story of my life and her life. Then . . . I'll see what she got and soon I'll have it." They all laughed.

The man didn't tell them that he had already told his woman to make friends with LaMarie, get her trust. So he could take LaMarie's love and then her money. He didn't want to put anything in the slow-thinkin minds of the other men.

C.C. just nodded and spit out the side of his mouth. (I just hate that spittin stuff, don't you? Men do it all the time!)

I think the next evenin or so, LaMarie went down there and was sittin on the bus bench with her little hat and white gloves. When it got dark, this man, C.C., went over and stood by the bench, watchin LaMarie. She didn't seem to pay him no mind. He decided to speak to her.

"May I ask you somethin, lady?"

She looked over at him. "What . . . do you want to ask me?"

"I been seein you for a couple of weeks now, and I just wondered. Do you work close to here and this is just the place where you catch your bus?"

LaMarie slightly smiled. "Nooo. I don't work."

C.C. put his foot up on the bench, "Well, what you doin sittin down here all the time."

She stopped smiling. "Is this your bench? I thought it blonged to the bus company."

"It's in front of my place of business and I been seein

you out here and wondered what a nice-lookin lady like you would be doin down in this part of town if she didn't have no business here."

LaMarie looked away. "Maybe I do have business here."

"I ain't seen you do none. What you lookin for? What you waitin for?"

"I don't think that's any of your business. I'll tend to my business and you tend to yours."

"Lady, I don't want to see nothin bad happen to you and you in a mighty good place for that to happen!"

"Don't you worry bout me."

C.C. took his foot down from the bench. "Somebody better."

"I'm a grown woman. I can . . ."

He interrupted her. "Anybody can be a fool. Even a grown woman. Stay way from down here. Stay home where you blong." The bus just happened along at that time. LaMarie got up in a bit of a huff, threw her nose up in the air (to show the nosy man she wasn't payin him no mind) and got on the bus. He started toward his shop, lookin back a last time. He saw LaMarie lookin through the window at him with a ugly frown and she even had her tongue stuck out at him, but she snatched that back in when she saw him lookin at her and stuck her nose up in the air again as the bus pulled off.

She stayed home for awhile, but after about two weeks LaMarie started goin down there again. About another month passed with her goin down there. One night she was waitin for the bus to go home and C.C. was lockin up the store early. He got in his car and drove slowly to the bus stop . . . and stopped. He leaned over to the window, said to LaMarie, "Hop in, I'll drive you home."

LaMarie shook her head no and said, "Thank you."

He replied, "I said get in. I want to talk a little business with you."

This time she said, "No. Thank you."

He raised his voice a little. "Well, what you out here for? Are you a fool? Get in, you'll be safe. I own that store over there you always see me in. I don't want no trade for myself, so I'm not gonna hurt you, and you goin home anyway."

She turned to look at the storefront then back at him and shook her head slowly, no.

C.C. got out of his car, walked around and opened the car door sayin, "Get in this car. Do I look like a fool? A killer? Don't make me look like a fool in front of all these people. They see me askin you to get in. So, get in! I will drive you home."

And LaMarie did.

The car was big, nice and warm and smelled good. She looked at C.C. out of the corner of her eye. What LaMarie saw was a man who needed a shave, with a beat-out hat on. His clothes were good clothes, but they needed cleanin or pressin. She looked down and saw his shoes were good . . . and shined like new money used to look. But, he was not her type, she thought to herself.

He asked, "What is your name?"

She answered, "LaMarie."

He already knew how she looked so he concentrated on drivin after she told him her address.

When they got to her house (The car took up the whole space in front of her house. Ms. Winch looked out the window when she heard a car parkin. Her eyes grew big as the car, I know.), he finished parkin and she started to jump out, but he took her arm and held her in. She tried to wriggle free, and he said, "Be still. Act like you a lady." She sat back to wait a minute.

Then he got out, walked around and opened her door.

She said, "Thank you. Good night."

But C.C. wasn't through. "I'm walkin you to your door."

He did, but when she opened the door and turned to say, "good night" again, he pushed past her into the house. (I was watchin out my window and I saw it.)

C.C. looked around at everything in the house. Walked through the house and came back to the living room and, finally, the front door. She had been followin him, tellin him, "Get out of my house, you don't have no right to do what you are doin." Stuff like that.

He looked down at her. "This your home?"

"Yes, now leave."

"You rentin or buyin?"

"I own this house. Now, please leave."

C.C. leaned against the door. "Where is your husband? Dead?"

"Yes, now please leave."

C.C. crossed his arms over his chest. "What you doin on that street all the time?"

LaMarie was exasperated. "None of your business. Now go."

"How long your husband been dead?"

"Almost a year. Will you please go?"

His voice softened, "You lonely out here, ain't you?"

LaMarie felt like cryin. "No! Yes! You better leave here now. I will call the police."

But he still wasn't through. He took off his coat and reached for her. It was so quick she didn't realize what was happenin, but she looked up and she was cross his lap and her dress was up and her drawers were down and he was whippin her behind . . . good! (I know it cause I was standin outside the window and heard it all. She was my friend, I went to see bout her!) I was bout to go in and help her when he stopped whippin her and said, "You keep your ass away from those streets! Every time I catch you down there I'm goin to whip your behind again, til you get sick of me. It ain't no plaything out there! It's dangerous! Anything can happen to you. You been lucky! But the better they get to know you, and know you alone, the more things gonna happen to you!"

LaMarie was cryin from anger and indignation, and embarrassed too, with her drawers down round her ankles. She had on a wig this night and it had done fell off. Her makeup was runnin, smeared. She screamed, "Get out of my house! I mean it!"

C.C. opened the door as he turned to her. "Look at all that stuff runnin all over you face. You don't need all that shit! You don't need that hair layin on the floor over there either. You don't preciate what you got! I'm leavin, but I don't want to have to bring you home off them streets

again. Now. Good night!" That big car engine made a big
smooth noise and he was gone.

I know LaMarie sniffled and stayed mad for awhile. I
hadn't tried to stop him because he was tellin her the truth,
what I wished she would do. I went on home cause she
really didn't need me. I waited for the next episode.

Next day LaMarie talked about how "He didn't scare
me. I'll do whatever I want to do! I'm grown!" All such
stuff as that. Her pride was hurt. But she didn't go down to
them streets for three or four weeks. Then she took to
blivin her own words and one night she got dressed up and
went. She was back home in about two hours though and
she was mad. Seems like he just came up to her with his
hand on his hip and looked at her til she got on the bus and
left. When I saw her and she told me, she said, "I don't
have to take that! This a free country!"

"Sometimes," I said.

Bout a week later, I was lookin out the window when
C.C.'s car drove up and parked. He sat there a minute, then
got out and went to LaMarie's door. She opened it, then
tried to close it, but he went on in anyway. I noticed his
clothes looked better this time. I saw Ms. Winch rush out
to work in her yard on that side of her house where she
could see better. (I went over to sit on LaMarie's porch, so I
could hear if she needs me.) I couldn't hear it all, but she
was hollerin at first.

"Why you comin to my house? I haven't been down
there near your place! You don't need to watch me! I'm a
grooooown woman!" You know, stuff such as that.

I couldn't hear him cause he was talkin in his normal
low voice. But she told me later he said, "I know you lonely

over here by yourself. Ain't you got no friends?" LaMarie didn't answer. So he continued to talk. "I came to take you for a drive."

In a little lower voice, LaMarie asked, "Why?"

His voice came up a little, "Now listen, I ain't lookin for no woman. I am fifty-two years old and I ain't never been married and ain't neither plannin on ever bein married. I ain't never wanted no trouble and from what I have seen, that's all a woman is. But I will take you for a ride. It's a nice day and all. I have put on a suit. My car ain't too clean, but a ride ain't gonna do nothin but get it dirty again anyway. So? Let's go."

LaMarie wanted to tell him "No! Get out of my house and don't come back here again!" But she WAS lonely. So she got dressed while he had a cup of coffee and a piece of homemade cake, then they went out, going for a drive. (I ran off the porch.) Later, she told me, "I had a good time, but it wasn't anything special."

I could see how some of LaMarie's plan was workin out. LaMarie was a live woman and she was makin life know it. Now my husband and I been married bout thirty-two years and we used to each other and romance ain't dead, but it lays over to the side a lot. I decided to go to the beauty shop and do somethin with myself. I know one thing, the next day, I met Ms. Winch at the beauty shop. We was both gettin our hair done.

Bout seven or eight days later, C.C. came back. Had a package in his hand when he went to the door this time. Flowers. They went for another drive, she said, then to dinner! and to a show! "We just friends, but I like him now. He ain't bad lookin. But he's never gonna get married and I ain't never gonna lay my body down side of his cause he really will think I'm too lonely and a hard-up fool on top of that."

Well, it got so that every time I looked up, he was there at her house at lunchtime. He wasn't lookin for nothin free cause he always came with a armload of grocery bags. When I would see her, she would tell me what I wanted to know. "We still ain't done nothin though. I'm too old to be a fool." I just looked at her, cause there's a fool on both ends of that stick.

He took her by his house one evenin. His apartment. LaMarie said it was neat and clean, small, but comfortable. "You could tell a woman didn't have no part in it. But I do think he needs a woman." I waited for her to tell me they hadn't done nothin yet, but she didn't say nothin.

Next day, I went down and bought me some fashion books and the next day after that I went and bought me a few nice clothes. Kinda stylish, but still not to look like I was tryin to catch nobody else. Just to put a little life back in my husband. I was pleased when my husband smiled at me and said, "You should buy more nice things, honey, I like to see you lookin good." After that, I bought a new bedspread and some fancy, modern sheets with rainbows on em.

I just happen to see Ms. Winch comin out in a few new dresses to go with her new hairstyle on her way to church . . . or somewhere.

Well, you know I had to notice C.C. when he started comin by after he closed his store. He started out walkin

casual and slow to get up to her door. Then he started
jumpin out the car and kinda hopped to it, gettin there.
When I would see LaMarie she was always lookin better.
Skin glowin, her own hair lookin pretty. Casual, but done
and all. Eyes so bright. She looked happy. She worked in
the yard more. Had the inside of the house painted again,
to look more like a home than a harem.

I saw a truck come by and pick up her kinda new twin
beds. Then I saw another truck come by and deliver a new
queen-size bed. She led em in, showin them the way and
where to put it. She was smilin, big, big, big.

Now, I was lookin better. And I noticed Ms. Winch
was smilin more now, didn't look so grumpty all the time.
Sometimes we went to the same church and my friends told
me Ms. Winch was lookin better and better and was gettin
a little attention from some of them old, old men in the
church. Said she was comin to the Bingo games. Ms.
Winch herself told me that she was goin down to the
YWCA for senior citizen exercise classes. Said, "And I ain't
no fool for doin it, cause I feel better. I feel like a million!"

Then . . . LaMarie told me her and C.C. were
thinkin about gettin married. She said, "I know he don't
have nothin but that little apartment and that store he rents
where they do gamblin in the back. But he is . . . he's
excitin, I guess. To me. We talk about everything under the
sun. Spencer didn't talk bout nothin but the news and medicine. C.C. reads. He got me readin more different kinds of
books." She leaned closer. "Even some of them books with
dirty pictures." She leaned back and laughed. When she
was settled down, she said, "He likes my cookin and I like
his. But he likes to go out to breakfast and dinner and

lunch a lot too. He likes to search out interestin things, right here in this city, that I never thought of. He spends his money, always bringin me somethin." She looked sad a moment, then said, "Spencer never did that, cept on a anniversary or somethin for both of us that we needed." Then she smiled again. "Me and C.C. play gin rummy . . . and checkers, when we sit up in the bed. And if I talk about somethin foolish I want to do, like go around the world, he don't try to kill my dreams. He just lets me have em and gives me a book on some place excitin to go to. He almost a rainbow."

I didn't dare compare him to my husband, cause I knew my husband did the best he could and he had made me happy. Maybe it was me that never gave him any new ideas. Maybe we had worn out all the old ones and settled now for grandchildren and a show now and then. If my marriage was not so excitin, it was as much my fault as my husband's, cause he sure was a good husband and tried to make me happy. I know that.

Another time, LaMarie said, "He ain't never had a home, I bet. A real one. His mama died and his daddy left him with a girlfriend and never came back. He stayed there til he was twelve, then he set out on his own cause the woman kept tellin him there wasn't no blood between them. He been alone ever since. No wife. No children that he know of."

One night, when we were havin a glass of wine together, she smiled that great big smile and said, "Retha, there is more to makin love than I ever knew, girl. He makes love to my whole body. Nothin weird, nothin freakish, just lovin. Slow, good, gentle, sweet, sweet (she closed

her eyes), deep lovin. I was lookin to find out about a climax. Sometimes I have two. Two! in one night. (She
opened her eyes.) But still, he is more than just that. That
ain't just only why I love him. I'm happy. I'm just all around
happy."

I smiled, cause I know what she means. I asked,
"What's your last name gonna be when you get married,
Miss LaMarie?"

She smiled like she had a secret. She said, "His name is
Ryder. C.C. Ryder." She laughed a very deep, sexy, feminine laugh. "I got me a C.C. Ryder, chile!"

Well, you know they got married. And you know what?
C.C. didn't own no property, but he had saved his money.
He told LaMarie, "You got a home, so we got a home. We
both got cars. I got a business, so we got a business. We
gonna take the money I have saved and go see the world
and we gonna take our room and board with us, cause I'm
too old to be worried with carryin suitcases and lookin for
the right place to eat. We travelin on a ship, a ocean liner.
First class!"

They went on a round-the-world trip!! Three month
honeymoon! A rich man couldn't a done more. The chile,
the woman, was happy! And so was the man! He finally
found somethin he could spend his money on, someone he
trusted, someone he wanted to live the rest of his life with.
That's heavy!

They came back full of love and life and all the interestin and wonderful things they had seen. My husband and
I love our presents from Africa and Greece. Then C.C.
went back to work and LaMarie went back to keepin the

house up, which she liked to do cause she loved a home. They lived together happily.

Ms. Winch still didn't find no man. She said she didn't see none she wanted. She had plenty company though. Men and women, cause she had made lots of new friends that needed friends too! You have to keep makin them regular, cause the older ones die and leave you.

C.C. Ryder and LaMarie went on with their travelin and homemakin for about twelve, fifteen years. I'm not sure cause we were all older and different problems take your attention. I know, as C.C. got older, they traveled less and he would take that money and buy LaMarie a little duplex or fourplex to bring her in a little income cause he was goin to sell that store-gamblin business. He said, "I don't want Marie to have to go nowhere near down them dirty streets!" She didn't care. Whatever that man C.C. did was alright with her. He had done made her happy.

He must have known he was sick a long time, why he was takin care of what to leave Marie, as he called her. (He didn't like the "La" much.)

Then, C.C. Ryder died. It broke LaMarie's heart and her life for a long, long time. She kept cryin, sayin, "C.C. Ryder look what you done done." She played that record all the time.

She was in her late fifties or early sixties now. I don't remember no more. She looked good cause she was healthy and she had been happy. After two or three months I asked her, as a joke, "Well, you goin on down to them streets again? Find you another husband?" I laughed a little.

LaMarie smiled. "No. I have had the best of two different worlds. A good man who left me secure in my house, even though the rest of my life with him was bare. And a good, good man who showed me the world in more ways than one. Loved me so good he took care me for after he died. He taught me about life. He built me a rainbow and we flew over it. I really know that. I got my rainbow. I don't want nobody else to touch me. Don't nobody want to anyway."

LaMarie slowly poured us a little glass of Dubonnet wine again, in some pretty little glasses. We was older now, it don't take much. And we was both takin medicine now for high blood pressure and such and we had to watch those things, but whats the hell?

She commence to talkin again after she lowered herself back into her chair. "He left me so many memories, I can coast on them forever. I'm doin alright. I'm satisfied." She tilted her head and smiled. "And to think he tried to keep me from comin down there! If I hadn't never gone down there, I never would have met him! Look what I'd a missed! I went down there, but I prayed a lot. I ain't sayin God found me no husband, but maybe God said, 'Let me get this fool out of this place fore somethin bad happens to her.' Cause when I think back on it now, I realize I could have been in serious trouble down there by myself. Wasn't but one good thing down there, and I got it!" We laughed and finished our wine in silence, just listenin to that low music to "C.C. Ryder, look what you done done."

We all older. My life has been added to alot. I have more good memories. I play the piano for the Senior Citizen dance of the month. Life don't have to be dull and dry. My life is so full I have to wring it out sometime. My grandbabies and now, some great-grandbabies! My husband is not always well now, but we takin care of him. He go with me sometimes when I play the piano and he laughs to himself when he sees them old men winkin at me up there on the stage. It ain't nothin, but it lets you know you are still a little attractive to somebody and you are a woman. Such things like that.

That's what I enjoy, bein a woman. In a way, that's why LaMarie did what she did. She was a woman. And let me tell you, even now, you may not feel like doin a lot of things you used to, but the moon and the stars are still out there. All your life. There is always some beauty in life. Look up . . . and get on with it. Build you a rainbow. Do it yourself! If you can't do that, build your mind near one. Learn how to fly. Then . . . soar a little.

Living Without a Life
or
(The Life You Live May Not Be Your Own)

Sometimes some people, good people, just let life carry them along. If they facing south, they go south. If they facing east, they go east. They don't have to be real dumb, they just wants a leader, somebody they can trust to live their life for em. Now, sometimes that all turns out okay, but this really ain't the kind of world where you can trust everybody to do your living. Whether they mean you right or wrong, they got their own life and they may not be thinking bout what you want and need!

I take a long look at some people and I will tell you what I mean. One night, some years back, a girl baby was born to a woman who did not want another child. She had tried to get rid of this one, but the chile came anyway. It was a weak little baby, small and looking sickly. They named her Audrey cause somebody just happened to laugh and say "Call her Audrey," and they didn't care either way so they named her Audrey.

Audrey grew up always a little hungry and mostly alone cause her brothers and sisters would sit her down and leave her soon as they got tired of her and the mama was gone . . . again. Her little behind was always full of sores from unchanged, stinging diapers. It took forever to finally get her potty-trained. She sit on that trainin pot so long sometimes til her little behind be shaped just like that pot when they take her off of it. Her stomach was usually empty of solid food and that bottle her mama and them kids tried to keep her on was always full of soured milk or plain water. How that chile kept breathing I don't know, but she did.

I was young, but I was home takin care of my mother who was a invalid, so I wasn't married. I wanted to be, but I didn't have time to do no courtin or nothin. I took to Audrey and would grab her whenever I could and feed her and clean her up best as I could. I grew to love that little girl, so I watched her as she grew up.

Audrey stayed small and thin as she grew up. She had a little roundish head with short, short hair and them kinda eyes that turn down on the outside corner so she look like she was always bout to cry. If you add that to the fact that she always had a bewildered look in her face . . . like she didn't know why she had been born (well, none of us do, but hers showed) then you know she was a sad-looking little girl. That's how she drew my heart to her.

She was smart in school though, when she went, which she usually didn't do cause wasn't nothin to wear or what she did have was laughed and teased at by the other kids and they wasn't all that hot off themselves!

Strange, to me, but she had a kinda personality that made her smile a lot, pretendin she was happy, I guess. She didn't know she was pretendin, but she was. Her little heart was always eager to follow a new friend, hopin "this one" wouldn't turn on her when somebody better came along.

She got tired of them school kids teasin her after she grew up a little and dropped out of school when she was bout fourteen or fifteen years old. I was watchin her, wonderin what she was gonna do cause I had always felt sorry for and liked that child. Been tryin to feed her for years, give her clothes and all, cause she didn't have no other way and I can understand that. Well, she went all round this neighborhood askin everybody in some business for a job. The old man what owns the community store decided to give her one. I guess he figured maybe she would pay for some of that food her family was always stealin or maybe she would stop em since she worked there. Anyway, she went to work.

She was steady on that job! Went every day! I don't know what she gave to her mama, I know she had to give her some, that's just the way things were. But she took to buyin herself some little nice things on time payments. New things. Hers only. Got her hair done now and again and just regular kept herself up. She was lookin a lot better and her smile wasn't so pretend anymore.

I watched her with the boys, but they didn't pay much tention to Audrey and it got to where she didn't expect it. But I noticed, sometimes when I be in the store, how her eyes follow them around with a little longin in em.

Then, round that time, a new family moved in the neighborhood and they had a son was a tall, hungry-lookin fellow (well, the whole family looked hungry) and, in time, he took to hangin round that store to walk Audrey home. Her little eyes almost stopped lookin like tears and got a little light in em. Good! I was glad! Cause Wardel, (that's his name) seemed to be a nice boy. He was studyin hard, stayin in school. A nice boy.

Audrey fell in love with Wardel and when he graduated, they got married. She was bout nineteen years old then and still workin at the store. He found him a job right away! I looked for a baby to show up, but didn't none come. They got them a little place and was just doin alright. I was proud of both of em! She stopped gettin new clothes and things, but I thought that was all part of bein newly married and tryin to make it.

A few years passed like that and still no baby. I thought he would keep that job and she might quit workin and settle down to bein a housewife, but he decided on goin back to school, only it was college this time. He dropped down to a part-time job, but Audrey got ANOTHER job and kept workin at the store too. I was tryin to be proud of her, but I wished she had gone back to school too, for herself. She just smiled happily and sent him on his way. He smiled back happily, and went.

I don't member what he was studyin, but it took him a long time, and during those four or five years, he began to look better and better, like a college man, you know, while she looked tireder and tireder like some drudge or somethin. They didn't never hardly see each other, and her eyes got that longin look back in em. I wanted to say something to em, but that was their business. I figured when he graduated, she could sit down and begin to look as good as he did. Catch up, you know?

Well, he graduated. Lookin real good. Audrey was workin so she couldn't go to the graduation things and all. She probly didn't have nothin to wear anyway. But my heart hurt for her. She never had been too strong and workin two jobs took a lot out of her. Her hair never did grow good and her eyes looked like little sideway teardrops. She just didn't look good at all. Still, I could see a lot of love for Wardel in them eyes. She told me, "Miz Honey, sometimes I can hardly breathe cause life just seems to get so big to me." I told her, "Keep takin your breaths, chile, deep breaths. The size of life can change on you. Sometimes air is thin, sometimes it's fat. Sometime you needs more air, sometimes less. Just breathe deep." I didn't know exactly what I was talkin bout, but it made sense to me.

Anyway, they been married bout seven years now, still didn't have a baby or their own home or nothin. She didn't stop workin two jobs when he graduated, cause he said it would take him awhile to get sit . . . u . . . ated in his new work. Audrey, seeing that he was coming home less and less even for the few minutes she could share with him between her jobs, decided to have a baby . . . to make home more homelike, you know?

He grumbled when she got pregnant, but when his son was born, he loved the son and buckled down to bein a good husband and father. Stayin home more, walkin em to church and all. Spendin a little money on em for clothes. I sure was glad.

He still kept his looks up though, and his clothes. Soon, he even bought a real house for his family. Audrey smiled again. She had a family. She was a mother. She tried to keep herself up, but she didn't know how to, very well, and didn't really have any girlfriends cause the ones that came to be her friend really came to be close to Wardel. He didn't help her cause he wasn't going to take her anywhere round his college friends anyway. I could see that.

After they had been married bout eighteen years, Wardel quit spendin any of his money on them and he start stayin out later and later at night. Sometimes he didn't come home for the whole weekend, or some weekdays either. Now, Audrey was bout thirty-seven years old, lookin ten years older. He was bout the same age as her, but looked ten years younger. Probly cause he had love in his life and she didn't have none in hers cept for their son, Woodrow, who they called "Woody." Woody was round bout eleven or twelve years old then.

It got so she could hardly breathe again (she said) cause she wanted and waited to hear Wardel's footsteps to see if he was coming home at night. So many times he didn't now. She had a house and a son, but she didn't have the family she wanted. Her man wasn't really there.

Well, Audrey wasn't no plain full-out fool, so one night she stood across the street from that big huge building where he worked and waited for him to come out and then she planned to follow him to wherever he was going to, to see why he did not come home. When he did come out, he had on different, even better clothes than he left home in. Them clothes were even sharper than his usual ones.

He walked right on past his new Cadillac car, leavin it at work, you see, and walked on down the street. His head was high, lips parted in a big smile, shoulders thrown back proudly and walkin like he was steppin off into heaven. Audrey followed him.

Now, Audrey was small, rather timid, and brown. No one paid any attention to her and Wardel never looked back. Used to doin whatever he wanted to, I guess.

Well, Wardel turned into one of them nice apartment buildings Audrey had never even been in (cause Wardel never took her out, you see). He turned in like he lived there hisself and was going home! He even had a key! Audrey stopped and blinked her eyes, wonderin if this was another office, as he waved at the uniformed man in the entrance hall and went on to a elevator, stepped in and disappeared. She did not know what to think cause she hadn't heard about him havin no new office and she didn't cheat on him so she had no practice at bein cheated on herself. She just stood there with her mouth hangin open, lookin confused. It's the kind of thing where "after" you know, you wonder how you could'a been such a fool. You know what I mean.

It was already kinda dark, so she moved over behind some large bushes in front of the building and scootched down in order not to be seen. She watched the colorful, richly dressed, laughin people come and go, in and out of the building for almost two hours! She finally just sat on the ground cause her legs were gettin numb and stiff from the cold. It was really cold too.

She was lookin down at the ground, trying to think through her confusion when she heard Wardel's voice. She looked between the stiff branches and leaves to see him walking down the pathway, laughin and talkin, with his arm around this pretty, pretty woman who had a fur stole over her shoulders, just under Wardel's arm. The woman had on sparklin earrings and a twinklin necklace and matchin bracelet. Audrey could even smell her perfume! Her dress was long like a formal gown and had a split up the side that showed a very pretty curved leg and a shapely foot in high-heeled gold sandals. Chile!

Audrey stood up, in spite of herself, but Wardel didn't see her cause his eyes were full of that woman, with his mouth smilin that handsome look of his. They high-stepped to the corner and into one of them cabs was waiting there and were driving away when Audrey came to herself and ran behind them, jumpin into the next cab, saying, "Can you follow that cab there, sir?"

"Can you pay?" Sir asked.

"Yes, sir, I blive I can," Audrey answered as she tried to keep her eye on Wardel's cab. The cabdriver grunted and pulled out. He followed them, but they only went three blocks and stopped in front of a lit-up nightclub. Wardel had stopped to pay as the lovely, slender woman strode into the club with her furs hanging from one shoulder, chile.

Audrey stopped her cab across the street and asked the cabman as she paid, "Are them diamonds on that woman there?"

The cabman laughed. "On any other woman I would say they ain't, but I know for a fact that Miss Ruby don't wear nothin but the real thing! The only thing I know is false on her is that wig she wearin. Yes, mam! Them are diamonds! And the fur is real too! Whatever it is, it's real!" He drove off laughin.

Audrey didn't cross the street right away, she watched the people going in the club, heard the loud laughter, the music coming out. She didn't have much money, but there was a $10 bill stuck in a secret place of her purse she was savin for something for Woody. She crushed the $10 bill in her hand as she thought, "Should I?" She waited til she thought the place would be kinda full and went to the door of the club. The man at the door looked at her clothes, but, then, all kinds came to hear Miss Ruby sing. He took her money, gave her $5.00 in change and turned to the next customer. She moved into the dark club stayin near the wall at the back. One of the waitresses pushed and pointed her to a table almost behind a well-decorated post and took her order for a beer. Even just a beer, it was $2.00. She asked the waitress for a straw as she flashed by and when she finally got one sat there sipping slowly. She looked around for Wardel. Ahhhhhh, there he was, close to the stage talkin to a few ladies and men. Buyin them drinks! While she had to save her money for necessities! Two jobs! How long had she been workin to help him spend his money over a bar?! And on another woman!?

While she waited, Audrey began to notice other things, like women leavin with men after talkin a minute or two. Money changin hands. Women comin back in straightenin their clothes, pattin their purses. Hair messed up a little.

Some women lookin mad, some men lookin mad. Some women lookin glad, some men lookin glad. Everybody seemed to be very busy. Audrey understood what was happenin. She just shook her head in shame for them.

Then, suddenly . . . the stage lights came on, a man came out in a classy suit, tellin a few jokes. And then he introduced a band and Miss Ruby! "One of the last few nights here," he said as he waved his arms. "Miss Ruby is goin on to better things, leavin us here. But we will see and hear Miss Ruby, with that voice of hers again, I am sure! And now, ladies and gentlemen . . ." Audrey didn't hear the rest because of all the applause was goin on and her mind had snapped into the fact that Miss Ruby was leavin soon. Her man, her husband, Wardel, would be safe! Ooohhh, I can't tell you how her little starved heart gathered that little piece of hope and smothered it in her breast.

The lights on the stage made Miss Ruby more beautiful than she really was and them diamonds just sparkled their behinds off. Audrey was blinded by what she thought she saw. The woman sang and moved her body in them suggestive sexy ways. She threw that wig hair around like she was born with it on her head. Audrey watched the woman look over at Wardel on all the best lovin lines and she seen Wardel standin with a drink in his hand and his mouth wide in a possessive smile, drinkin that woman in. His eyes glittered like the diamonds on Miss Ruby's ears, throat and arm. Audrey's heart just sucked all the air out of her and dropped down to the soles of her feet, like a kite slowly fallin to earth when all the air is gone.

Audrey left after the first show. She was filled with fear, and envy, jealousy and pain. Her little teardrop eyes ran tears as she walked all the way back to her home. The one good thought was Miss Ruby was leaving. She picked her son up from her sister's house and finished walking home. Later, as she held her son in her arms and listened to his gentle snoring, she decided in her heart-tired way not to mention anything to Wardel.

But Wardel mentioned it to her a few days later. He came home to pack what he wanted to take with him that he hadn't already taken away. He was leavin with Miss Ruby!

Audrey cried, "But our house? Us?"

Wardel said, "Keep it . . . til I come back."

Audrey cried, "But our family? Our son?"

Wardel said, "Well. I love my son. But you his mother and you got a job. Two! You're gonna take care of him."

Audrey said, "But . . . what will we do? What will you do?"

As he walked out the door, Wardel said, "Live! I'll be living! I can get a job anywhere and I might not even have to do that!"

Audrey watched him get into his new car and drive away. She held her throat with both hands. She could barely breathe.

Now, sometimes what looks like bad luck is really good luck. Of course, she survived. I told her, "Look, you got a whole life you can build it like you want to. Go on back to school. I'll help you all I can. Soon your son be grown enough, send him to college too. You all can work your way through. Thirty-eight, thirty-nine or forty ain't old . . . if you got your health." But her heart hurt and it got in the way of her mind. Time passed though, and that helped.

One of the first things she did was go look at some diamond earrings. Ohhhhh, they was high-priced! She couldn't even begin to look at a necklace or a bracelet! Then, she went to look at furs . . . from outside the store, through the windows. They was priced high too.

After her heart got its wind back, she took a deep breath and decided she needed more money now, then she would get them diamonds and a fur, just like Miss Ruby, and win her a man too. Or, maybe, she would go find Wardel and get him back. I just shook my head cause who would want him . . . back? But that little money she made on both her jobs, one, a stock clerk, one, a sorter in a laundry, they didn't pay no money enough for her needs and her dreams. And our little town seemed dull with no future to it, with Wardel gone. So, she didn't exactly plan a way, she followed a way. A woman goin after her man.

She needed money, fast. She didn't want to do what she had seen the women in the club doing, she just didn't want to. But she wanted Wardel back so she decided she would go find him, get another job, get the things she was dreamin of, then come on back home. She checked the club to see where Miss Ruby had gone, took her son to her sister's, which I thought was the third wrong move. She rented her house out, leaving me in charge of care of it and the tenants. I was supposed to give the extra money to her sister for her son cause she didn't trust her sister to care for the house right. I'd a rather trust her with my house than my son, but . . .

She got her little short hair done . . . and packed. I

almost cried when she stood in front of me, come to say good-by. She looked so little and alone. And she was having trouble breathing. I told her, "You ain't thought about this good enough, Audrey. You just doin somethin cause it came up. Walkin into somethin blind. Life is more important than that. You got to know bout what you doin much as you can. You got a son countin on you. You countin on your own self to look out for you, but you ain't through thinkin bout what you doin yet. Life ain't so cold as to leave you completely out of it. Wait . . . and think!" That's funny, cause I was still givin my life to my mama, wonderin what life was ever gonna hold for me.

Audrey smiled in her little sad way, said, "I'm goin after my husband. I ain't comin home without my man. We are married." We said a few more things, but she was intent on going. Anyway, she left for the bus station, walkin, with the suitcase banging gainst her little thin hip. Bewildered.

She got to the new city, was a big place, and Miss Ruby and Wardel had already gone on. Didn't nobody know by that time where they was then. She followed confused directions and found her a little room she could afford and went straight out to get a job. She ended up a waitress in a little breakfast place. Didn't pay much, you know that, but she was nice and she made pretty good on tips. In time, she went to town and paid down on some diamond earrings and a fur. She was dreamin, hopin, and breathin. Well? What else you gonna do?

What she thought would take a year, turned into two years. She was still payin on the diamonds and the fur, but it just looked like she wasn't never gonna get them things out. The store man told her, "Go on, take em home with you. I trust you. You'll pay." But she didn't want to do that. "Thank you, sir, but I don't want to owe nobody. I got a son gonna be ready for college soon. I don't need no debts. I'll pay it off soon, I promise." The nice store man didn't stop chargin interest, which would have helped. Audrey just kept workin and payin.

Audrey was gettin tired of everything. No home, no son with her, no nothing. No money. Time was slow and she was gettin in a hurry. Once in a while she thought of the money them girls made on the streets, but that was too low-life for her.

She had noticed them streetworkin girls comin in and out of the restaurant and they seem to be havin a good time. She knew a couple of the girls, talked with em when she was at work, so she knew they weren't really havin a good time. Plenty shit goes on between the high, false laughters. Anyway, she was waiting for Wardel to come back through. She didn't want any other man to touch her body. She was keepin herself clean. She wanted respect. She actually still thought she would get her husband back.

She still hadn't seen Wardel and when she heard from me, I told her I had heard he had been killed over that same woman, Miss Ruby, when she found a new man and tried to quit Wardel and he didn't want to go. Dead, chile, in all his fine new clothes, sittin in his gettin-old Cadillac.

It had been some years, but she still grieved for her lost marriage. Now she would never have her same home again and her man was gone. She had no dreams then, except for them diamonds and that fur. More time went by while she thought her life stood still.

Then she start payin tention to a nice-looking young

man who came in to eat. Well, he made her pay tention to
him. He was a workin, quiet man. Name of Louis. Always
tended to his own business. He came in for a coupla
months, then he asked to take Audrey to a show. He was
bout fifteen years younger than she was and he sure was
good-looking. He could have anybody, she thought. She
sure didn't have nothin he had to lie to her for. So she
spent a little of her savings for a new little outfit and went.

Now, it had been a long time since Audrey had a man
in her life. Breathing wasn't no problem now. He came
back again and again. Soon they were talkin bout dreams
and things. Hers first, then his, all his. I don't know everything, but seemed he wanted to save enough money to go
to a smaller town, open a business, marry and settle down.
"That's my whole dream," he said. "That's all I was workin
for, til I met you. Now you have taken my heart and here I
am spending money I should be saving, to take you out
cause I'm falling in love with you."

So with all that love right in her lap, Audrey agreed
when he suggested they move in together in order to save a
little more money. He moved to her place, of course, and
she continued to pay her rent. She washed and tended to
his clothes, with love. She cooked for him, kept their bed
clean, kept the cubbards full. With her love and money. He
was savin. She wasn't. When she, hesitantly, told him that,
he asked her what she made and how much did she save.
She told him cause he was her man, wasn't he? She told
him about the diamonds and the fur. He laughed and
hugged her. He suggested they put their money together
and thereby they would both be saving more. He told her
just to keep on payin on her things, she'd get em out one

day and show them off when he took her home with him or to whatever place they decided to settle down and start their business. Their dream now. Chile, you talk about happy! Audrey was. Breathin real good.

Then, one day soon after that talk and the joint bank account had been opened, she came home to find Louis crying. Really crying! She rushed to him, asking him to tell her what was wrong. He wouldn't tell her at first, but after she pleaded a while, he told her, "It don't look like I'm ever going to have my dream. I'm not ever going to be able to do the things for you I want to, that you deserve. We're just saving too slow. It's going to take too long for us to get to be happy."

Well, I'm not going to try to tell you everything cause I don't know everything. I do know that about two months after he moved in, he was thinkin out loud, wishing Audrey made as much money as some of them women who were hangin out on the streets. "Just thinking," he said. Then, too, Audrey remembered hearing, over the time she had been workin round the prostitutes, "Women don't have no power over nothin but they ass and ain't no sense in givin it away if it be worth money to you! If you sittin on a gold mine, that's your power, your bizness! Ain't nobody else givin they bizness away! So sell it! Own your own body and money!"

To me, that's a lie, cause how can you own yourself when anybody can have you for a dollar or two? Your whole body! Even your face. ANYBODY!? And I bet, I know, a prostitute don't even get to keep that dollar! Now!

Soon Audrey had quit her little waitress job and was on the street with the other women she use to shake her head at! She was going on forty-four or forty-five years old. No, that ain't old, but it depends on what you plan to do! If it makes twenty-year-old women look like they are thirty in five years, forty in seven or eight years, fifty in ten years . . . what is it going to do to somebody who is already over forty? They say you can take care yourself and it won't ruin you, but I'll tell you what I think . . . rubber tires wear out in a year or so, when you usin them all the time. A woman ain't nothin but flesh and blood, what you think happens to her . . . thing? And all them different sizes? Chile, chile, chile.

I wondered what was happening to her breathin now. I pictured her little soul in her tiny body holdin its hands up to its throat, barely breathing at all.

They saved money. Least she did have sense enough to get her earrings and her fur out the stores. She even put down on a diamond bracelet and soon got that out. She didn't never get to wear em, cause Louis was too tired to take her out, and she was always workin when he went out for some "air." If she did put them on and take herself out to eat somewhere, people thought they were rhinestones. But she knew they were diamonds. That must have had to be enough. Her little sad eyes got sadder and sadder. Sometimes, at night, when she went to bed, alone, cause Louis worked on the graveyard shift now, she could hardly breathe at all.

Audrey got to know her new job pretty well. The other men and women didn't bother her too much cause she was older and quiet and no real competition. But she learned that women out there can be vicious and even real violent! You may think you goin to them for some pleasure, but you can get robbed, mugged, swindled, beaten and even killed! They don't just do that to strangers, they even do that to each other! They think they smart cause they don't pay taxes, but the lawyers who try to keep them out of jail get all the money the tax man don't! Louis was talkin "One more year, baby." He was still nice to her, she thought. He gave her little cheap gifts, but after all, it's the thought that counts . . . she thought.

After the fourth year with him, he said, "One more year, baby. We will be ready. We'll get us a brand-new car (he drove a sturdy old car), and drive to your home in style! We'll get us a fine wardrobe and everyone will know your ex-husband, Wardel, was a fool and what he missed by bein such a fool! (she had told him about that). But you're my woman now! One more year and we won't ever have to work for anybody again!"

Now, I got to stop here a minute. Every woman knows how she looks and how old she is. She got to know something bout how the world works! When you have a younger man, you got to wonder sometimes, "Why does he love me?" I'm not sayin he can't, cause it happens for true. But you got to do your own wonderin bout your own self's life! Cause it ain't usual. And a woman ought to ask herself why . . . if she a little bitty, tired, nice-looking, older woman who done already lost a man to a hot-looking woman. But even more than that! When I was growin up, my mama told me, and I knew it was true then and it's true now, if a man loves you . . . he don't want NO OTHER man to put his hands on you! And I don't care what all these new modern people lie to themselves about, I know that is true today!

Plus, Louis didn't take her nowhere either. Said, "We got a future. We'll go out when we have all the money we need." Money is a hard thing to mix up in your love. First get the love . . . then mix up the money if you want to. And love ain't just words, love is deeds. Good deeds. Anyway . . . Audrey smiled through her little tear-shaped eyes and went on out to "work."

Now, one thing . . . Audrey had come upon an older man who had a strange need. It took a long time for people to fill this need. It seems Audrey could do it in less time than most and it still took her bout three hours to do it. This man paid $20 every twenty minutes. And he needed it once a week, sometimes twice. The man must'a had a lotta money. Audrey decided she wanted to surprise Louis with a bundle of extra money when they made their grand exit out of town, so she put all this special money aside, saved it. She smiled when she thought of it. "We have only one more year and then I'll surprise him with all this money!" It made her happy to do that. Well, sometimes so many things in your life can be such a big ugly that a little ugly can make you kinda happy.

Audrey and her son, Woody, wrote each other through me and I told her how he was doin when I wrote. He was through school and tryin to start college, but he fell in some kinda love, got married. Audrey didn't come home. I didn't like her so much after that, but I tried to understand that she was tryin to live her life and was thinkin she was goin to do a lot for him when she DID come home. Only thing was, this was the time he needed her. He was tryin to live his life and he needed a grown mother or father to help him learn how to think. I don't know. It wasn't my business noway.

My mama had died by then and I was alone, so Audrey and Woody was kinda my family. I tried to help him, but I wasn't his mama. That's who he needed. He wasn't bad, he just didn't have no way to know things, I guess. I guess maybe Audrey thought he had a few years he could lose cause he was young, but his mama didn't have them years to lose no more. She was at a last minute scramble tryin to make money and hold Louis. Mothers shouldn't count on bein able to do the important things later in their life, cause kids die young sometimes.

Well, anyway. Louis had to take trips to his "home" now and again. He never did take the bank savings book and no money Audrey knew of except what he needed for the trip. He talked about their marriage, but she had to work and they/he couldn't take the time off.

Audrey did call home at least once a month though. When she discovered she had a grandchild she did rush home to see it and her son and his wife. She felt like a natural woman. She felt good. She didn't take too much money, but she took some of her surprise money and gave it to her son to help out with his family. She could tell he was not happy with his wife or life, but Audrey was not too happy with hers either and didn't know what to do about either one. I was pretty mad about the way her son was left out, but I knew Audrey didn't know what she was doin. Hell, how many people do?

Audrey was going on forty-nine years old. Each "one" year had turned into several. She was showing her age, but it wasn't really her age, it was her life. She was going out in the wind, rain, knee-deep in the snow, all night (she hated to go home to a empty house). Standing, in the summer, out in the heat of the sun that built up all day and lasted all night. She was better than a mailman. But she loved Louis and loved to see him smile at the money she brought home, which was less and less cause Audrey was getting older and older. So he smiled and she worked. Out in the weather, alone each night and you know what can happen to a woman, a person in the dark of night. And they saved money.

Finally, the time came. They were going to leave in one week. They had thousands in the bank, the bankbook said so and Audrey knew it because she loved to deposit the money in the bank and hear the teller say what the balance was.

Louis "let" her talk him into getting the new car sooner than they had planned. She wanted a Cadillac like Wardel had, but Louis wanted a Buick. "I don't want no pimp's car," he said, "I'm not a pimp! I'm going to be a husband. Husbands have Buicks and Oldsmobiles." So he got a brand-new off-the-floor Buick. She was so excited, she wrote me, "I'm gonna celebrate my fiftieth birthday by coming home in a brand-new Buick!" I know she smiled and her eyes lit up.

Now . . . Number 1, Audrey was a woman. Number 2, Audrey ain't never really had too much . . . from birth. Number 3, Her heart was in need, her mind was in need, her soul longed to be happy. Truly happy. She musta thought, "I'm almost fifty years old now. I ain't got too much longer to live maybe. At least I can be happy these next few little years." She musta smiled through her teardrop eyes . . . ignorin her difficulty in breathin, and counted money harder.

Finally, it was her last night to be in the big city. Tomorrow they would leave for home, for good. To her grandchildren (there was one more now, though Woody and his wife had separated), to her own home. She thought, "How lucky I am to have a young, hardworkin man, a house rented out, a new car and a savings account. Yea, and a diamond bracelet and earrings and a fur. PLUS, I got a fat sock filled up with $8000 I have saved to surprise Louis with. I'll open it up on the road when we stop to eat or somethin!" She looked forward to his happy face when he heard about the extra money. That night she said to herself, "This the LAST night I'm gonna have to get out here and face all these crazy people. I'm tired of em, TIRED of em. I hate em. I'm even bout to hate myself! I don't never want another man's hands on me but my husband's." But Louis had suggested they should get every last dime before they left. He smiled down at her. "I want us to work this one last night, baby." So, out she went for her one last night of work.

It was a dark, dark Thursday night, streets kinda empty. Snow was on the ground and Audrey was standin knee-deep in it. She was huddled up, shiverin, in a thick coat and low boots the snow kept fallin in. She just noticed all the car lights automaticly, then she saw Louis in his brand-new Buick. He drove slowly by the spot where she worked. She bent down to see him better, thinkin he would stop and they could go on home. He bent low in the car so he could see her better, and waved to her. She could see his smile in the flickerin lights. He kept drivin slow for another little piece. She started walkin toward him, then the car picked up speed and moved smoothly on up the road.

Her excitement was so much she forgot the cold snow, she thought, "Hell, we already got bout $32,000 saved and I got that other $8000, what I need to stand out here for? She pulled her coat tight around her little thin shoulders and trudged through the snow . . . home.

The apartment was neat, but Louis always helped keep it that way. Her bags sat by the closet where she had left them, but his were gone. "Did he put his in the car already?" *Her heart began pounding lightly in her breast.* She turned to see if his things were gone from the bathroom. *Her heart, not wanting to, but pounding just a little louder. Her breathing coming difficult and a little faster.* Tears seemed like they had been waiting to run from her tear-shaped eyes. His things were gone from the bathroom. She rushed to the drawers, pulled them open . . . Empty! She backed onto the bed, holdin her throat, choakin on her sobs, holdin them back because this just couldn't be true! Something rattled as she sat on the bed. A note.

The note said, "It was good for both of us while it lasted. Don't look for me. I won't be there. Louis." No love, no sincerely yours. No affection. No Nothin.

Now, he had left all her valuables behind, the diamond necklace, the bracelet, the fur. Her $8000 was safe. But he had taken the most important things, the hope, the love, the dreams, the future. She was empty, empty as she lay there for the rest of that night starin at the gray ceiling and the walls closing in on her. *Barely breathing at all.*

Audrey stayed there, like that, for two days, until Sunday. Then she slowly and sadly picked up her bags, said good-by to the apartment where I guess she had been happy, and left. "I'm goin home anyway! This ain't my life no more. Never was a life! I'm sick of bein a got-damned fool!" She went home on a bus.

She went straight to her sister's and heard all the excuses about Audrey's house not bein kept up and the fact that I didn't send her sister all the money I collected. Well, I didn't. I gave it to her son, Woody who gave it to his father-in-law who was the one kept his two kids since his wife was gone. Now! Audrey patted her $8000 she had put in her brassiere. She did not mention it to her sister. Wants and needs were everywhere. She looked at her sister's man who was a gambler. A big ole dumb thing with no manners, no money and no job. She started to think, "He sure ain't nothin!" Then she thought of herself and her men. "Well, at least Louis was clean and worked. A liar and a thief ain't all that come in a package. The best liars don't show it at all."

She was anxious to see her son. Didn't nobody know exactly where he was since him and his wife broke up, but I knew Woody went to see his kids three or four times a week. Her sister said, "Sure was glad they granddaddy took em in cause I didn't have no place for em." Audrey found out where the grandfather lived, then decided to sleep one night and go over there. She slept in her clothes on a broken couch, using her suitcase for a pillow so she could keep her hands on all her valuables. She planned to come to my house after that night.

The next morning she went to find her grandchildren. "I'm late, but they still my grandchildren. If I help anybody now, it will be them. I think." She carried her bag with her.

Her sister asked, "You taken your bag with you?"

"Yes, I might find a room."

"What's wrong with you stayin here? I could use the rent money!!"

"I'll see what happens. I don't want to bother you all."

"Won't bother us none. You can help with the food cause we broke for a minute. I'm your sister. You know I ain't gonna let you down."

"We'll see," Audrey said over her shoulder as she walked out the door carrying her bag.

Her sister followed her, "Well, don't give somebody else your money. I can sure use it. We done hit a bad luck streak. What's in that bag you got to carry it with you?"

Audrey stopped, turned around, "Nothin. Just everything I got to show for ten years' livin. Just nothin."

Her sister backed into her house, "Go on then. It be bout seven blocks. Bett'a try to eat over there, cause, you know . . . See you later."

Audrey was the most lonely, saddest, forlorn, miserable woman you have ever seen. She walked, leaning to one side with the weight of the suitcase. Her little worn feet in the cheap shoes she had bought, savin money for her dream. One of em had split down the back of the heel durin her travelin. Her little cheap coat from the secondhand store had an uneven hem and bits of the lining hung down below the imitation wool or whatever. She hadn't bought anything new for herself cause she thought she was savin for the "Dream." She thought she was holdin her head up, but it was hangin down and the tear-shaped eyes looked ahead of her with no joy, no hope, and as far as she could see . . . no future.

She walked all the way, passin her own old home. She stopped in front of it, sat her suitcase down, just staring at the house. The house need work. The TLC kind of work. All she could say was, "Wardel dead. House dyin. I'm dyin." *It was getting real hard to breathe.* She whispered, "Well, house, I'm home. I got a little money. We'll get you fixed up." She picked up the suitcase and kept on walkin on her way.

Audrey came to a big, old two-storied house. Had a little storefront to what would have been a basement otherwise and the huge backyard was full of all kinds of things that looked like junk. She walked slowly up to the steps. "Poor kids. Poor everybody. Poor me." She took a deep breath and struggled up them steps with that suitcase. She would have laughed had she not been so tired, so disgusted with life. "Here I am worryin over a suitcase cause it has a fur and a few diamonds in it. Probly ain't worth nothin. But they one of the reasons I'm in this place in life. I can't let em go now! I paid too much for em!" She reached the top of the stairs. "I ain't gonna let me go no more either!"

She was startin to ring the bell when she heard a child screaming inside the house. She rang. She heard somebody crying and a voice shouting, "You are gonna eat that cereal, NOW! You better!" Then the door opened. A slender, graying, older man stood there in a apron. His face all frowned up, but his eyes bright. "Yes, mam! What can I do for you?"

"Good mornin. I came to see the kids."

"What kids? Whose kids? Who are you?"

"My son's kids. Woody's children."

"That your son? Well, you ain't got much! And I can't say nothin cause I ain't got much either! He married my daughter and she gone too! Come on in. What's that you got there? Here, let me help you. Come on in, I told you. Have some cereal with us. If these your grandchildren, see can you make em eat!"

Audrey walked in slowly, followin the man carryin her bag. He was medium height, slim, but kinda solid and strong. Caramel-colored. Needed a shave or had a beard of mingled gray and black hair. Was slightly bald in front or his hair just grew far back from his face. Medium full pretty lips and a nose with a flat bridge. Then, his eyes. His eyes were golden brown, large, soft and warm. Audrey smiled her hesitant smile and turned to look at her grandchildren.

They were not dressed so neatly and there were a few little holes in their T-shirts, pants and rompers, but they were clean. Their little stomachs were plump and round, filled with food. Their mouths were smiling and their eyes were bright.

"EAT." Audrey almost jumped as the man strode past her, dropping the suitcase. The children didn't jump, they were used to him. They were staring, smiling at Audrey. Audrey's heart smiled back.

"They're gonna eat, sir." Audrey smiled and took her coat off, throwin it over a chair. He took it and hung it in the hall on a coat hook. "You're gonna eat, aren't you?" She began to feed them and they began to eat, still lookin up at her in wonder.

Later, over coffee, they talked. It seems Woody and Burgess' daughter, Alma, had separated. Woody came over pretty often, bringin a few dollars.

"I don't know what we did wrong, but my daughter don't seem to want to do nothin but live in them bars. And Woody is right in there with her, but he does work. I don't know what she does. I'm scared to think about it. Anyway, these my grandchildren and I got tired of seeing em left here and there and everywhere, so I went and got em and brought em on home with me. I got this big, ole empty house. Used to be a home. Now, it's a home again. I just hope I live, God willin, til they can do for themselves . . . or their mama and papa grow up and get some sense. I told my daughter, 'Don't bring nare another one, cause I can't take it!' I'm stretching every which way I can, and, thank God, we makin it."

Audrey shook her head, sadly. "Where is your wife?"

"My wife is dead. About eight years now. This would have made her happy, to have her grandchildren around, but her daughter would have made her sad. Soooo . . . . . But where you been?"

Audrey sat back in her chair, folded her hands in her lap, smiled at Burgess and said, "I been tryin."

"Tryin to what?"

"Tryin to live. To survive. To be . . . happy. To breathe."

Burgess smiled, "Well, you look alright. Little peaked
. . . and sad. Like you ain't been winnin in the game of
life." He reached for more coffee. "But, hell, almost the
whole world looks like that."

Audrey smiled weakly. "I'm gettin out the game of life."

"Where you goin? Got to stay in the game! Game won't
let you quit!"

"Well, I'm goin to try to help my son and my grandchildren now, with their lives." Her voice became almost
unbearably sad. "I'm old."

Burgess laughed. "You ain't old! You just tired, is all."
He looked around the kitchen. "I could use some help
around here. These kids need a mother's touch."

Audrey's eyes were pleadin and grateful, chile. Her
smile went deeper.

He continued, "Where you livin?"

"I'm goin to my friend's house (That's me!) and then I
got to find a place while I get my own place fixed up."

"Your friend a man?"

"A woman friend."

"Stay here! This is a big house. I got rooms I don't
never go in, don't need."

"I could rent one while I fix my house up. Then I could
be around the babies. I want to be round my grandchildren.
I . . . missed a big part of Woody's growin up. It's probly
my fault he don't know how to have a real family . . . a
real home."

Burgess shook his head slowly. "My wife and I stayed
together, made a real home for my daughter and she still
don't know how to make a real home for her kids. Don't
nobody know where to put the blame. And you don't need

to rent a room nowhere, you can HAVE one of mine. You can use the money you were goin to spend on rent, for food. I make enough to keep things goin. Fact is, I'm sposed to be on a job right now."

Audrey sighed and asked, "What kind of work you do?"

"I do a little carpenterin, lay carpet and fix appliances round the house. Got a little junk in my yard I fix up and sell sometime tween my other jobs." He smiled. "I'm good! Just ain't gonna work no regular job, cause I got my grandbabies and I want to know they are taken care of. I don't want no liars, thieves, whores and dope addicts nor unwed mothers and fathers in my family if I can help it. So I try to monitor everything I can where they're concerned."

Audrey frowned, her nerves jumped at what he said, but what he said was what she wanted for her grandchildren too. She said, "Well, I got a job for you. You can fix up my house. It needs a lot. I'll help with everything and live here til I can move into my own house. I can try to do a better job on my grandchildren than I did on my own child. And I got in my mind a little dream left. I always wanted a store. A little grocery store.

"With appliances for sell in it! Good! We're off to a good start!"

And they were. He never tried to have sex with her. All Audrey did was work in that house and yard and love her grandchildren. She still had that bewildered look about her, but we talked sometimes and I told her I thought she was doin somethin real and decent with her life now. I said, "Audrey, all most of your life you ain't never just sat down and thought about what you really wanted for yourself. You just took things that came up. You've done a few things that

came out right, but you sure have done some things that
have left you nothing to show for your life but pain. You
got some years left, I blive, you got to be more careful with
yourself. Don't get no older and still be confused about life.
You ain't got time." She listened to me cause she knew I
cared about her.

Several months later, Audrey's house was finished. Burgess'
yard and storefront was cleaned up and neat. Audrey
laughed more, fattened up a little, got to wear her diamonds and fur cause Burgess took her out on the town to
hear jazz sometimes, or some wonderful blues singer. She
began to have a life. I was glad to have my little friend back
and see her doin so well.

Now . . . I had always known Burgess. He had always
been married and a snotty little man that tended to his
business. He wasn't loose with his love or time. But I noticed as time passed he was pattin, or huggin, or reachin out
to help Audrey. And lots of love was surroundin them
grandkids of theirs, so I knew some of it had to spill over
on them grandparents.

One night they finished up the work at Audrey's house
and they lit the fireplace and sat down on the floor drinkin
a little warm beer and talking. This was just fore she was
goin to move into her own house. Now, Audrey was doin
better, but her heart was still sad. This a little woman who
never had had no real love. And EVERYBODY knows
how most EVERYBODY feel bout this love business. Ain't
that true?! Give me a 'Amen.' I'm old now for sure, and
don't want nobody, but I stillllll miss love.

Anyway, they was talkin and it sounded to Audrey like
he was tryin to say somethin special to her. Like he wanted
her to stay with him. She took a sip of her beer, tilted her
head and said, "Burge, there are some things I have not told
you about me."

He took a drink of his beer and said, "I know that."

She took another sip. "I . . . I been . . . a . . . a
prostitute."

He leaned back on his elbows. "I know that."

She turned to look at him.

He went on, "I always knew that from when you first
came home. But, now, I know you. All that in your past is
your business. If I had thought you was no good, I wouldn't
let you stay round them children. Their life is more important to me. For whatever reason you did anything, you
didn't become a prostitute because you liked it, did you? Or
cause you was born to be one or nothing else I can think of,
did you? Maybe you was stupid for a minute. Lots of people get that way sometime. But I blive you are what you
were in the beginnin and the way you are now. I don't blive
I'd ever want to get married again, but . . . maybe I will.
And you feel the same way bout OUR grandchildren as I
do. They need a family. We are a family. Sooooo . . . I
never thought I'd have a virgin anyway. I married mine and
. . . she gone." His voice faded on out. Then, he asked,
"Did you do EVERYTHING or . . . ANYTHING for
money?"

Audrey whispered, barely breathing, soft as the sound
of the flames in the fireplace, "No. I did some, but I
wouldn't, couldn't do anything and everything. I just

thought I was makin a dream. I didn't know I was spendin one. And my son too. Lost him."

Audrey cried softly. Til the flames burned low. Burgess let her.

Then . . . later . . . she cried in his arms, still sittin front of that fireplace. And that was that. Audrey still had trouble breathin, but only a little trouble breathin after that night cause her life was better than it had ever been. But she was scared bout her needless past keepin her from a future.

One thing Audrey told me when we was alone one day. "I don't think Burgess gonna marry me. I'm shamed of what I did to myself and to my son. I don't think I want to use this body again. I don't blive I will ever have sex again. It ain't never brought me no real joy in my life."

I told her, "Listen here, woman. That thing ain't sick. Ain't scared of the dark. Didn't tear or break. It done gone through everything you put it through. And that thing is still lookin for a home. This here is a different kind of man, Burgess is. You done took the two wrong ones. Where is your good sense? Ain't you ever gonna do somethin RIGHT for yourself? At your age? You don't think you can love Burgess, don't marry him. But if you think you love him . . . you better jump up on your horse, try to get Burgess and head for the sunset, cause its sunsettin time in your life."

Today? Well, they done all moved into her house. Then they fixed his house up and rented all the rooms out, doing real good. They fixed that storefront up and Audrey got her grocery store and Burgess got "a few household appliances" in it too. The children got a home. Woody comin over more and more to help raise his own kids. Audrey's face still looks a little scared sometimes when I catch her lookin off into space. But with all the love surroundin her, she been breathin real strong and steady. I blive she got the kind of future she wants now. At last, she did it all for herself. And them kids, too!

And I got to go, cause I likes goin over there to help. You know they my family too. We done made us a family, chile! Burgess got plenty old friends. Some of em is single and lonely . . . like me. I look good and healthy. Took care of myself. I see em smilin at me! One of em makes my breathin feel kinda funny too. I loved my mama and I ain't sorry I spent the most part of my life carin for her. That was MY choice, my life. But if I was to have somebody, get some love, I'd be mighty happy more. It ain't never too late. You see Audrey gettin her own life now. Long as you're breathing, chile. So, I'm busy. Gettin some more of mine. So . . . Bye now.

The Way It Is

Now there is one thing I am sure about in life and that is you can't be sure of nothing. That's just the way it is. I am sure about something else too . . . and that is I am sure I don't want to do nothin but what I WANT to do. No time. At all. So don't ask me to. And that's just the way that is too!

I am almost seventy years old and I done had me a pretty good life. Oh, it had some hard times in it. My family was poor and that's how I grew up . . . poor. Watched my father work hisself to death for us kids in the South. We was five of us. Then I watched him work hisself to death in the North. He still stayed poor. Then . . . I watched my mother and older brothers work to support us

til each one of us young ones grew up and was ready to get out in life and make our own way. That's just the way it was. I don't care how well off anybody is, livin is work. Ain't no rose gardens less you till, plant, water, cut back, prune, clean and take care your own. Work at it. That's just the way it is. I'm tellin you!

I married when I was bout seventeen. I wasn't lazy and tryin to get away from home, I just fell in love. Ohhhhh, yes. Clifton. I call him Cliff. He was a good man. A good man. We loved together and we worked together. The first ten years was the hardest. But we made it. We wanted a baby, but the only one we got didn't live. He died when I birthed him. Ambilical cord round his neck. My son. He died. Didn't never no more ever come. But we loved each other, Cliff and me, so we just went right on workin together on our married life. It was a good life. He was sweet. Always bringin me little presents. Perfume, scarfs, pretty nightgowns. Cheap, but pretty gowns. Last bout through four nights of our lovin. We was passion, honey.

We fussed and things, but he never hit me but once. Slapped me cause some man was at the bus stop how I got to work. Me and that man talked every morning, laughing and such. Well, good grief! On cold, early, drab, dreary mornings on your way to a job you don't like noway, the world don't always look so good, so a good laugh and a little easy talk makes the world look better. Didn't mean nothin! Cliff, hiding round the corner watchin me! Peekin! Stalkin!

When I got home that one evening, both my arms full of bags of groceries for him to eat, Cliff slapped me so hard

I peed . . . almost shit, so I know it can be true when somebody say they got the . . . stuffin slapped out of them! I didn't say nothin, couldn't, but I didn't like it and could feel how I didn't like it all the way down to my toes. I was mad! While I was cookin and cryin (very quietly), he was walkin round with his chest all poked out. I was thinkin, wonderin if this was the kind of life I wanted to live all my life. I knew it wasn't! I knew this was a real important thing for me. See, almost everything you do sets your life. I wasn't goin to let Cliff get set in the ways of hittin on me!

After we had eaten dinner, I sat a big pot of water on to boil. He was listenin to the radio, readin the paper as best he could, then he went on to bed with me still messin round in the kitchen. He come to say he was goin and put his hand, that hand that had slapped me, on my behind, rubbin it. That made me madder. I knew he was thinkin we was gonna make some hot passion love that night cause he thought I was feelin sorry and shamed and wanted to make up to him. Wellll, I did want to make up to him, cause he my husband and I love him, but I don't want to make up to him less I'm sure he know how to love me back! So I took a long time til I knew he had dozed off to sleep.

I took my little bath and put on my best nightgown, such as it was. Then I got that water off the stove. (I had had to keep addin water to it that had boiled away.) Oh, it was hot, hot! Then I went to that bed and held it over his body. I left the blankets on him cause I didn't want to burn him too hard, just enough to teach him my lesson. I tapped him on his shoulder to wake him up. (Sides I want him to be able to move out from under that burnin water.) He opened his eyes and I waited til they focused on me . . . good.

I poured that water all over him and got out the way. He got up huffin and puffin and shoutin. I threw that pot on the floor, hard, to get his attention. When I had it, I said, "Clifton, I love you. You is usually sweet and gentle with me. But long as you live, don't you never put your hand on me to hurt me again less you ready to leave me, cause I ain't stayin with no man who don't treat me like I'm his own body just like them marriage vows say!"

His mouth was hangin open and his eyes was poppin out his head. The blanket was steamin where he had left it behind. I took the pot back to the kitchen, got the dry, clean sheets (we only had two sets) and a pad. I stripped the bed, said "Help me." He jumped to it. We made the bed together (for the first time). He hung the blanket in the bathroom to dry while I went to get my Bible and find the words they say at the weddin. We covered ourselves up with towels and coats and things, then we sat up in bed while I read the weddin ceremony over again, leanin on the "Cherish" and "One body. Treat it as you do your own." Honey, we stayed in the bed the whole weekend. Lovin, eatin, talkin and all them good things. We slept in each other's arms. He understood me. He never did hit me again and we were married over fifty years! We loved each other. That's just the way it was.

My husband was good to me, in all ways, chile. That's just the way it was. I didn't want for nothin he could afford. It got to where we both cooked after the water episode. Most times he help me in the kitchen so we could both get to listen to the radio and, later on, look at TV after we got one. He bought me the best he could. Well, I was good to him too! You see?

Anyway, after we was married bout fifteen or sixteen years, we had done saved up to buy us a house. It wasn't much to anybody but us, but we sure loved our house. It made itself like a member of our family. We had a garden, food and flowers, birds and things. We both had family, but they was kind of stretched out and we liked to keep to ourselves anyway. It seemed our love got along better that way.

Soooooo . . . all in all, we had a good life. We watched each other change with the years. He sure did watch me change, and it looked like I did the most changing. This world is fixed so women look like they do the most changin gettin old. They got so many ways for women to get ugly sometimes. Why they want old to mean ugly? Anyway, we sure did grow ooooold together.

We grew so old he got sick and I lost my Cliff. Lost my Cliff, you all. Oh, I can't tell you, the hole, the great big, empty body I carried around, without him. My right arm, my right hand, leg and body was gone. Gone. Well, I had had him fifty years. It could have been less, much less. So I had to satisfy myself with that. And since I blive in the Bible and God, I told myself I would see and be with my husband again. Yea, I blive it. And it helped sometime.

But, otherwise, I felt good. We had taken such good care of each other that I felt good. I looked good even for my age. Oh, a few little things always go wrong, wear out, that's just the way it is. But on the whole, I felt good. I walked plenty, didn't need to run. Ate good. More raw vegetables and such what they say is good for you, cause I didn't have the heart to cook much. Maybe a pot of beans or greens and corn bread on a Monday and stretch that out over a week. Maybe bake a chicken on Sunday, stretch that too.

When I got tired of my own fixins, I could afford to take myself out to eat. That's just the way we planned it for both of us. We planned early to be able to do special, good things for ourselves when we got too old to work and was livin out the rest of our lives. It's terrible to get old and have NO money. Be poor and too old to work. Save me Jesus! So we planned to be able to do some of whatever we wanted. So that's just naturally the way I do it.

Oh, but my chile, I must tell you, I was so lonely. So lonely sometime I wanted to hurry up and get on way from here and join Cliff. But I wasn't sure that was gonna happen, so I didn't rush myself. Sometimes I'd turn to talk to him when I watched TV or came into my house, callin his name, "Cliff? Cliff?" Never no answer anymore. I was low, low and still empty. Hadn't filled myself up with myself yet. Couldn't.

I got a friend, Tonya. (She gave herself that name.) She knows lots of older men who live over there where she does, in the senior citizen place. She tried introducing me to some of them men. I did kind of like one, for company. But a week later, before we even had a chance to really talk, he died. That was enough for me. I'm tired of death.

So, life goes on, it surely do. One day I was sittin in a restaurant eating a evening meal and this man came up to my table. I looked at him and thought, "Who is this old man?" til I remembered I was old too. He said, "Good evenin, mam." And I thought, "Mam?" See, I'm old, but that young girl that once was me is still runnin round, livin, in my head, won't leave. Sides, I don't want her to.

I said, "Good evenin" back.

He smiled and said, "I see you in here sometimes when I come here." (I said to myself, "Ain't no other way to do it." But I smiled.) He said, "You are always by yourself. I'm always lookin out for you, but you don't come too regular." I smiled, but I really wanted to eat my food while it was hot. He went on talkin. "My name is Collin. I promised myself the next time you came in, if you was still alone, I was going to ask you could I join you at your table and treat you to your dinner."

I just looked in his face cause I didn't know what to say. This was like romance and I wasn't in practice with a stranger. He pointed to a chair and smiled. "Can I sit here with you if I behave myself?" I smiled and nodded yes. As Collin sat down, he said, "I'm a perfectionist and that's why I like you. You look like perfection." I felt a little uncomfortable, but I smiled. I guess I wasn't listenin either. I didn't let him pay for my meal, and he didn't put up much fight about it. We parted friendly like.

Over the next couple of months I went there to eat a couple of times. He was usually there and I got used to eatin and talkin with him. We went for short walks as he said we should after we ate. I knew that, I did that, walked every day after I ate. But what the hecks, let him go on and live. I never did invite him to my home though. I don't know why, just didn't.

I kinda thought I was lucky finding and meetin a older man who was single, without the help of my friend Tonya.

She always tellin me bout how much they socialize, sex and all. She always talkin bout sex. Welllll, I reckon it ain't over til it's over! She always lookin for somebody, a man. She tell me bout some of the men who love her but can't get . . . ready. Or she engaged one day and next week he dead, or gone on to some other older woman's apartment. Or bout the retired preacher who done tasted all the ladies and got nerve to have three or four women. All such stuff as that goin on. Now, I wasn't thinkin bout no sex, I don't think. I had done had the best and I am more interested in Quality than Quantity. And the one time I had let her lead me into one of them old men, I told you, he died. But here I was minding my own business and here come a man out the blue lookin for me! Life won't leave you alone, chile, til you're dead.

Welllll, Collin didn't have a home of his own. His wife had died and his kids were livin in it now. He lived in a small co-op apartment. I didn't see how he could do that. I wouldn't give up my home. It was still part of my family, you know. But everybody got to do their own thing. Anyway, he commence to coming over to my house and I cook dinners and we sit around watchin TV and talkin. I liked that. My loneliness wasn't so hard to bear no more. The man could be sweet and make me feel so comfortable.

I don't know how to tell you. I thought I had already been through the change and had my good sense in place, but we got married because I thought we could make these last few years good for each other. Lawdy clawdy! Married! Chile, chile, chile.

Now we had never talked about it before for some reason, but the man, my new husband, Collin, had a real big idea of what a man was and what a woman was supposed to be. When he was taking me out to eat the first week or so, he said we was on our honeymoon. After that, he said he wanted more home cookin, so I smiled and, on Sunday, baked a chicken and made other little one day things. Monday I cooked beans and rice with corn bread and served some of that chicken. Tuesday we had the same, a little salad and all. Wednesday, the same, a little Jell-O dessert and all, you know. Thursday, the same. I smiled and served it and washed the dishes all by myself cause he was on HIS honeymoon, you know. The next Sunday I baked a roast beef with little one day things: baked potato, salad, green beans or something like that. Everything was goin long alright, I thought.

He had a few things that worried me, but I know what married life means, so I didn't worry too hard. Like, if I ironed his shirt, he would tell me to do certain parts of it over. "I like my things ironed perfectly smooth," he would say. Even when I made the bed, when he got into it later, he would say, "This sheet is wrinkled, Melly. I like my sheets perfectly smooth." Well, okay. He like me to run his bathwater. Well, that ain't too much work, so I did it. But when he said, too many times, "This water too hot! I like the tempture perfect at the body tempture." I began to think one of us was crazy and I didn't want it to be me.

Anyway, soon after, I cooked a good meal on Sunday and we had the same thing on Monday. We had roast beef and greens and corn bread with a few additions for change, you know? He mentioned the way I baked my roast could be better, but I let that slide cause I didn't give a hot damn. I been eatin my roasts all my life. I'm satisfied.

Then, after I washed dishes, I handed him a dish towel, cause I was kinda tired from doin all this for two people and he said, "I don't want to dry no dishes." I looked at him handin me the towel back, and said, "Well, sweetheart." (Cause he really was. Old as he was, when the lights went out, he was more than I needed. But it seemed like it was a job well done, stead of real love given back and forth like I was used to with Cliff.) I said, "Well, sweetheart, you can wash them if you rather do that."

He said, "I'm a man. I ain't sposed to be doin no kitchen work. This is woman's work!"

I said, as I still held the towel out to him, "You don't have no job that is 'man's work' to do. So what are you gonna do for your part?"

He said, "I done already worked all my life. I'm through. It's time for me to rest and read, poke around and sleep, watch TV, go for walks and things like that."

I said, with a smile so it wouldn't look like I was mad cause we was still on our honeymoon but the moon was goin down, chile, "You didn't spend all your years workin for me. So now, you need to try to help me make a home for you. We sposed to work this here stuff together."

He smiled. "Your husband, your FIRST husband, spoiled you! He loved you more than you loved him. He didn't make you take the responsibility of bein a whole woman!"

I said, smile gone now, "Me and my FIRST husband loved each other. Wasn't no lovin more or lovin less. We just loved. And he was so much man he didn't need pieces of me to make up for what he lacked." I was talkin bout my

home, my stove, my bed, my refrigerator, my washin machine, my yard and everything else Collin didn't have.

He turned to go, sayin, "Well, things are diffrent now.
You my wife. I'm the man of this house. He don't live here
no more."

I said to God, "Stop me! Stop me! Don't let me put this
fryin pan up side this man's head. I might kill him cause he
old, and I accidently smash one of them blood vessels that
done wrapped itself too tight round his brain. Help me,
God!"

In a flash my life passed before my eyes and at the end I
saw myself with him and I saw myself alone . . . again. I
thought of bein alone again and I was glad! I said to him,
"No, no, YOU don't live here no more. I'm sick of all your
perfection mess. You go on back to that perfect apartment
of yours and do your own perfect cookin, perfect cleanin,
perfect washin and perfect ironin. Cause I didn't take care
of myself, with my husband's help, all these years, restin up
to take care of you!" Chile, the marriage wasn't even three
weeks' old! We was still on our honeymoon! But the moon
was going down fast!

He tried to talk to me, his voice done changed and he
was treatin Ms. Woman like maybe she was important after
all! But it didn't matter no more, no how. I was busy packin
his perfect clothes in his imperfect bags.

He said, "My apartment is gone, Melly, you know that.
And I don't see why we can't take care this better than that.
This ain't nothin but a little family tiff. We're sure grown
enough to settle our marriage without breakin it up. People
will say . . ."

Still packin his stuff, I said, "I'm no perfectionist! I don't care what people say. You got a place you gave to your son. It's still your house. You worked all your life for that one. I worked for this one." Then I sat his bags by the front door, said, "Come get the rest of your things tomorrow. I'll have em ready."

He left, still talkin bout what we could do, should do. But it had already taken me seventy years (almost) to know that, and I was doin what I knew I should do. Yes, mam. I watched him walk away, leanin sideways with that suitcase and his perfection behind, and I can tell you right now, what he did, makin love, when the lights go down low, didn't even make me have second thoughts. My lights is turned up way more than they are turned down low!

My life had been peaceful, safe, quiet and restful. I had done invited trouble in and I had done put trouble out. Life sure ain't borin no matter how old you are!

That night I was layin up in my bed looking at my TV and eatin some good candy out of a box I have, when Tonya called to see "How the newlyweds were doin." I told her what all had happened and that Collin was gone, I had done put him out.

She said, "Melly! Are you crazy? I know that man. That's a good man! You betta hold on to him, girl! And you told me he can still make love? Good!? And you gonna let him go!? Are you a fool, Melly!?"

Before I hung up the phone, I told her, "Listen, Tooonya! I don't need no fool to be tellin me that I am a fool! You ain't even asked me why I put him out. I know when I'm happy and when I'm not. And ain't nothin hangin off a man gonna decide my life for me. I done had aplenty of that from Cliff! And it was better than good! And ain't no woman, old as you are and still flappin her legs and can't get enough of nothin gonna tell me I'm a fool bout how I run my life! Now, let me let you go talk to your man fore he dies or fore you die! Good-by, Toooonya!" And I hung up the phone and went back to lookin at TV and eatin out of my box of candy.

I got my divorce as soon as I could. I was at the age where I could die any minute and there were people in my family I wanted to leave my things to. Now! My sister got children and grandchildren that are my nieces and nephews and I got some favorites of my own!

The lady at the divorce desk looked at me so strange because I am almost seventy years old. She ask me, "Are you sure, at your age, you want to do this?"

I answered her, "It's because I am my age that I want to do this. Every minute counts. Young woman, if I don't know what I'm doin now, you at your age can not tell me cause you don't know what you're doin yet. If you did, I blive you'd be sitting in some college somewhere instead of at this desk depending on somebody for your pay. When I was your age, we couldn't . . . didn't have the same op- portunities you got now. You need to fix your life early so you don't have to stay with nobody you don't want. Now . . . where do I sign?"

Then . . . I went home to my house that is my family, ate me some string beans and roast turkey and dressing with candied yams. I'm gonna stretch it all week . . . cause I feel like it. Tomorrow I may take myself out to that new restaurant I read about . . . cause I am able. All my life I been with somebody, and that was good. Now I am alone, but that ain't the end of the world. That can be good too! I can do whatever I want to . . . within reason. May take one of them senior citizen boat trips and honeymoon with my own soul. There is all different kinds of love in this world. May go get one of my grandnieces or nephews. They're my family too. May do anything! That's the way I was plannin it. You know what I mean? That's just the way it is.

Now . . . I felt good, but I felt bad too. I was glad Collin was gone but I missed SOMEbody. I wasn't lonely but I was lonely. One minute I was on top of the world, feelin smart and all and the next minute I was laid out under the world. Then little by little I began to feel better longer.

Bout that time my usual doctor's appointment came up and since I was feeling pretty good, I went. After he asked several questions bout all my business and the marriage and the divorce came out, that doctor told me I was in a trauma or somethin. To me, I didn't feel bad at all, but he gave me a shot and some tranquil pills and sent me home to go to bed and rest. But I wasn't tired! Cept for the days I took his tranquil pills! So I put them in my "Sometime" drawer and went on livin!

Then one of my friends called me to tell me about our church revival coming up. Revival plus reunion days. All the old members comin to visit and all. I decided I'd go, cause you can't go wrong going where God hangs around.

Now, since it was going to be a reunion and I was almost seventy years old, I decided to make myself look as good as possible to show all my old friends (and enemies) that would be there that I was still holdin my own.

I went to the hairdresser for my hair and got a facial to iron a few of my wrinkles out. (I don't have too many wrinkles anyway.) I wanted a massage but I ain't goin to get naked and show my body to nobody.

I didn't intend to buy no new clothes cause I got plenty I never get to wear, but on my way home I passed and looked into a store window and saw the prettiest white silk blouse with ruffles at the neck and cuffs. Ohhh, just really pretty, honey. And a long white skirt with nice slim lines down to the floor. It had a red velvet belt and a small red rose on the breast. I loved it cause I always wanted to wear somethin like that. I went in, tried it on and bought it. $125.00! I frowned all the way home, but I held that package tight under my arms. I loved it!

When the day of the reunion revival came, my hair had done fallen out of curls, but I combed it back smooth and the few curls left just curled around back of my neck and it still looked good! I still looked good! I sailed out my house to get into my friend's car just'a grinning and lookin good! You hear me?! Good, chile!

We got there even with all her bad drivin (cause she can't see all that good no more), parked and waltzed in, cause my friend thought she was lookin good and smellin good also, like me. She doin the best she can. I guess I am too. I know I am too.

Well, as usual, everybody greetin everybody. We seen some people we hadn't seen in years and months. Then we found a seat and let people find us.

Now, I am not gonna lie to you. It was nice but after a

while I got tired of saying hello to people two or three times cause they had forgot we already talked already. And then, the ice had melted in the punch and the sandwitches wilted a bit and the choir had already sang and people was just walkin round. The preacher had already preached his speech and was comin back for the Farewell speech when this gentleman came over and sat next to me in the seat that just happen to be empty. I didn't pay him much mind cause I was watchin a tiny little punch spot on my new dress.

He leaned toward me and spoke, I turned to him, lookin up into a smiling face. He asked me, "Didn't they used to call you 'Melly' in school?"

I turned with a smile, to look at him better and guess what I saw? A tall, good-lookin, silver-haired, slim, but healthy bodied, well-dressed man. With all his teeth, false or not, lookin good and bright eyes behind some fancy frames. My smile went wider. I said in my best low voice, "Yes, they did call me Melly. My name is Melody."

He leaned closer toward me and whispered, "I remember you perfectly because when we were in school I had a terrific crush on you." He leaned back, smiling at me and then laughed, a low warm laughter. I laughed too, hold it long as you can, my mind told me. But my heart wasn't eager. Just settled back and began to really enjoy the reunion.

He kept that smile blazin in my eyes, said, "You have not changed. You still have your warmth and sense of humor."

I laughed softly, "Oh yes I have changed. I hope I didn't look like this when I was . . . ?"

He spoke right up, "Fourteen going on fifteen. But I didn't just mean your looks."

"Oh?"

"I meant in your relaxed manner. I always relaxed around you. I was shy with girls, but you always relaxed me, like a friend instead of a girl."

My mind flashed over all the things that would have changed his mind about me if he had seen me. Like that hot water and my Cliff.

He went on talkin, "You always seemed so in control of yourself."

I coughed a little, "Well I tried to be. When you lose control you don't have no self left."

He laughed softly. "You're right, you're right. Well, where is your husband? Is he here? I remember you married Clifford."

"He . . . passed away."

"Oh, Melly, I'm sorry to hear that."

"I'm sorry to tell it."

"So . . . You're alone now?"

I didn't want to tell anymore about me. "Is your wife here?"

"No. She passed away also. Three years ago."

"I'm sorry."

"Well, death makes us all sad." He cheered up. "BUT! We are here . . . alone!"

I laughed that low laugh again. I hoped it was sexy, but didn't mean sex. "Tryin," I said.

He stood, "Would you like more punch?"

I looked up at him, he's tall. "I'd like to know your name. And I'd have more punch if it had some ice in it."

"My name is Randolph. Randolph Conners. I had hoped you would remember. And you shall have ice in your punch if I have to go to the North Pole for it!"

(I like this kind of man!) I said, "No, don't go to the North Pole. You might not get back in time to talk anymore."

He made a slight bow. Said, "Ms. Melody, I'll get back, but in case you leave, give me your address so I can find you again. I'll only be in town another few days."

I laughed that low laughter again. "Certainly. It would be . . . a pleasure."

I did. And gave him my phone number too! I usually write so bad, but you should have seen how clear them letters and numbers were, honey!

Well, I'm not gonna run you through all of it, cause you all probly think older folks don't have no romance noway. But we do, we do. A heart is a heart. Where there is a way, there is a will.

For the few days that Randolph was in town, he courted me. He took me out to breakfast and we talked all day. Next day I cooked breakfast and we talked. He took me out to lunch. He took me out to dinner. He took me to lunch the last day and we had dinner in his rooms at the hotel that evening. Wasn't none of that sex stuff to it. We had too much to learn about each other it seemed. We talked and talked and then we sat silent sometimes too.

Randolph had gone on to college for accounting and

tax business. That's why he still worked at his age, eighty-one years old. He had his own businesses, long established. He had married and lived with his wife for thirty-three years. Til she died. That man fixed his lips and told me he came back to build a new life and find old me. Oh! Ain't the heart a strange, wonderful thing?! A marvelous, marvelous thing. I felt like a princess in them fairy tales I read as a child.

Anyway, time came, he left. I missed that man more than I missed Collin, EVER! Ain't that a shame?! At my age, fallin in love. Well, it ain't your business, but I had done fallen in love, honey.

When he came back two weeks later, he proposed and before he was through askin, I accepted. Me, with my crazy quick self. Saw the stars again.

We married, chile. We married.

We bought a new home in the city where his business was. He did, anyway. I moved back there.

We walk every mornin and every evenin . . . for the joy of it. He loves to dance and I do too, only I never did too much of it before. He plays golf. Now, I'm learnin too. I like it, the beautiful walks and all. He loves it. I cook and we spread it over the week or we go out cause all this walkin and fresh air has made it easier for me to get up and go! He has taught me about concerts and symphonies and even the ballet. He opened my mind to music. We are blessed.

Yes, we make love. These two old bodies are warm and comfortable to each other. It's a close, thank you for the blessin, lovemakin. He ain't tryin to be a trapeze artist and I ain't tryin to be Mata Hari. We just lovin each other.

You know, not even in my most wildest dreams did I ever blive I would have a life like this startin at my age. You just can't tell about life. You can't never give up. You just have to be wise as you can. Cause I got the wrong one once after Cliff left me, but now I got the right one. And you know every day is a blessin, cause it might be the last one.

You know, when I thank God for my blessin, I always remember to ask him for one for you. Are you ready? I mean, ALL ready?

I'm happy. And if I die this way, I'll die happy. It seems the best, though God bless Cliff, it seems the best was saved for last. I don't know what else to say. That's just the way it is.

Right now, I have talked so much I got hungry again. I goin to get up and make me a sliced turkey sandwich on toasted wheatberry bread smoothed over with a little fat-free mayonnaise and pieces of crisp, fresh lettuce and fat round slices of tomato. I'll have a glass of ice cold milk or ice cold beer. Then I'll go to sleep and take a nap and get ready for Randy to come home. God willin I keep my health. That's just the way it is!

Livin and Learnin

Sometimes in this life, you be so busy trying to live, in fact, you don't give a lotta thought to where you goin in the long run. But I found out from my own real life experience, you better do it . . . You better think about where you taking yourself in life.

I said something the other day that brought a lot of memories into my mind. Made me think! People say life is hard, but I truly believe that some people make they life hard. Just keep makin the same mistakes over and over. Runs down into generations. I don't want that for me!

When I said what I said that reminded me of the past, I was talkin to my fourteen-year-old daughter. She tryin to court and I happen to see one of her friend-boys. I have to

pay tention to her, cause see, this is a city we livin in and it's all kind of people here. Mostly the wrong kind! When my mama was raising me and havin trouble, she said one day it would be my turn. So I'm watching for it!

When I heard myself talkin to my daughter, I realized I was saying what my grandmama told my mama and what my mama told me long ago. Almost the same words. (And all of us were right.) Cause my mama had fallen in love with one of them "mannish bums" who my grandmama recognized on sight. My father.

The boy I was talkin to my daughter about, he look like a ole slick-head bum to me, so I asked my daughter, "Who is that slick-head bum hangin round you? That mannish boy don't look like he mean nobody no good!" She rolled her eyes at me just fore she decided to look innocent. I kept on talkin, cause, now, I am a mother. "You better leave that boy alone cause he ain't gonna mean nothin but trouble!" Well, now, you do get to where you know em when you see em! But let me tell you why all this came about, from the beginning.

My mama didn't pay her mother no mind, caused she loved him she thought. Then she got pregnant with me and when my mama told that boy they was going to glorify their love with a little blessin from heaven and would have to get married, he left town and stayed gone!

I know my mama caught hell! And she had to have me cause she couldn't run off nowhere and leave her body behind like a daddy can. And Grandmama never let my mama forget what she had told her in the beginin. (Also told her the day was comin when it would be her turn, she'd see!)

After I was born we still lived with my grandmama, naturally, cause where was a fifteen-year-old girl goin? Grandmama was good though. She made my mama finish high school so she could get a decent job and raise me. Mama worked in a factory for years.

When I was bout seven years old, Mama got sick of hearin bout how she had ruined her life and, since she was making a almost-decent salary, we moved out to a kitchenette apartment. (I know all this cause some I heard and some I remember.)

My mother couldn't court too much cause we had to sleep in the same bed. She was a good and fair mother to me. (I came first.) Her heart never jumped up and acted like a fool again, like it had with my daddy, cause her life had been too hard raisin a child all by herself. And her mama's words musta sunk in too. There were so many.

She had boyfriends though. When I was bout ten or so, she said she was thinkin of getting married. She had two friends who had asked her. She asked me which one I liked. Wasn't that nice? Cause, she said, I had to live with him too.

She had been goin out with both of them a long time. One was Mr. Jones, a tall, long-faced, older man, who seemed very stiff, dressed neat, but cheap, no taste at all. Always askin me bout my schoolwork, homework and all. Didn't laugh much, and his smile really was cracked. I had read bout them kinda smiles, but with him, I really did see a cracked, dry smile. I think he had a big home and some money. He was always givin me quarters and half-dollars and bringin Mama candy, which I ate. Mama was always quiet round him. I liked him cause I could see he would make our life better. I liked them quarters and half-dollars.

The other one, Mr. Evans, was a medium tall, lazin, laughin nice man. He worked a job. Dressed real nice. He asked bout my schoolwork, but didn't dwell on it. He never gave me any money, but he took us to shows and games and bought us a lotta hamburgers and things. He ate a lotta Mr. Jones' candy, too! He and Mama could laugh about almost anything! Mama was always playin and laughin when she was round him.

Now, when all this marryin stuff came up, she asked me which one I liked the best for a father. Naturally, I picked Mr. Jones who brought the candy and gave me money. Mama looked at me, kinda sad, a long time as I bit into another piece of Mr. Jones' candy. Said, "You are just thinkin of yourself." She sighed real heavy. "You not thinking of my happiness. Life is more than just a box of candy and a quarter."

I swallowed that good candy and said, "Well, you ask me who I liked, and I know Mr. Jones will give us a bigger house and a better livin you always complainin bout."

She said right back, "A person needs to marry somebody who can make the livin worth livin. If you ever ask me that question, I will like the one I think will make you the happiest, not the one who will make ME the happiest."

I reached for some more candy. She slapped my hand away, hard. Then I kept my mouth shut. I'm good at that. I had sense. Then.

Mama married that laughing man . . . and I'm glad. Cause, now, as I look back over all these years they have been married, they've worked and finally got their own house, gave me a stepsister who I love. She musta picked the right one. Cause if she had married Mr. Jones, her smile might a been dry and cracked by now, like his. As it is, she and Evans still laugh together. She smiles a lot, big smiles. That is until she gets to me. But I'll get to that later.

After my mama married, we got a bigger place to live in. I had my own room and I was alone a lot. I hear them laughin and talkin . . . havin fun. I want to have some fun too! So I was always makin friends with somebody. Anybody. As I got older, my grandmama always say I was a fast-tailed girl, but I was a virgin til I was fifteen and a half years old. I didn't mean to give it up then. I planned to wait til I got married like my mama always talk to me about. But, chile, I got foolish and forgot.

Now . . . when you are young, you don't think bout all the reasons older people have for choosin friends. You just like to have fun. So, when I was fifteen or so . . . I had a friend who really was a fast-tailed womanish girl, bout my age. My mama worried bout me and her together, but I really liked Honey B. She was doin such excitin things! When other girls be goin to the library or somethin, Honey B be goin to get some gum and cigarettes at a store that was attached to a cocktail bar. She would stand and listen to all that fast talk and have men look at her and say, "Pig meat" or "Jail-bait." Sometime they pull her hair or pat her cheeks and arms. She got offered money too, on the sly. But she didn't want to be no prostitute, she just liked havin fun! When I went with her I just watch and grin. I'm good at that. Besides, I didn't want em touchin me. I move out the way when they reach out to pull my hair or somethin.

But when they ask do we want a soda pop? I always say "Yes!" Lord, we drank plenty soda pops. Sometime they sneaked us drinks, real drinks, in a soda bottle, and we'd be a little high. Honey B liked that. I didn't. Wonder did they think they was doin us a favor? Now I know, they just want to see us act a fool, or see how fast we get in the gutter. Then they could say they always knew we wasn't gonna be nothin! Whole lotta people are good at sayin things like that!

I didn't do that all the time, just sometime when school be borin.

I also had a real nice boyfriend, name of Donald. Played sports and everything. He wasn't the best, but he played. He was what Honey B called a square. Didn't even smoke. He studied hard and had a job after school. Rode a bike he bought hisself, til he saved enough to buy a little ole car. He was good at savin. Honey B made me think he was borin, wasn't excitin to my life. I thought I was so good at everything, I shoulda been good at takin care of my own business!

The night that changed my life was when Donald was graduating and he asked me to his prom. My mama and daddy dressed me to look like a angel. All in pink satin and organdy. Well I was only fifteen and a half, so I was a angel. I went to the prom with Donald, all fresh, smooth, clean and pretty.

Honey B wasn't invited by anybody to the prom. She stole in when it was all crowded. Now, even I noticed, she looked older than the rest of us. The teachers looked at her funny. They knew by the way she was dressed she was different. But she was my age! She was my friend, but I like to died when she headed straight for me. She told me she was goin off to a party, way off in some classy place, and she had come after me! After me! I didn't know whether to be mad or glad.

She said, "Leave that ole square date of yours." She grabbed and tasted my drink, frowned. Said, "This ole dumb punch and square music! You betta come on to the swingin party I'm goin to. We gon meet some real fiiine young men! Hep! Girl, some of them men there will put these here to shame! Come on, girl! Let's go where a real party is!" Then she looked at my pretty pink formal. I started to smile, caused I liked the way I looked. She frowned a big ugly frown. "Girl! Where you get that ole fashioned rag? Off one of your dolls? Oh, hell! I don't know if I want to be seen with you! Dressed like that!" All of a sudden my heart hurt and I hated that dress my mama had worried over.

My life has proved I'm very good at being dumb. You know I left with her. Left that poor boy Donald to be embarrassed and confused when he couldn't find me. Honey B made it seem like such fun. A game! You meet people like that . . . people who want to make you think life is a game. Well, it ain't! Life is real real.

Anyway, I left. A friend of hers sat outside waiting for us. I didn't even have sense enough to wonder how she knew I'd come. I didn't wonder bout nothin! Like . . . Honey B. Why did Honey B need me to come with her? She knew where all the hep people and places were and she had the invitation to the "best" party where all the fine men were! Why did she need me to leave that prom in that pretty dress, with my beau who was a nice, decent beau?

Well . . . she couldn't have done it without me bein a fool.

Anyway, the party was at a nice house. Music all bluesy, jazzy and slow. Real drinks flowin. There were no gardenia corsages, but perfume filled the room from the sexy-dressed women. Everybody was older than us. And I looked like a nut with ruffles in that pink organdy prom gown.

I tried to sit and be quiet and not think of what my mama would say when I got home without Donald. But Honey B kept bringin me drinks, strong drinks, which I drank out of nervousness til I wasn't nervous anymore. There was this man who had come by bout three times to ask for a dance, but I didn't want to stand up and stand out in that dress of mine. But finally my liquor said "yes."

We danced. Oh, chile, he danced different from what all my younger boyfriends had. He moved slow and very close. He held me different, somehow. When I tilted my head back to focus my eyes and see him in that dark room, he looked deep into my eyes, different. He talked real softly in my ear. Had a deep sexy voice. Even his laugh was sexy. He squeezed me even tighter every once in a while. Chile, the man had a natural-born sexy way! I don't have to lie to you! I didn't even really know what sexy was, but I was learnin. He smelled good. His shoulder was smooth with some good material, and it was a strong shoulder, and warm. I remember the song we danced to. "There Will Never Be Another You." It became our song. To me.

When the music stopped, he didn't let go. Just held me. I know I looked stupid, rolling my eyes wonderin what next to do. I started to be embarrassed, but wasn't nobody payin no attention to us. So my liquor said "just relax" and I did. After bout three dances he led me to the bar and got me another drink. Then we had another dance, then another drink, then another dance.

By that time I was almost out of my birdbrain mind counta all that attention he was givin me. He was good-lookin and the other ladies kept passin by sayin "Hi there" with beautiful smiles, far as I could see em. And them were older, grown women more his style.

Now . . . I know you know this man. You may not know him good as I do, but you have met him. I know it. Him and his type are good at things like this.

Out of the clear, blue sky I started to feelin sick. I was shamed and I know I looked like a crazy chile. I wanted him to go away, so I could be sick all by myself, but he wouldn't. He was takin me toward the bathroom when I threw up, chile, all over me and him, even tho he tried to jump out the way!

Oh Lord! I could have died! Just died! Everybody kinda laughed like somethin stunk! He was upset, but he kept his cool. He led me out of there, wipin his clothes and holdin on to me with one hand leading me out. I didn't see Honey B nowhere. I was so sick and confused, well drunk. I let him lead me out. I wanted to go home. I told him where I lived.

I didn't pay any attention to where we were drivin cause I had my head out the window most of the time and my eyes closed, layin back when my stomach let me. When I did look up, he was parking in front of his apartment. He told me not to worry, that I needed to get cleaned up before

I went home lookin a mess. I went in, cause I already told you I was good at being a fool. I was too young for all this and didn't know it.

The man had me take my clothes off! Made me! In the nicest way. Ain't no man had ever seen me with no clothes on in my life! He not only took my clothes off. He bathed me! Bathed me and took all that vomit off. Then he carried me to his bed and took my virginity off, too. I was still a little drunk, but I was soberin up fast. When he was through, he got me up, put me back in my damp clothes and took me home and left me on the sidewalk. He drove off without even seeing if I got in the house right.

Now, I'm goin to tell you the truth. I was smilin cause I thought everything had been so romantic! A grown man! Liked me! Loved me, even! I had been bathed . . . and . . . and . . . loved. I was a loved woman. Wasn't no star in the sky as bright as that comet flyin through my head that night!

When I hit those steps though, I was so glad my mama was sleep when I went in! Because I looked like I had been in a tornado right after I came out the great flood and a big earthquake. It was early, early morning. Sky was gettin light!

You know I should have hated him. Maybe you also know I didn't. I just thought about him, a lot, and blushed, every time. I waited, real romantic like, for him to call me, to check on me, to like me, to want to see me again. But he didn't. I even went and bought that song, "There Will Never Be Another You," and played it over and over.

So . . . after two weeks, I went to find him. Oh Lord,

I wish something had fallen on me, like good sense, and stopped me.

I asked Honey B. I knew his first name was Webb. (Wasn't that romantic?) Her friend knew who had been dancing with me, so I got his number. I called him. My heart overflowin with love and anticipation or somethin just as dangerous.

That man, Webb, answered and spoke just as nice to me as he would to a stranger. Not excited and glad to hear from me, just casually said he was pleased I called him. I told him I thought he might have been tryin to reach me and I wanted to give him my number. He hesitated a minute then said, "Fine." I waited for him to ask to see me again. He didn't. I was too ashamed to ask him so after a few minutes we hung up. I stood staring at the phone, not understanding a damn thing. I wondered what I had done wrong.

My conscience whipped me for bout three days, then I whipped it right back. I called him again. Chile, I called him every day for two weeks! Sometimes he was busy, sometimes he was out, sometimes he talked a minute or two. He still didn't ask me out.

Finally, my wits, which were always at their end round bout that time, made me ask him to take me somewhere. I got up the nerve to ask him that one time, but he laughed as he said, "I'm pretty busy right now, maybe sometime." That didn't even hurt me bad enough to make me stop askin. It didn't take as much time to get up the nerve the second time cause I was in too deep. I don't know if he planned it that way, but he couldn't have planned it better, if he did!

I asked him so many times, he finally agreed to go out. We did. It was just sposed to be for a picture show and hamburgers. But we went to his place after . . . for you know what. I hadn't planned to do that again, but I never said a word, just did it. And I liked it again. And I loved him.

My schoolwork began to suffer. Got bad is what it did! Started missin tests and classes. I had always liked to have fun, but I still did good in school cause my mom and dad wanted me to. They helped me and depended on me to do the only thing I had to do; get good grades in school to work for my future. I really had wanted to be something special when I grew up. But now, I thought I had found my future already. I knew what I was goin to do with my life. Give it to Webb. Let him take care of me. Give him babies. Raise em in our own little house we would have someday. I sure was good at being a fool.

By time another month had passed I loved that man so hard, I couldn't see straight! The touch of his skin thrilled me. The shape of his head was the handsomest thing in the world to me. He looked at me and when his eyes were on me, little thrills just shot all through me. Even my nose got wet! When he talked to me, I always seem to say dumb things. Nervous! Chile, I lived that man. But he was always so hard to reach, so hard to get. I had to BEG him to see me sometime.

I got me a douche bag. Hid it. Stole perfume, sexy, older underclothes. Hid em. Lay awake half the night, many nights, dreamin of Webb and holdin my body where I wanted him to hold it. Dreamin, dreamin all the time. Didn't hear nothin nobody said to me. Went through all the motions goin to school, comin home, goin to the store, anything. I was mostly miserable, but didn't just quite know it. I thought it was loooove.

That man was so cool. He never did grab me or hold me and say he loved me. But I told him I loved him all the time. Every chance I got! So I told myself he loved me . . . and made up a hundred reasons he would try not to let me know he loved me. Well, that ain't the way you do it. But I was a fool. And good at it.

Do you know! . . . I started hangin round outside that man's house to see who he had with him when he told me he was busy!? I got what I came for. When I saw him with those other women, I like to have lost my mind!

Once I saw him go in his place with another woman and I threw rocks at his window til he came out cursing. He had a robe on, and nothin underneath! I went walkin home cryin. I was gettin good at that.

Another time, when he went with somebody, I rang the bell, long and steady, til he answered and snatched me in, cussin and tellin me how I was makin the OTHER woman nervous! Me! I was sposed to be his woman! I was just sixteen then.

Once I took a knife and cut up his car tires. That was a long hard job. Them tires was hard! The next time, I scratched up all his fenders and doors. He might be inside screwin some woman, but I was outside screwin up his car and you know I knew he loved his car.

Webb invited me over the next day after that car scratchin business. I walked in his door and he slapped me so hard I heard bells through my eyes and saw things with my ears! But I didn't care. You hear me? I didn't care bout him beatin up on my body! My only body! Just wanted him to do somethin to me! Anything! I even, still, wanted to make love. He smiled a funny, strange kind of smile, then he made love to me. Then he put me out. I walked home all wet, blue, smellin and smilin. And head still hurtin from that slap.

Oh, I wanted that man to love me like I loved him. I wouldn't, couldn't, believe he didn't love me.

One of the times he did call me and want to see me, which made my body feel like a whole concert playin inside my head as I ran to him, was also a terrible time. Cause when he drove me home, my mama was waiting behind the door. When we pulled up, she ran out and asked him who he was.

He took a deep, bored breath. Said, "Ask your daughter, baby." To my mama!

She was angry. "I'm askin you!"

He smiled, "Nobody. I'm nobody."

She snapped, "You a old nobody to be messin with my child!" He was about thirty-eight years old.

He kept smilin. "I belive you got more than a 'child' here."

She leaned toward him. "I am sure you know! But I bet you betta leave her alone!"

He stopped smilin, said, "Lady, if you can just get her to leave ME alone, I'd be glad!"

My neck snapped when I turned so fast to look at him. My heart broke. My head bent down.

My mama looked at me. "This man ain't got shit for you! Do you hear him? He don't want you! He don't mean nothin but trouble for you! You fool!" Oh, and all such things like that, that hurt, stung, tore, ripped my heart. And all my little dreams.

My dad, who had walked over to my mother, said to my bowed head, "If a man cares for you, he respects you, wants everybody else to respect you."

Well, I just didn't pay him no mind. My body was remembering all the good feelins that Webb had given it. I didn't really hear either one of my mama nor dad til . . . one of them said, "If that man loved you, he would want to marry you! He would come in here and meet us and treat you like a lady. He wouldn't have you runnin out in them streets after him like a dog! Makin you run after him! He would marry you! I bet you haven't heard from him! He knows YOU're gonna call him!"

The words stuck in some crack in my brain. "Marry you . . . marry you . . . marry you!" Well, that was the answer! I wanted that man. I looooved Webb. I just KNEW he loved me back. He had to understand that.

But he didn't understand that. He mostly hung up on me when I called him. I took money from my mama's purse, stole, to buy him presents so I could get a chance to talk to him. That helped, cause he liked presents.

I would say, "Hi!"

He would say, "Oh, Jesus."

I would say, "I'm . . . I'm out by your house. I was gonna stop by."

He would say, "Tilla (that's my name), I'm busy right now. I'm gonna be busy a week or two. I'll call you when I have time."

Then I would say, "I've got a present for you. I wanted to give it to you . . . today."

Then he would say, "Well . . . okay. Come by . . . but only for a minute. I really have a lot of things to do."

I mostly always got us ended up in bed. Makin love. At least I was.

Then I would have to take some more money, get another present, so he would say, "Well . . . okay," and let me in again.

Finally, I did what I wanted to do. Tried so hard to do. I was still sixteen years old. I got pregnant by Webb. Mmmh, mmmh, mmmh! Chile, chile. Lord, I pity little foolish women with hearts.

My mama liked to died. Not only because I was remindin her of her pain in raisin me, but because she knew what my pain was gonna be. My dad liked to died. He thought he should try to fight Webb or somethin, but he really didn't know what to do. Mama talked to him, he quieted down. Webb liked to died! He said he couldn't make babies.

My mama turned out to be my only ally. She took Webb's telephone number from me, called him, told him I was a minor and she would have him arrested! He said he would come by.

He got there.

They sat. They talked.

He tried to lie.

They talked some more.

He lied.

They threatened.

They asked me. I told the truth. It was his baby. There had never been anyone else. There never would be anyone else.

They threatened some more.

We got engaged and married, all in one day.

I felt my dreams had come true. I had my man! I had my Webb. I thought I had been good at what I did. What I was was good and mistaken.

Webb wanted me to stay home with my mama and be married to him for the baby's sake. Lord, that man didn't want me.

But Mama made me go. Said, "You wanted it, you got it. No matter what I told you, you forgot about me and chose him. Now you go with him til you get enough! I'll be here if you need me, but don't come here to stay til you are good and through with him! You are a fool. That Donald boy, in your age class, wants to make somethin of himself. He liked you, but you treated him like a fool. Now, you gonna find yourself in somethin like deep shit." She broke down and cried then.

I cried, "Oh, Mama." Held her and cried. But in the back of my mind and heart was the joy I was feelin, knowing I was gonna be with Webb all the days of my life. I wanted a long, long life.

Mama wasn't through though, said, "You gonna wake up one day and find out that you can't let your behind do your thinkin! You better think with your head . . . and let your behind stick to sittin til you find somebody it can sit RIGHT with!" She wiped a tear from her face and some from mine. "You bout to have a baby, child. One day, sooner than you think, it's gonna be your turn. You gonna learn what I mean."

Chile . . . I took my foolish hot behind and ran happily to my miserable future with that man I loved . . .

Webb. If I could have just seen into the future I would have saved a lot of tears from runnin down my face. And, oh, the pain I could have saved! But I didn't. I was good at doing the wrong things. I still thought, I KNEW, I could MAKE him love me!

But . . . I didn't. Couldn't. And I tried for a long, long time.

Let me tell you what he put me through. No! What I put myself through. Cause he never promised me life. Nor nothin.

Maybe I deserved what I got, cause I asked for it. Maybe not as bad as it was . . . but . . . I did stay . . . I did ask for it. From the beginnin when he NEVER said he loved me. When he was searchin for his own life. Wasn't his fault he was handsome . . . spoke well . . . acted loving, and made good love. He didn't mean to be punished for that. Hell, he hadn't done nothin but be hisself! But he was, in a way, a liar. He was lyin when he was lovin. He knew what women wanted. What they would think. He led them to that. And he helped them to think and feel what he would never say, so he would be blameless. He made them think he thought what they wanted him to think. So he was, naturally, loved by them women. A liar at love.

Marriage was sposed to be different. Before we married, we use to separate at daybreak . . . me, sneakin into my house. I thought I could hold him all day if I was married to him, was able. But I thought wrong. Cause after we married he wasn't ever hardly home at daybreak . . . or he was just comin in.

(CRAZY!) I was gone out of my mind! He took my brain and turned it, twisted, stepped on it. Stumped on my heart, my thoughts. He could make me feel more like a fool, a slave, a dog, than anything in this world. Whatever I said was dumb, whatever I did was wrong, whatever I thought was unnecessary.

Tell me, are you crazy when you try to hold on to the one you love? When they don't want you? Yet? You don't have to tell me now.

One time we talked. One time . . . when he wasn't "too tired, too sleepy, too sick, too busy," again.

I was in a soft, tired, lovin mood. Seems like I always was. I put "our" special record on, "There Will Never Be Another You." As it played for lovers, I said, "You know, I love you." Hands and arms reachin for him.

He was as sarcastic as usual. He moved away from me, said, "Yea . . . you been tellin me."

I began to whine. I hated it when I did it, but couldn't quit. "I love you. Why can't you stay home with me? Love me?"

He sighed. "Cause I don't love you. Been showing you from the beginning. Never have."

Naturally, still whining, I said, "But I love you."

"Naturally," he said. "But that don't make me love YOU." Still sarcastic.

He got up to leave the room I had cornered him in. I wasn't through though, hadn't had enough, yet.

"Baby." I reached out, again, to touch the man I loved. "Webb, we could be so happy together, if you would just love me like you should. Like I love you. I'm your wife."

He moved away from me, saying, "Girl, that was what YOU wanted. I know what you want cause I want it too. I want to love somebody like you do. My way. For me. You can't make me love you . . . cause love don't be made. Love is given freely. And . . . I want the person I love to love me back freely. I don't want to have to MAKE nobody love me, like you try to do."

I tried to say something, anything to make him stop, cause he was hurtin me, again. "But, Webb . . ."

But he didn't stop. "Tilla, I tried to tell you I didn't want you for no wife. You didn't want to hear that. All you knew was what you wanted. Well, now you got me and what I give you. It's all you ever had and I not giving you any more than I have for you. It's all I'll ever give, which is almost nothin." The record music came to the end. Then he left the house again and I didn't see him for two days.

We now had two babies. Girl first, boy second. I loved my babies. When my first baby was born, Webb wasn't there. Didn't see her til my mama brought me home. I know he loved that baby, but he didn't spend much time with her. When my second baby was born, he didn't come til the second day in the hospital. He did help take care of our daughter though. I lay in that hospital bed, in pain, and pretended ours was a natural, happy home now. I get sick when I allow myself to think of how I was!

Once, I decided I would make him jealous. Then he would see how much he loved me. Mmmh, mmmh. I ran Honey B down, cause I didn't know nowhere to go and didn't have no new friends. She was still doin the same things, havin a good time. She said it was good.

We went out. I didn't look too good. My stomach plump under that satin skirt Honey B loaned me cause I didn't have no clothes to fit me. She put a low-cut blouse on me, with my breast showin at the top, full of milk anyway, which kept runnin out a little. I shoulda been home feedin my baby boy. High-heel shoes that was too small. I felt ugly. I was.

Honey B said, "Wellllll, you'll be all right. Somebody out here will fall in love wit cha!" But they didn't. They couldn't.

I didn't like strange men touchin on me. Didn't like the way they held me and tried to roll against my stomach and thighs. I only went once. It didn't work out and Webb never gave my absence a second thought. He might not even'a known I was gone out. Cause my mama kept my babies.

Another time, I decided to call Donald. He wasn't hard to find cause he was still livin at home, going to college, bout to graduate again. I bet he had somebody better to take to his prom this time. He seemed glad to hear from me, but couldn't understand what I wanted with him. I didn't know either. He did tell me though, that Honey B called him, a lot! But he didn't care for her company. Honey B always said he was ugly and square! Well!! So much for friends!

I gave up after that. I was a mother and a wife. I decided to settle down at that and try to be happy . . . til I could do better. I spent my nights up with my babies all by myself, sick or well. I spent many nights, hundreds, sittin by the window, waiting, waiting, waiting for my heart to come home.

I also began to spend nights standing outside some woman's house, all I could locate, watchin to see when Webb came out. Sometimes I saw him. I made scenes, whinin and cryin. Fightin even. We fought on the streets, endin with him drivin off and me gettin on some bus, a wreck, goin home to whine some more.

I spent my little young life waitin, waitin, waitin for that man to love me. I wasted my time. Ten good years.

Webb worked and took care of us til the babies were four and five years old, then he told me I better get a job or something cause he needed help. Said he couldn't take care everybody's needs and his too. So I got a part-time job. He brought less money home then. I even gave him some of mine for awhile, til I decided something else came first. Me! I guess you say, "At last!"

After a few more years, he settled down to a regular woman. Gildy. She was bout thirty-five years old. (He was bout forty-six then.) I looked at myself and I could see why. My skin was dry and looked moldy, from all those cigarettes I smoked waitin for him to come home. Liquor will beat you out and I used it to be able to go to sleep nights. I was almost skin and bones cause I never had a appetite. My clothes were a mess cause I never got nothin new and what I had was old and ironed out. Gildy was always lookin fresh and pretty. She was a mellow, good-lookin woman. A adultress, to me.

I knew her house cause I had stood cross the street from it enough times, holdin my babies' hands. (Yea, I even took them with me when I couldn't find a sitter.) When I couldn't do that, I just called on the phone til they took the phone off the hook. I kept tryin to give up and not do those things, but seem like I couldn't quit, no way I tried.

Bout that time, my mama and grandmama wanted to give my children music lessons. Piano for her, flute for him. I came out of my tired confusion long enough to agree. I

don't remember the day they moved the piano in though.
But I do know, one day, early on, I happened to be sittin
there when my daughter was gettin a lesson. Some piece of
my mind woke up and listened. I got interested. I started
being there at all her lessons and practicin myself when she
was through. In five months or so, I was playing better than
she was, cause I practiced more.

Practicing seemed to take my mind away from Webb. I
loved music anyway. I started going with my son to his
lessons. Hell, another five months and I could toot a few
simple tunes on the flute. I remember my mama couldn't
get me to take no lessons when I was young. I thought it
was borin. Now music filled some of my mind and Webb
didn't have it all.

I started payin more attention to other things the kids
were doin. Got to play volleyball and baseball, go to pic-
nics, met some nice people. That took my mind off Webb
some more. I began to gain a little weight and felt way
better in my mind. I start lookin a little good and that did
me a lot of good.

Another thing I noticed, the parents of my children's
friends. They was all something special. The mothers
mostly all had gone to some kind of college or skill school.
They had special training and good jobs. My daughter was
always kinda complainin that I just worked in a kitchen. I'd
listen to her and think, "Hell, you oughta be glad YOU
ain't workin in a kitchen. Be glad I'm working anywhere!"

That's the way my life was round about then. Just
nothin much. Then one day, I was gettin the bus home
from work. Worked full time then. Just doin lower slave
work at that restaurant, not even a waitress. No personality

I guess, all dried up. Anyway, I had sat down at the bus stop that evening, lookin tired and haggy. I noticed these people comin down the street.

A older man and a older-lookin woman was coming toward the bus stop. She had a frown on her face and was saying words like little snakes and little crocodiles and termites and things. He was saying words like pretty flowers, but they was just pretty weeds. They was talkin bout money. She had a uniform in a clear plastic bag over her arm. I could see the little white apron. He was askin her for money. He begged and she fought every new argument with facts about their needs, bills and such. Finally she gave up and, turnin her back to him, she went into her purse. Dug way, way down and come up with a few crumpled dollar bills, not wantin to see her money go away from her, I guess. He grinned and took them little dollar bills, turnin to go without a "thank you." She hollered after him, "I know what chu gonna do with it!" She lowered her voice. "Bastard!"

I forgot myself and stared at her. She looked at me and rolled her eyes away. She was mad. She rolled her eyes back to me, said, "What you starin at?! If I don't give it to him, he gon steal it! That man don't worry bout nothin! He spect me to do the worrin. He don't keep no job! Yes, he do; I'm his job! He keep me workin! Humph!" She looked away, she looked back. "I use to think I loved him. Now, I just done got too old and everybody needs somebody! I wish I knew then what I know now!" She looked away, then back at me. "You only young once, honey. Heist your ass up and do somethin for yourself! Get somebody who loves YOU! If somebody just havta be the slave, make him

YOUR slave fore he makes you his! Cause if you don't look
out . . . you'll be the slave! How old are you?" She didn't
wait for no answer. "Bein a young fool can be fun, but
young fools turn into old fools, and it ain't no fun no
more!" She gripped her purse hard and tight and looked off
down the gutter til the bus came.

When we got on the bus, the driver frowned as she
counted out pennies, nickels and dimes to him for the fare.
Then she sat down and looked ready to kill or cry. I sat
down, thinkin and watchin the gutters whiz by, like time.

Another day, not too long after that, same bus stop, I
was movin to my seat when someone said, "Tilla? Tilla?" I
sure didn't want to see nobody, tired as I was and lookin
bad too! It was a old school friend of mine, Maxine.

Now I was bout twenty-six years old, so she was too.
But, chile, we look so different. She was dressed like a older
college woman, fresh, young and bright. I was dressed like a
tired slave, looked way older than her. She told me she was
bout to graduate from law school college and she would be
a lawyer. A lawyer! Why I was as smart as she was when we
was in school!

She said, I remember cause I can't forget, "And what
are you doing with yourself?"

I looked down. "I got two children. A girl and a boy."

She laughed. "Well, any woman can do that, Tilla. I
mean, what else are you doing?"

I didn't laugh. "Well, any woman can't have the ones I
have. I'm glad I have them."

She smiled. "That's good. Are you married? Who did
you marry?"

I didn't smile. "Yes, I'm married. Almost ten years now.

You don't know him." Then I thought. Or maybe you do.
"You sure are goin to make a good lawyer, cause you sure
ask a lot of questions!"

She preened. "I have to practice. I intend to be good!
But didn't you ever have something else you wanted to do?
Something special you wanted to be? I dreamed of being a
lawyer all my life."

I sat thinkin a minute or two.

She said, "Humph, you didn't have a dream?"

I answered, at last. "My husband was my dream."

She laughed. "Well, you must be happy then."

When I didn't say nothin and didn't laugh, she said,
"Maybe you have another dream? After him and your children?"

I looked down at my bleached, calloused, sore hands.
Didn't say nothin.

She did though. Said, "You don't look happy to me.
Maybe you need another dream. One day the children will
be gone. He may be dead. That's when you will need a
dream all your own. He may even leave you broke! You
need another dream that makes money!"

I laughed to myself. He kept me broke!

She got up to go. Sayin, "You don't look happy, Tilla,
you don't even look mildly satisfied. Get yourself a dream.
It's your life."

As she was passin my knees, I said, "I'll get one! Next
time you see me I'll have me a dream!"

She pat my shoulder and said, "Good! Every life needs
one." Then she was gone.

I didn't move over cause I didn't want anybody sittin

beside me. I wanted to think, alone, as I looked down in the gutters whizin by, like my life.

Here I was on my way home to try to rest enough to be ready to get back to a lowly third class kitchen worker!! Jesus, Mary and Joseph. I got off that bus thinkin bout that and I thought about it a loooooong time. Ain't stopped yet. Called the school board to see bout me makin up my school graduation. They told me "three months." It was work, it was struggle, it was hard. My kids helped. In three months, I had it!

Stopped off, another day, to pick up a catalogue for classes at the junior college. Not long after that I registered in college. Now! Smile, smile, smile. Business administration and computer science. Two things I didn't know nothin about! But I'm smart. And gettin good at it!

I learned so much, I heard so much. Met people, men and women, struggling just like I was. But we were making it! The hard way, too!

Not too long after that, ramblin round in my mind that was pretty busy lately, I decided to give Webb a divorce. The next time I saw him, I told him.

Said, "Webb, I'm not gonna try to hold you anymore. You want to go down and get your divorce, go ahead."

He looked at me a minute or two. "What's bringing this on?"

I put my book down and looked at him. "I just think you oughta be free to do what you really want to do."

He laughed. "That would make you free to do what you want to do, too. Have you found another poor fool you want?"

I didn't feel like laughin. "I just want us both to be free. Right now, you the only one free."

He frowned, looked at his fingernails I kept manicured. "I don't know. I'll think about it . . . let you know."

That made me mad! I said, "Ain't no thinkin to be done. You don't really live here no way. You just get some of your clothes washed and ironed and you eat here sometime. And make love, well . . . have sex with me sometime. I thought you wanted to be free!?"

He frowned harder. "I said I'm not sure. My kids are getting older," he went on, "I'm gettin older. And you make a good home. I'm not so sure I need a divorce . . . to be free."

Madder, I said, "Well, I do need a divorce . . . and I mean to be free. I'm . . . I'm gettin a dream for myself! And you aren't in it! I'll get a divorce if I have to pay for it myself."

He started leavin, sayin, "Well, you sure will have to. But I don't believe you. This is just something new you're trying, to get me to stay home more."

I quieted myself down, followed him to the door. "This is no home and you are no husband. These are real kids, cause I had em, not you. So they are mine. And I want to be free. Gildy got you anyway, all these years. Now, I want you to leave. You don't spend much time nor money here . . . so we won't miss you."

He was standing at the front door. He laughed, bent down and slapped my behind. Well, I did something I had wanted to do for years. I reached waaaay back, gathered my strength and slapped the livin shit out of him before I thought about he might hit me back. I KNOW it hurt! My hand stung and I know his face did! He looked at me a long time, seem like ages. Then he left. Never raised a hand. I packed what few things he had there. Waited for him to come home.

Well, chile, life just don't wait for nothin! When he came home, they brought him. The ambulance. He had been in a accident and was all broke up and bandaged. I showed em to the bedroom. Later that night I lay down in my children's room, we couldn't afford separate rooms for them, least I couldn't. I lay thinkin about my life. Wasn't it a mess!

My daughter had to stay home from school to tend him, cause I HAD to work. I tended him at night. He had to have bedpans and such, or he would wet the bed. I could never rest. He had to be fed, had to be bathed and teeth washed and all everything.

Bout two weeks into all that work and answerin the phone that always hung up, I rented a wheelchair, in his name, put him in it, called a cab, put his bags in it and took him over to Gildy's. Yes, I did.

Her house was below the street level, had a walk-way down the slope leadin straight to her front door, where I saw her peepin out the side of the little curtain. She was watchin me, with great big eyes, standin up there with him, lookin down at her and her door. He was tremblin and breathin hard, tryin to kick his feet and push his behind way back in that seat. Scared I was gonna push him down that hill. I started to, can't lie, but my heart wouldn't let me. On accounta God, not no feelin I had for Webb; I didn't feel anything for Webb anymore!

Lord, forgive me, but I couldn't help stretchin my arms

out, tiltin that chair over the edge, pretendin I was gonna let him go. I looked down at her, still peepin, her mouth open now. But I didn't do it. I walked him down the slope, came back, got his bags, sat them beside him.

I smiled, gently, into his big scared eyes. Said, "Well, Webb, you here to stay at last. You been tryin to live here a long time. Now you can. This your home. You don't live where I live no more." My mad came up and so did my voice. "She got the best of you when you were well . . . now she can have the rest of you til you go to hell. I'm not takin no more leavins! I turned to leave, but there was one more thing to say. Quoting "our" song, I said, "Webb? There will NEVER, NEVER, NEVER be another you!" Then I left. Walkin proud! And free. Free! Chile, I felt like the world had dropped off my shoulders.

One thing though. I told God, "God, I was gonna leave him before he had his accident so I don't need to feel guilty now . . . and I don't."

When I turned back, one last time, the woman Gildy hadn't opened the door yet! She must didn't want him, sick. Well, she had him. Somebody had him. Anybody could have him! But . . . not . . . I.

Webb bein gone didn't make any big difference in our lives. The kids missed him, but didn't say nothin about, "Mama, take Daddy back." We kept right on doin with and doing without. I went on to school, struggled with my job, life and children. They helped me. Already I live better, speak better, am closer and better with my children and feel better. I'm doing better all around.

Three years have passed now. I'll be graduating from college soon!!

Oh! Let me tell you this first. I went to our high school reunion dance. Alone. Saw Donald. His wife had passed away a year ago. We talked. The years had been good to him. He really looked good to me. I knew I looked healthy, fresh and good too. He held my hand an extra long time and we smiled a lot at each other. Then, guess what? Honey B came in! Yes! Honey B, still the same. Still alone. Saw me talkin to Donald and came straight toward me. I excused myself to Donald and moved toward her. I even smiled at her. She opened her mouth, full of missing teeth gaps, and told me, "Girl! You ain't progress none! Still talkin to that ole square."

I turned and went to the ladies' room. She made me have to go there. She followed me, still talkin and wavin to people, some who didn't even recognize her. Got in the bathroom, still tellin me how "I need to go to this club with her and really live, meet some real men."

I came out that toilet, flushed, my history zooming through my head. Honey B was still waiting for me, standing alone. I walked up to her, said, "Honey B, what's going on in your life? How have you been?"

She laughed. "Still havin fun, girl. Doin my thing."

I laughed a little. "What is your thing?"

She laughed again. "Partyin! What you doin when you leave here?"

I sighed. "Going home to study. Got an important exam coming up."

She looked shocked. "Study?! You ain't in school."

I nodded, "Yes, I am. In college. Getting ready to graduate with my master's. What else you doin besides partying?"

She tilted her head and smiled an empty, sad smile, "Ain't nothin else to do."

"You get married? Have kids?" I smiled at her.

She shook her head, "Giiiirl, I was sposed to get married, but somethin happened every time. I got three kids though. They at my mama's house. She keeps em. What about you? What's all this bout college, chile? I thought you'd be glad as I was to get outta any kinda school!"

Still smiling, I said, "Oh, I have two big children. I keep em at home though. Trying to get them ready for college, too. I'm doing . . . better."

She laughed a half-hearted laugh. "Sure must be borin. You don't have no fun! I always did have to teach you to relax and have fun. Why don't we do somethin sometime? Tonight?"

I tilted my head and looked serious. "I am doing something. I have a dream that I am making come true. That's what you need, Honey B. You need a dream."

She waved her hand at me. "I'm doin alright."

I waved her hand away. "You can't be. You're doing the same thing you were doin fourteen years ago. What are you going to be doing next year, in ten years? You need a dream, Honey B. Get yourself a dream. Life will be a lot more fun to live. You may think what I do is hard, but I know what you do is way harder than my life. And it can't be satisfying you. When I get through following my dream, I'll BE somewhere." I started to walk away from my old friend, but turned back one more time. "Get yourself a dream, Honey B, I know you got one somewhere."

Then I went to find Donald to tell him I was going home because I had some studying to do. So he would know it wasn't a repeat performance of the past with Honey B. Because I was putting together another dream with love in it. He asked when he could call. I thought he would. Then, I went on home to study.

Now I'm about to graduate. Got a dance coming up. Donald calls often. When he called the last time, I asked him to be my date. He said, "Yes." Laughing.

Well, my mama says I got some sense now. Yes, I'm getting better at it. Well, you live . . . and you live.

But today . . . what started me to telling you my story, I saw the boy my daughter was walking home from school with. A slick-head, crafty-lookin bum! When I got her in the house, I asked her, "What is that slick-head bum doing hanging around you? He doesn't look like he is good for nothing! He sure doesn't mean you any good!"

Then I looked into her eyes, saw the past there . . . and, maybe, the future.

Here we go again. But this time . . . I'm ready . . . I think. At least I am thinking, and I'll know what to do in time, I hope. Thinking and hoping. Having sense. I'm getting good at that!

Please, God, let my daughter have some sense. Cause, oh God! It's her turn. That means it's my turn. And I'm coming up fighting for her.

Sure Is a Shame

You know, it's a fact and I seen it, sometimes when you think you taking a bite out of life, chewing hard on it, life be done taken a bite out of you and done already swallowed. Sho is a shame, sho is.

Like my neighbors cross the way there. Inez and Fred. That's their house. They been married a long time. Her good luck and his bad.

Long time ago, when I was in high school, my family lived next door to Inez' family. Inez used to pull her youngest sister, Gartha, around by the nose practicly, cause Gartha just bout worshiped Inez. Anyway, we was kinda friends, not best friends, but kinda friends and sometimes I would go over to their house. It was a poor, little bare

house, most everybody's was, but it was never too clean nor happy. Their daddy was gone, but their mama was still there. Mama Lil. And Mama Lil was always fussin bout somethin. Mostly men.

Mama Lil liked to drink and smoke while she sat at the kitchen table and talk bout life and men. I didn't blive everything she said, but I was sittin up there lookin in her mouth, listenin to everything she said, just like Inez and Gartha. She would talk bout their daddy too. He came by to see em sometimes, but Mama Lil would always fuss, cuss and holler at him and try to get his money, so he didn't come by much.

Mama Lil say things like, "A man ain't shit! He just a dog! You can't let him get way with nothin! He'll walk all over you, blive me when I tell you! All they want is one thing . . . that coochie down tween your legs and then they be done gone off after another one!" (My mama said somethin about what most men want, but she said it different.)

Mama Lil said, "Don't never tell a man he looks good cause he will lose his mind, honey! Sho will! He'll go out and try to look good to all the women then! And he'll go up-side your head if you try to look good! And once he get you to start havin them babies, it's all over then! He don't want you no more, he wants somethin new! Oh yea! Somethin young! Men ain't shit! Don't you ever trust no man! They'll hurt you! They'll let you down every time! Ain't no mother's son worth a good hot damn! Blive me when I tell you! I hate em! I ain't never gonna work to help no man do nothin! Don't never give your money to no man! The lyin good-for-nothin bastards!"

Now, see, I didn't blive everything Mama Lil said. Cause I loved my daddy. He always was comin by to see us and always takin us somewhere. My mama didn't have to fight him bout no money. And I had brothers and uncles I loved. They laughed a lot and was always doin somethin for us or bringin a little somethin to make you feel good. I loved em!

Anyway, pretty soon my life was full of books and courtin, dresses and all them things like that, so I didn't go over Inez' very much at all. Neither Inez nor Gartha laughed and smiled much, so it wasn't much fun at their house. Inez would go out with Fred some, but she said she didn't really like him, was just waitin for a real love to come along. Gartha didn't have nobody courtin her, she just follow round behind Inez. Sho was a shame!

I was gettin round pretty good and I fell in love with a boy named Buster and he fell in love with me. We planned to get married. We were near graduation and we both come from kinda poor homes so we both worked. We even saved our money together. I opened the account and we put the money in. When we finally did get married, we were able to put that money down on a little house. This one we still in! It's where we started our family. It ain't big or nothin, but it's ours. And you know our kids start comin right away, even early. (smile) We sho was happy!

Inez wasn't nothin much to look at in school, had a hateful attitude, but a real nice body, pretty legs and such like that. But Fred sure loved that girl. She was sure glad cause the other boys didn't pay her much mind. She was like sweet sugar to him until she found out how much he loved her and how much he would take, then she took to being a little mean. Even to making him do things for her in front of her girlfriends so they would see how much she was loved. Fred just took it with a smile, saying, "That's Inez."

Now everybody was gettin graduated and married and such like that, but nobody still didn't pay no attention to Inez so she married Fred. Not too long after that, Gartha got married. She was still tryin to do everything Inez did. I don't know how Gartha got that man, Pete, cause everybody knew he was in love and goin steady with another girl. They say she lied bout bein pregnant. Whichever way she did it, she got him. Then she "lost" the baby, she said. Pete had really wanted his baby and he was going to leave and go back to his real love, so Gartha got pregnant "again" and this time she had a baby girl. Pete loved his child and he did work hard for them both, and I don't know if he was ever in love with Gartha or not. But I do know he was a foster home child and he wanted a big family of his own. They finally got a house too. Not as big or as nice as Inez' turned out to be, but they got one.

Fred was workin his hands to the bone for Inez. That very house, right there where I showed you, he built that house with his own two hands. She might'a handed him a hammer or a nail, but he sure nuff built it. Just like she wanted it. Took a year or two to finish, cause they didn't have much money. She wouldn't work, said, "A woman's place is in the home." Well, I guess she was right cause that's where a lot of em is. When they finally moved in, she got that house straightened out and then proceeded to keep him from enjoying the fruit of his labor. The Bible talks about that you know. Sho was a shame.

Friends could sit in Inez' dining room whenever they dropped in and she would serve em something. Fred had to eat in the kitchen if it wasn't a special gathering. She let other outside people smoke in her house, club ladies and such, you know. Fred would light a cigarette and she be fannin all around him, fussing. And he had to have his own special ashtray cause she wanted to keep all the rest of em clean. He cleaned his own. If he went to work and left a butt in it, it was still there when he came home.

Fred couldn't bring his friends home to watch a sports game or play cards cause she didn't like em. "Too trashy," she said. "And I just hate them ole football and baseball and basketball games! Only a moron would sit up and look at them things all day! It's a waste of time!" Whose? Musta been hers, cause Fred liked things like that and such. I don't always watch em, but I make bets with my husband on em and that makes something between us we can share. Now, that don't mean I'm right, it just means my husband is happy and I have peace in my house.

As usual, Gartha followed Inez. Gartha commence to treat Pete like he was a fool dog. Pete kept workin, but he spent a lot of time in them streets. Just came home to bring Gartha enough money to help with the baby and the house. He spent the rest of it any way he wanted to. Mama Lil said, "I told you so!" Gartha's house wasn't too clean either. She was always over to her mother's house sittin at the kitchen table smokin and drinkin a little, talkin bout how low-down men were. I guess history do repeat itself cause people buildin the same history every day.

I know I sound like a gossip, but I sure am not. I just study life. I had children I was raising, still do, and I had to watch life so I might know how to explain it when the time came I needed to. I knew there was some men like Mama Lil talked about, but I knew they wasn't all that way. Sho is the truth!

Now, even though Fred was workin for both of them, he had to wash his own work clothes by hand or at some launderette cause Inez said, "I don't want all that dirt in my washing machine!" When he sit down to try to read a newspaper after a thrown together dinner and maybe doze off, cause he's tired, you know, she wake him up to clean them papers up from round him. And I know he had to clean up the kitchen after his self-made breakfast fore he go to work, cause my husband sometimes waited for him to give him a lift. To me, his days started out wrong. But what do I know?

Fred never, honest to God, he never forgot her birthday nor nothin. Always had a surprise present or somethin for her. He must'a marked his calendar. She kept her calendar for other appointments, I guess, cause she never got him nothin, cept maybe for Christmas when everybody got somethin. Sho was a shame. Sometime my husband didn't always remember either, but he mostly did, cause I make big hints and such, you know. When he did forget, he just tell me to go get something I like. Some women don't like that, but I can live with it cause then I go get something I REALLY wanted that he might never think of.

Lord, Inez had all kinds of clothes. Fred worked two jobs sometimes, like when she wanted a mink jacket? She laughed, said, "Gets him out the house and keeps him busy, steada sittin up lookin at these dumb games or somethin!" Yes, she had all kinds of clothes. Even that fur that tried to pass as mink. Fred had one good suit and all the rest was work clothes. He didn't say nothin cept, "Inez looks good when she all dressed up!" and he look proud. She just roll her eyes at him like he a fool. Sho was a shame.

She didn't want no babies, no children. Said, right in front of Fred, "Honey, if them babies come here looking like Fred, I'd die. I'm not going to be guilty of bringing no such babies into this here world." I didn't think he was ugly. I thought he was nice-lookin and I know some other women did too. And even if she thought he was ugly, he was her ugly. Sho was a shame. Sometimes I think maybe she just didn't want to share the spotlight with no child. My husband didn't look no better than Fred did and we had four children. (smile) Beautiful children.

It was a shame cause every kid on this street, over the years, had something Fred had made for em or given them. He played ball in the street and that empty lot with em, til Inez call him in the house. "I got something you can do round here with all that energy. Mow the lawn or something." They had the best-lookin lawn in the community cause it seem he rather stay outside than be in the house with Inez on weekends when he be home.

When they wasn't havin company for dinner on Sundays Inez fix that hardworkin man leftovers or some lunch meat sandwiches with a cup of soup. And even after he done worked all day sometime and come home tired. And

she been home all day! Sho was a shame. On my husband's
day off, I cook him a good meal, or sometimes he cooks a
real good meal. I don't never feel like no fool cause he is
MY husband and treats me better than right. And I don't
think he's no fool for doin it. If you don't treat what blongs
to you right, who you gonna do it for?

Sometime I'd see Pete and Gartha come over to Inez
and Fred's house with their daughter and when they get out
their car, you can hear them squabblin all way cross the
street. The child would have her head bent down, but she
be walkin, holdin both their hands. I understand Pete don't
hit Gartha though. Gartha too big. And, anyway, none of
Mama Lil's kids play that hittin stuff. I don't blive in it
either and didn't raise my daughters to take no hittin mess.
Sho is the truth!

Now . . . I know all about this woman's liberated
thing and such, but I know one thing, when you have
somebody love you and try to do everything to please you,
they are liberating you too! Everybody sposed to have a
hand in liberating themself! If you don't want to kiss nobody's behind, then don't keep puttin your behind in their
face! Cause that's wrong and sho a shame!

One time, I remember, Inez broke her arm. I don't
know what she was doin to break it. I know she kept her
house clean, but how you gonna break your arm cleanin
house? Oh, I guess you can fall or somethin, but, you
know? Anyway . . . that sling thing stayed on her arm
bout six months and Fred had to come home from work
and clean the house . . . to her specifications! She had to
have it clean clean! Cleaner than when she did it herself.
He did it.

Now, maybe her friends mighta helped her, but they was eatin and gossipin and going-out friends, not heart friends. I helped her a couple of days, but I had a husband and four children so I already had plenty to do. Anyway, Fred did it. For six months or such. He sure was a nice man, a good man. Sho was a shame. Then, one day I was outside getting my mail and I saw her open the door for the mailman and she used that arm just as good as she want to. Wasn't no sling on her arm or in sight. She musta forgot to put it on before she opened the door. Later on that day I saw her and the sling was back on. That arm had been well, chile, and I know it! Bout a month after that Fred came home early one day, sick, and caught her with the thing off and that was the end of the broken arm.

When somebody tryin to do what you are tryin to do and you been friends, you pay attention to how life is turning out. I never did talk about her to nobody but my husband, and he didn't care nothin bout nobody's business. But Inez talked about Fred all the time cept she never did say nothing except all the things she thought was wrong with him. Said he couldn't do nothin right, he was so stupid. Or she should'a married somebody else cause he didn't have no class, no culture. She tore him down. I didn't say nothin cause I didn't agree with her. I liked Fred. Only reason I'm tellin you is cause you don't know neither none of us. And . . . I felt sorry for Fred. Sho was a shame to me.

I don't know whatever else happened in their house, like their bedroom or nothin, but after about ten years or such, Fred got him a pretty lady who was washin her clothes over at that same laundromat Inez made him use. I guess Inez didn't give him much of that sex stuff either, you know. Lovin, chile. (I got more than my husband ever gonna need and I help him know that.) (smile)

Fred and that lady started keepin company, pretty regular. When Inez began to wonder why he was late from work more and more, she buzzed around and found out bout that woman. She went down to that woman's job, cussed her out and wanted to fight! After that she trailed Fred all the time in her car. She driving, him walking. He didn't keep the lady or the lady didn't keep him, I don't know. I do know he told my husband, "Sometime a man can't be happy in the house and can't be happy out the house. What can he do?" My husband SAID he said, "I don't have that problem so I don't know." Anyway, if that was true, it sho was a shame.

Quiet as it was kept, I knew Pete had another woman too. The woman even had a baby for Pete cause Gartha didn't want no more children. I do know Pete was a good father to the daughter Gartha had.

Not long after that, Fred started building him a add-on room. Just a little one. She made him use cheaper, second-class wood and things. Said, "It's too expensive and you don't even need it!" He did it all, then bought cheap curtains and a used big chair. He fought for a TV of his own. The room had a door to the outside so his friends could come in the back way and not disturb Inez when they came to watch the games. Inez wouldn't let him "eat up all my food!" so he bought a little refrigerator and stocked it up with all kinds of things for games; lunch meat, beers, Cokes, potato chips and all such as that. She told him, "Let them men bring their own food! You spending too much money!" Them men wasn't there all the time neither, cause they visited each other in turns. Fred just couldn't satisfy Inez. Sho was a shame.

Later, more things happened, or didn't happen, but I had my own family growin up and other things to look after, so I don't know everything. Sure always thought it was a shame that the man couldn't enjoy the life he worked so hard for. He was gettin older and he didn't smile so much, cept at the kids round here. Fred just kept workin and almost lived in that back add-on room.

Well the years passed that way. Back bent as he walked down the street to home. Frownin a little, head bent down. I guess Fred was thinkin bout his life and it wasn't happy at all. One day when they had been married about twenty-five years (still no children yet) he came home and went to sit in his little room. Didn't turn on the TV or radio. He got a plate of cold lunch meat out of the icebox and sat down, forgettin to eat, starin off a million miles into space right there in that little room. There were tear streaks down his face when they found him. He died right there . . . that day. Sho was a shame. The man had never really lived where he wanted to, like he wanted to.

Well, hooonney, Inez went to pieces. Allll to pieces. I mean, she fell out! Her life bout fell apart. She took it pretty good the first day, but that night! And all the rest of them days and nights! She looked at that expensive coffin (she insisted!) as they lowered it into the ground and she looked so hurt and confused . . . and alone. Alone, chile! Seems like she had never thought of death and Fred. But he was gone. Gone!

His old girlfriend came, crying, so he must have been nice to her too. Poor Fred. Sho was a shame.

Naturly the days passed, naturly the nights followed and Inez was mi-ser-aBLE. No new man rushed over there like she thought they would with her "fine" self. I don't mean to sound ugly, but you know what I mean. Her life was more lonely every day. Every day she had the blues!

Well, Pete didn't die, but Pete said to himself, "Life is too short!" and he left Gartha. Left that unclean, unhappy home. Their daughter was grown and he had three younger ones over at his girlfriend's house. (That first girl he had loved in school.) They called him "Daddy" out loud everywhere.

Gartha liked to went crazy! She whooped and hollered and went on about "I gave him the best years of my life! I been a good wife! I gave up plenty good chances for Pete and now he done left me for some young whore!" (The girl was wrong to go with a married man, but she wasn't a whore and she wasn't young. She was Gartha's age. She had been raisin the children and waitin through the years cause she loved Pete.) I heard Pete said back, "You haven't ever given anybody your best nothin! You ain't ever had a best nothin! I gave you the best years of MY life!" Then he was gone, from Gartha anyway. Naturally, life went on for everybody.

Well . . . bout two months later Inez came over to my house. She was breakin. She had already been a little gray, but now her hair was almost all gray. New lines of tears or frowns was deep in her face. "Oh, Ella," she said to me, "I miss him. I miss Fred. I lay in that bed at night or sit in that house wishing I could hear Fred rambling round in the kitchen, in his little room, just anywhere. I wish him and his friends was back there in that room or anywhere else he

want to be in that house. I wish I could just smell his
smoke, see his cigarette ashes all over. I don't care. I wish
he was there, hungry, so I could fix him somethin to eat
. . . drink . . . anything! Even wish I could wash his
clothes. Ohhh, Ella, I miss him. I miss Fred. I can't sleep
since he been gone." She said a lot more things, but I can't
remember all of it. Sure is a shame. It was too late for all of
it.

Soon after that day I went over cross the high grass of
her overgrown lawn to take her a plate of food and she had
the TV on to a game and the radio on to another game, just
blastin! Was even a cigarette burnin, smokin, layin in one of
her beautiful ashtrays! She sat there crying from the bottom
of her body. "I'm alone. Fred is gone. My good, good man
is gone."

Then Gartha came in and I always left when Gartha
came and started cryin bout how she had been treated bad
by Pete and life. Cause I knew she could have kept what
Pete's other woman had if she had listened to her heart
instead of old bitter women who twist and stretch the truth,
sometime, til it covers up all their own mistakes. Both
Mama Lil's daughters had missed out on life by listenin to
her talk. They should'a looked to see what kind of woman
she was! What would a good man who loves peace and a
happy home want with Mama Lil for? I may be wrong, but
I think you get what you attracts to yourself and what you
choose. And you don't get what you don't attract! Or
choose! I may be wrong, but I don't think so. I hate to see
people unhappy, but you know, sometimes it's our choice
anyway.

So I left there . . . sad for Inez, mean as I knew she

had been to Fred. They could'a had such a beautiful life. All I could say was, "Sho is a shame." Two people's lives messed up! I just couldn't stop sighin and sayin, "Sho was a shame."

I finally forgot about it a little when my husband came home and hit me on my behind while I was fixin up his dinner. I had done fed my two grandkids early and put them to bed til their parents came to pick them up. When he hit me on my behind, I know what that means. (smile) Inez' life just sorta flew outta my mind cause the best thing, I blive, that you can do in your life is tend to your own business. I have always tried to take care mine. And I blive . . . that's why I got some business to tend to. (smile) Sho is a blessing and a joy!

The Bank of Life

You know, you can do just so much livin til you gets to a point when you get tired of it. That's where I am. I done got to the place where I just watch life. Use to do it sittin in there lookin at the television, but that got to lookin like they was gonna kill up the whole human race, so I had to get away from all that blood and killin. They either killin or tryin to make love. People what don't even know each other in real life nor in the play neither, makin love anyway. So I been comin on out here on my porch, between my marriages, sittin and watching these live folks do their business. Yea, for a long time now.

Like next door. Which is the easiest I can see cause it's the closest. Some people, the Dells, been livin there bout

thirty, forty years. I ain't sure cause I ain't all that old myself, but it's the same house like ours. The houses are medium size, but they got these big ole long yards. This was
my mama and daddy's house. They dead and gone now,
rest em, Lord. I know my mama is restin in the Lord, but I
don't know bout my daddy cause he was a hell raiser. Blived
in whippin everybody, I can sure tell you that.

Anyway, the one who I'm gonna tell you about, still
livin in that house, is named Roberta. Roberta Dell was the
onliest child her mama had that lived so they sure nuff
loved her and took such good care of her, they like to run
even me crazy! She always had to stay in the house, or if
they let her out, she had to just sit on the porch, quiet like.
Just watch us other kids play. Couldn't even get them little
raggidy clothes dirty. Sometime some child go over and sit
a minute to talk and Roberta be so glad . . . til her mama
come out and sit and rock, then the visitin child would go
away to play and Roberta be alone with her mama again.

Her daddy drank a bit, but everybody's daddy drank a
bit! When he come home Saturday nights full of liquor
sometime, you'd hear some hollerin and shoutin . . . by
the daddy! And in the backyard you could hear Roberta
cryin, beggin him not to hurt her mama. He must not'a
hurt her, she didn't never go to no hospital or nothin. Just
next day, Sunday, everything be the same again and they be
on their way to church.

Roberta was a dark black person with the kind of hair
you could wet, grease and plait and it would look smooth
with pretty waves in it. But we hadn't done got to that
Black was Beautiful part yet, so Roberta sure didn't think
she was beautiful even though her mama thought so. She

was beautiful though, well . . . mostly pretty anyway.
Cause it's hard for anybody to be beautiful no matter what
color they are. On television they can do anything with
makeup and they do! I bet if we saw them same women
walkin down the street without all that makeup on, we
wouldn't even notice em and might even think they was
ugly. No, chile, beautiful is hard to come by. Well, sides
myself. I sure could'a been.

Anyway . . . Roberta had these nerves and things
from never bein able to do nothin like a real child, so she
look like a thin, hard razor blade or somethin. Though her
face was round a bit, she always seemed to be sharp and
long. I don't remember her body none cause I didn't have
them kind'a glands would notice her body. The only thing I
look on women for is to see is her legs bigger'n mine.

Roberta went on through school like the rest of us. Me,
I went far as I could go, til I got married, then I left. My
family didn't make no fuss cause they had too many to send
to school and too little money to do it with anyway.
Roberta finished though, up to the twelfth grade, then her
daddy died and her mama had a stroke. I guess the mama
was so glad to be free of him it was too much for her. I
shouldn't say that but I blive it's like that sometime. I can
sure tell you that!

Roberta quit school and went on to work without a
whimper bout havin to take care herself til her mama and
daddy's Social Security and pensions come through for her.
Well, she didn't know nothin else to do, I guess. We didn't
never hear nothin bout no insurance or nothin and we
didn't know if the house was paid off or nothin like that
and we didn't ask cause we didn't want to hear no bad news

and we couldn't help her if she had'a needed us. I can sure
tell you that!

Now, Roberta had gone through all her schoolin without a boyfriend cause she was always so tensed up tight
and all . . . and shy too, so . . . what else? I bet that girl
was still a virgin when she got to be bout twenty-five
years old. Her mama died then . . . and Roberta was all
alone.

When the news got around pretty good that she was
single over here and had a house all her own, probly paid
for, some men came to court her. (Cause I done told you
she wasn't ugly. Far from it!) Nothin seemed to come of
none of them men.

Now, Roberta was a churchgoin woman. Not too
much, just every Sunday. But she was lonely and didn't
know how to change life for herself. Sometimes she just
come out and stand on the porch and smile over at us. By
that time I had done divorced my first husband already. I
had a few kids then, and was gettin ready to get married for
the second time. (I shouldn'ta done that one either, cause
all I got for it was another baby.) But she would smile and
walk over, sometimes, and we would try to talk. But, well,
she didn't know nothin to talk to me about. She didn't do
no night life, didn't have no men friends I was interested in,
so what could I talk about? Cept to ask, "When you gonna
get married, girl?" She would blush, much as a black skin
can, and it can!

I'd offer her a drink or somethin, but she say she didn't
drink. (I thought that was what she needed to loosen her
up some.) Me, I stayed loose. Then she'd play with the kids

awhile, said, "I love children," then she go on back to her house and go inside. She had fixed that house up kinda nice and that big ole, long yard too, but to just fix it up to go sit inside and look at it didn't seem to make no sense to me. Course, she had a house of her own and I didn't, so . . .

Sometimes, some of them older men came over . . . from the church, you know. But somethin in her mind told her she wanted love and she must didn't think them old ones could give it to her. See there? How wrong can you be? I've known some older men could run a young man outta town. Old age don't make everybody weak. Who you think these husky, healthy, good-lovin men turn in to? Yes, chile. But Roberta didn't have no way of knowin that, so most of em just faded away.

Then . . . a man I knew, Earl Western, friend of my new husband start visitin us. A real playboy man, bout thirty-five or so, done been married before, but wasn't no woman gonna keep him (with him runnin through every women round here, with track shoes!). Earl start comin over to see me bout every day. Well, I had had a little sport with him fore I got engaged, but didn't nobody know it, of course. Anyway, Roberta came outside one of them days and started workin in her garden. He asked about her. Well, she was a woman and that's what he liked!

He leaned back in his porch chair and ask me, "Where her husband?"

I leaned back in mine and answered, "Ain't got none."

He smiled. "Ain't got none? A pretty woman like that?"

I laughed. "What you thinkin bout, boy? You gonna sit on my porch and ask me bout another woman?"

He sat up straight and laughed that aside. "Well, who she livin with? Her mama?" He started to lean back again.

I smiled slowly. "Noooo, her mama and daddy dead. She all alone."

He shot forward again. "Alone?! She rentin?"

I was gettin bored talkin bout Roberta. "Naw, that's all hers . . . now."

He turned complete round to look in my face. "Who . . . is her man?"

I raised up then. "Man, what you want to know all her business for? Don't be settin up here on my porch askin me bout no other woman! When you sittin here talkin to me, ain't no other woman!"

He pushed that aside too. "Do she work?"

"I'll invite her over while you go get some more beer"— I hit him on his knee with my empty beer can—"then you can ask her for yourself." Well, he didn't go get no beer and I didn't get to invite her over cause he so cheap, he jumped up and went to help her lift somethin in her garden and introduced hisself!

He gave that woman the BIG rush, chile. Every day he was there, bringin things and doin things. He was really workin on her, and since he was big and strong AND good-lookin . . . well. Little by little he got into her good graces. He always left right around nine or ten o'clock at night, so I know she wasn't sleepin with him cause there was no home for him to rush off to and she didn't have nobody there to spoil any plan she made for the night. I know the other

women he was seein then and that's who he went off to
sleep with when he was through bein a "nice" man over at
Roberta's.

Now, a woman like Roberta couldn't help fallin in love
with a man like Earl. The rotten always seem to get the
good. Look at me. Both my husbands was rotten, that's
why I left them. Least that's why we separated our lives
anyway!

Earl and Roberta got married, chile. They "eloped"
cause he didn't want nobody gettin no invitation spreadin
the news and then somebody tellin Roberta, or them other
women either, bout his business. He didn't want nothin to
mess up his plans, present or future either.

After they got married, he kept his regular job, but he
didn't do no more yard work or nothin round the house.
And instead of leavin that house at ten o'clock at night, he
start to coming home at ten or eleven or twelve o'clock at
night. Even later on the weekends!

Roberta looked so happy and bright, soft and womanish before they got married. Shining in what she thought
was their love. I wanted to tell her, "Honey, he lookin for a
free home and a cook." But you can't magine how happy
she looked and how hard it would'a been to tell her something that would make her unhappy and, plus, she wasn't
goin to blive it anyway! You know how you have a hard,
hard time tellin somebody in love to have some sense bout
what they doin! She didn't have no friends to help her
think!

Over the next thirteen years she went through solid
hell! He never did bring his pay home, less it was a emer-

gency. Women called on the phone day and night. He gave them the number hisself! Some of them no-heart women even came to the door askin for him! Two times with babies! Babies Roberta never seemed to have cause she was so tight and tense and more like a razor blade every year! Her nerves was on her side, if you ask me, cause to have his baby would'a put another lock to his side.

I heard her once when they argued, well, he argued, she cried. With a voice just full of tears, she told him, "I have a heart under these breasts you never touch. My blood runs hot in my body just like them other women! What's wrong with me for you?" I didn't hear his answer. Then she said, "What's between man and woman, husband and wife, is supposed to be beautiful. Why does ours have to be so ugly? Am I ugly to you?" I heard her moan clean over to my porch. "Am . . . I . . . ugly to . . . you? Why can't I have your babies? You make me so bluuuue. So bluuuue."

That hurt me to my bones! See, cause I know! I know what it feel like to have the blues. And this child had the blues with a hundred blue-black "u's" in it. See? When a man fool around on the outside even just a little bit, his woman or his wife think, right away, that something is wrong with her! That something is missin, that she ain't as good as the other woman or why would he turn to the other woman?! Then, sometimes she get so disgusted with her life she just lets herself go. She changes her body too. She get fatter or thinner, harder or stupider even. Stops laughin, or even smilin, til they find somebody what puts that love for their own self back in them. I seen it happen to men too, when their women cheat on them. That cheatin stuff is a bitch with a capital "B." The real Blues is a Bitch! Some

people can sing about the blues. Most people don't feel like
no singin when they have em. I can sure tell you that!

But Roberta wasn't the type of woman to find somebody else for herself and cheat back on Earl. She just got
sadder and sadder. She got that bent-over look like her
heart was too heavy to carry. It got to be a long time between times she try to fix herself up to go to church even.
And a unhappy woman makes a unhappy uncared for home
and it turns into a sorry-lookin house. Little by little
Roberta's house got that way. That ole long yard just full of
dead flowers and weeds. And I do know she laid awake
many a night, many a year lookin at the ceilin . . . alone.

But the quiet in the night didn't tell her nothin and I
sure couldn't tell her nothin cause I was in the middle of
gettin married for the third time, tryin to be "happy" again.
I knew my new marriage didn't have much of a chance
cause my power to get any which man I wanted was cut
down some. A mighty big some. I was tired! And lookin
wore out from them men in my life! This husband-to-be
was kinda my last hope, though I didn't like to think so.

Anyway, I couldn't go backward in life so I was tryin to
go forward! My mama was gone and I sure wished I had
her back to help me think and remind me of some of them
things she said that I threw out of my mind when I thought
I was smarter than she was, chile. I know one thing she said
to all her children. Said, "I want you to remember there is a
Bank of Life. Just like banks for savin money. Whilst you
be livin, you be savin up all the good things and all the bad
things you do in Life. They gonna be there in that bank!
Sometime you can go get somethin when you need it, but
most time you got to wait. Then you don't have to go get

nothin, it comes to you all by itself, all what you done put in that bank. Don't care if you ready to draw it out or not, it comes. Sometimes a little bit at a time, sometimes a lot. You got to pay your dues, too. So you be careful how you live and what goes in that Bank of Life. You are going to get it back . . . someday. I can sure tell you that!" I sure remember that and I wonder what else I got coming.

Anyway, Earl didn't feel nothing, comin and goin as he pleased. No rent to pay, no food to buy, no utilities and such. Hell, he was in heaven. He never did beat up on Roberta, sides slappin her once or twice when she grab on his clothes as he goin out the door to try to keep him home. But it's some people, if they have to take a beatin, rather take a body beatin then a heart beatin. Your feelings can just be crushed up and bruised up and stepped all over and if you love somebody, Lord chile, it's a pain you can't hardly bear when you know they gonna be layin their body down side somebody else! Roberta was takin it though! Heartache, comin and goin!

I, me, who wasn't doin so well either, I felt so sorry for her. I told her once, "Why don't you get that child-man out of your house?!"

She answered, "The Lord is my friend and I can't do nothin He said don't do. He don't like divorces."

Well, I like to died! I said, "That man, Earl, done made a whole game out of adultry! The Lord said you could leave a person, get a divorce, for that!" She just sighed one of them heavy sighs. So, I asked her, "You love him . . . that much?"

She sighed again, said, "No . . . not really . . . any-

more. Just that I don't know what to do. When my Lord
wants me to change, I'll know it and I'll do it. Sides, Earl is
all I got."

I grunted to myself. "Huh, you ain't got him." On my
way home I told the Lord, "Listen, Lord, I know You busy
and all, but You got somebody down here dependin on You
and You need to do somethin for her cause she don't just
SAY she love You, she proves it!" Then I went on bout my
business. It wasn't doin too good itself. I was bout to divorce again and this time I had been true to him. My
friends was helpin me get through my mess with plenty
beer and wine. My kids was grown, gettin grown and I was
gettin older. But lookin back, you know I was as lonely as
Roberta . . . in a different way, but lonely is lonely,
honey.

Anyway . . . soon after that Earl got the prostrate
glands or something and was pretty shocked and miserable
bout the whole thing. He couldn't make love like he
wanted to. But soon as he was able he would be out in the
streets again. He be comin home drunk a lot. And still
takin medicine! Then all that medicine and that liquor
mixed up one day . . . he had a heart attack or a stroke,
one. His life just almost stopped! While he was still
breathin! Job lost . . . money gone and you know he ain't
saved none. But Roberta came through. She took care of
that cheatin, worthless man and I do mean worthless, cause
he was already worth nothin before he got sick.

The doctor told him he might get better with a operation, but he didn't have no money so he told Roberta they
would have to sell the house. The Lord must'a spoke to

Roberta cause she shook her head "no." He tried to sit up and cuss, but she told him not to excite himself, he better eat some soup instead. And that was that about the house.

Money was hard, so times was hard for Roberta. Them little pensions her parents had left only could cover so much and the medicine kind'a ate a big chunk of it. She spent it willinly, but when it was gone, it was gone and somethin else that would'a should'a been paid, wasn't. She didn't know nothin bout how to go about a lotta things, like gettin no money from the state for help.

Now, I had a woman friend, Alotta. Ohhhhhh, that woman was a hip-shakin, man-stalkin woman. Anyway, her husband, Ronald, was leaving her. See, that rotten one, good one, again. I knew he was a nice man who had got caught up with Alotta some way and I knew he needed a place to live and he could pay. Well, I liked him, not for myself, but just cause he was nice. So I told Roberta about him rentin a room from her, then I told him, too. He went to see her and I looked up one day soon after and he was movin in the spare room as a roomer.

Ronald started out bein a lot of help cause he was a roofer and knew how to work on a house. That ole house needed some fixin by now. It ended up with Roberta cookin and doin little things for him. She didn't seem to mind cause she was already cookin for ole sicky anyway. Had to carry it to Earl in bed and everything. Always what the doctor ordered, always fixed real nice.

Roberta even sat there talkin to him or readin the newspaper to him while he looked mad at life. Finally he would tell her to stop talkin or readin. "You bore me, Roberta." He told her that! He hurt her and he'd a been lost without her! He never did tell her the food was good or thank her for readin to him. Just took it as his due. It's some fools in this world, you hear me?!

Wasn't long before Roberta took his food in to him and left, then he could hear her and Ronald talkin and laughin together in the kitchen. Somethin Earl never did do with her since after the elopement. Earl would bang on his tray real loud a lot. She'd come runnin to see what he needed and it never was nothin! He just didn't want to hear them in there enjoyin their meal without him.

Then Earl tried to get her to put Ronald out! But she wouldn't. Said she needed the money and that sometimes Ronald took off work to take her around to all them offices they make you go to, to get some money to help her, Earl and all. They did it, too. They finally got it!

One day Earl really did try to make her make Ronald move then, cause HE said THEY didn't need Ronald no more. He demanded, as man of the house, that Ronald move. But Roberta never had had no life with smiles and laughs in many, many years. Not much laughter mostly through her whole life. She told Earl that, and she also said, "I got someone to help me in the yard and in the house. I got someone to talk to, to help me think about life. He never forgets I'm a woman and it ain't got nothin to do with sex and I feel glad about feelin like a woman. He helps me with my problems. I can't put him out, I need him. I know he may go anytime, but I'm gonna rent that room to him as long as he wants it." She didn't fuss, didn't shout, didn't stomp her foot. Roberta just meant what she said.

Earl said, "Well, come in here and talk and laugh with ME! He ain't your man, your husband! I am!"

Well, Roberta went to get all the papers she had saved over the years with all them ladies' phone numbers and addresses and gave them to him, then handed him the telephone. Said, "Call them. I bore you." When she was gone Earl looked through them papers, but he knew them ladies did not want to hear from no sick man who needed help and didn't have NO money. None!

Then he try workin on Roberta again. Earl was always telling her, "Now I'm home all the time with you like you always been askin me, and now, you don't appreciate it!" Roberta wouldn't say nothin, she just go on and wash his dirty behind or change his sheets and give him his pills, and that would make Earl so mad.

She was still sleepin with him at that time. Listenin to him gasp and snore at night, even turn him over sometimes, and he had nerve to say, "I'm home now and I want you to be glad and happy. We private. I want you to put Ronald out." To get away from all his fussin, she started not sleepin with him sometimes and that made him mad, too. She never answered him when he accused her of sleepin with Ronald. (She wasn't.) That made him mad too. But, somehow, Earl knew wasn't no sense in dyin bout it.

Well, they say all the time bout what goes around, comes around.

Roberta was not tryin to be mean to Earl. She was just hungry for kindness and company. Earl never gave her any for years, and now he didn't want nobody else to! Just

wanted her stuck up in there with him and his sick ole . . .
butt. Didn't want her to have nothin. Now, I'm gonna tell
you the truth. What Ronald and Roberta was doin was
nothing! That woman hadn't even thought about sleepin
with that man. Maybe Ronald did, well, I mean . . . you
know, but Roberta didn't.

I got single bout that time and been single ever since. I
was sick of men. And seem like I had lost all my gettin
power. Maybe . . . I'll try again . . . sometimes, after I
rest awhile. But I wasn't bored, I was watchin Roberta.

You know, day by day, night by night, with someone who
helps you, someone who makes you laugh . . . Lookin
up from the rows of that little vegetable garden Ronald
helped Roberta plant, lookin up from your plate and a
nice steak someone done bought you . . . stuff like that
can't do nothing but bring love. I can sure tell you
that.

Ronald liked music and he had a record collection.
That was the one thing he would spend a little money on.
Music began to flow through that house. Earl used to love
music, be snappin his fingers and all, but no more. He
didn't like it in his house and told Roberta bout it. Told her
to cut that noise off. But she said, "We like it, but I will
shut your door so it don't bother you . . ." and she did.
But I bet that bothered Earl more.

One day Roberta's bank made a little payout. It was
evenin and Roberta hadn't turned the lights on yet. Ronald
was just sittin there restin after a full day's work and a bath.

He put some soft music on, was nice and slow. Ronald asked Roberta, who NEVER danced, to dance. He had to teach her so he taught her his way. Now, while he was holdin her, they was talkin and, somehow, when they turned their heads they almost kissed. Their lips brushed together, anyway. On the days followin, Roberta changed. Her skin softened, her face smoothed, her features rounded. In fact, her whole body rounded, like a woman. The woman was beautiful! Even me, I can say so.

I don't know when Ronald and Roberta tried . . . IT, but I know things surely changed around there, right on along with Roberta. Everything seemed to be all better. Yard and all! Them lit up windows in that house looked like they was smilin!

Now, time was passin fast. My hip-swingin friend, Alotta, who was gettin older just like I was, was findin out that it wasn't so much HER them men had been after. It was just that what she had was free and I ain't got to tell you it's a mighty poor woman who can't GIVE some away. I don't think there is any. So, of course, they ran after her for a long while. Cause her husband had been taken care of her, them men didn't have to. That made her look better too. But things was changin for Alotta, just like for everybody else, cause there was plenty new, younger girls out there that thought sex was love and they was just'a givin it away too! Alotta was just startin to think about tryin to see Ronald again, thinkin she could get that good man, her ex-man, back.

In fact, she was on her way over to his house that
evenin when she came steppin out of the Good Time Bar
and Grill and a man stepped up to her and handed her the
divorce papers. She opened the papers and lost her balance,
stumbled on the curb and broke one of them five inch
heels. She limped on down the street talkin to that paper
cause she just knew Ronald wasn't going to really divorce
her. But he sure did!

Love curled around in Roberta's brain too and changed
her mind about divorce. Cause next thing, somebody served
Earl his papers in his bed and he tried to get up to cuss at
Roberta and put Ronald out. That didn't work too good, so
he tried to have another heart attack! But the divorce papers stayed. Now, Earl was scared he would have no where
to go. When you don't have much money, people don't
always treat you right out there in this world, you know. I
can sure tell you that! But Roberta said, "We'll take care of
you, Earl, til you die or we die." But her and Ronald looked
happy, younger and healthy.

Well, Earl, the man didn't want to think of dyin. He
wanted that warm body he had moved away from, so many
times, for so many years. He wanted that body to still keep
him warm in his ole sick age. But Roberta had done moved
all the way out of their old room and left him to hisself.
Ronald was sleepin on the couch, wouldn't let Roberta be
uncomfortable. He was a man, chile. When all the divorces
were over Ronald and Roberta got married.

NOW Ronald's ex-wife is not having any fun too much
without somebody to fall back on. She got to find somebody to love her for real, again, and they don't come

too easy, you know? The Bank of Life was callin in her dues! Ask me! Cause I know about it! Ain't I payin mine?

Around that time Ronald started carryin a lotta wood to the backyard. He was buildin a long hallway and another room on to the back of the house, FOR EARL! So Earl was IN the house, only, he was OUTSIDE the house at the same time! Have mercy!

Now . . . Earl lays back there, even WAY back there now, and listens to his ex-wife squeal, moan and holler up under another man. All them squeals of delight and passionate moans he never did stay home long enough to make her feel like doin.

Every time Ronald and Roberta have another baby and time come they want that child to have a room of its own, Ronald builds another room in back of the last one. Earl been moved further back three times now. They got three children. I know Earl prays they won't have no more, cause he be on the next street then. Oh, Roberta takes care of him, feedin, cleanin and all. But, hell! His life now is listenin to somebody else's lovin!

You know, I look at Ronald and Roberta, and I think, "Hot damn! Them people are happy!" Then I think some more. When I get through payin my dues to the Bank of Life, will I get one more chance? Just one more chance? I been takin care of myself. I don't look so beat, so tired, anymore.

Maybe . . . I had the wrong friends. Roberta's friend is still the Lord. You can say He looked out for her by tellin her what to put into the Bank of Life. They still puttin it there, together. I'm gettin older, but . . . I'm learnin, I'm learnin. And I'm courtin the Bank of Life. Ain't no sense in a good woman bein alone if she don't want to. I'm tryin to be careful now bout what I put in the Bank of Life. Hear me, Lord.

Yellow House Road

It's some strange things in this here world. Strange things! They be under your nose sometime, but you don't see em, don't think of em. I guess wherever there be people with their brains always workin, anything can happen. Thinking! There be power in a brain, you just got to work on it, is all.

Right now, I'm thinking of MLee. Her mama couldn't read or spell good, but her own name was Lee and she knew the letter "M," so when MLee was born, she just put the "M" in front of Lee and had MLee. Sounded like "Emily," so that was fine for her.

MLee was reared up with thirteen other children; she was round bout the middle child so she had her own kind of life. That's what each child gets anyway. She had a little,

mighty little, schoolin cause there was always some work to do with all them babies actin out or cryin and Mother was tired. Sure was.

MLee left home when she was bout fourteen, getting married to some ole big-mouth boy named Alec who said he loved her and would build her a nice home and take care of her. She had her first baby, a boy, at fifteen and the second one, a girl, at sixteen years old. She could spell much better than her mother so she named her son West, and her daughter Northa. Then, when she was pregnant again and didn't like to have sex, Alec went out to relieve hisself and brought some ole disease home to give her and she lost the baby. The doctor say she probly wouldn't have no more kids. By that time MLee didn't care. She said, "I got two. That's plenty for me, cause Alec ain't built me no house yet noway and I don't need nothin else to worry bout."

Alec didn't seem to be nobody you could love long. Sometimes he wasn't worth a tack that fell off the wall and got stepped on. He liked to hit MLee, at first. Use to come in the house mad cause he couldn't find no work or he done drank up the little money they had and needed real bad. She fought him back though, with anything she could get her hands on. Once he got his head hurt real bad, stitches and all. He stopped hittin on her so much after that. Sometimes he could be nice to her and his children, but not enough times. He wasn't all bad, maybe, but he sure wasn't much good.

Anyway, there she was in this same ole country town with two kids and him and nowhere to go and nothin to get there with. She sure wasn't goin home out there on the other side of town to her mother and all them children and grandchildren round there. Her little space she had taken up when she was home closed right on up when she left. Wasn't no place for her there no more.

Somehow Alec worked hard and MLee saved hard and they bought a little ole house that was already old when they bought it. Had a fence and a small barn or shed, whatever you want to call it. The wind and rain had done worn and chipped all the color off it and it had turned a old yellow color. The barn-shed was missing pieces of the roof off and some wood slats were missin and it leaned to the side like it was real tired. She didn't never get no new furniture, just made do with what she found and what was given to her. I guess every once in a while she worked and paid for somethin that didn't cost much. She could really cook, don't know how she learned so good. Some people just kinda born cookin good. That's how they paid for that cow and them chickens they got.

Anyway, she raised them kids good as she could. She sewed all their clothes. She grew most their food. They lived. Alec always lookin for work, find it sometimes. He helped her work the little garden back of the house so they be sure to eat, but he didn't do much else. Anything come up like the cow run off, chickens get out, kids get in trouble, something break down in the house, he always say, "Tell my wife" or "Tell your mama!" He thought he was gettin outta work, but he was gettin out of manhood.

MLee always talked bout her kids going to school and she tried to keep them there. She sure did want em to go to college. At least, one of em. But when West was sixteen years old, he lied about his age and went to join the Navy,

said, "I'm gonna make my own life and I want'a see the
world." That's what they told him, "Join the Navy and See
the World." I hoped that he would, but I don't blive nothin
white folks say bout what they gonna help you do.

Now, when you live far from everything cept the same
people every day, sometimes you ain't got nothin to do
except the one thing most everybody can do and that is
have sex. That's what most the older folks talk bout sittin
round on their porches and the children grow up, listen and
takin it for granted that that's what you do! And these boys,
if they can't talk good enough to talk up on a job, they sure
can talk good enough to talk up on some sex. Northa got
pregnant and left to get married when she was sixteen.
MLee tried to talk her into havin the baby if she want it,
just keep on goin to school, maybe college and MLee
would take care the baby for her. But Northa ask her,
"With what?"

MLee didn't have no answer cept, "We can try."

Northa answered, "You try, Mama. I'm gone." And
was gone.

MLee was only bout thirty-two or thirty-three years
old then, but she really did look like a old woman. Her
years wasn't many, but they was hard . . . and empty. So
her face had a lotta pain in it that centered in her eyes. And
her body looked tight, tight, tight.

MLee said to me, "I'm through. Everything I was tryin
to work so hard for is gone. I will not let Alec touch me in
bed, so that's gone too. I'm gettin old. I will just wait to die
now." At thirty-three years old!! Before she gave all the way
up, she did some work cookin for a lady and bought herself

a brand-new rockin chair. First brand-new thing she ever
had. All hers. She put that rockin chair on the yellow porch
of that yellow house and sat in it all day after she'd tend to
her garden and things. Just sittin there watchin that yellow
road and tryin to keep her chickens safe inside the rickety
yellow fence. She be there rain or shine.

The country round here is sparse, neighbors not too
near. Not too many trees and things. The sun just burns em
up. You got to plant and water regular. All the trees MLee
planted got knocked down or rutted by Alec draggin something through the yard or the kids playin. When her kids
was growin up, she had tried to plant a tree on each side of
the porch so she would have some shade. The trees never
did make it and grow. Just burnt up. Nobody remembered
to water them or nothin to fight that sun when MLee be
gone tryin to work and come home so tired. One did grow
one time when she was home sick. But when she went back
to work, everybody say they watered it, but they didn't. So
. . . it died too.

So, now, I would see her sittin in the hot, hot sun,
fannin with a handkerchief or a clean rag, movin that chair
back, little by little to stay out the direct sun. Alec had the
back of the house; MLee wanted to stay in the front so she
could watch the world not inside her house. Them chickens
was her company, her friends. If one get out, she go chase it
back in again. If she hear squawkin, she go see bout it and
come on back to her rockin chair, turn her head and look
up that long, long, dusty yellow road again, all day.

I told her, "I'll help you plant them trees now. You need
em if you gonna sit out here in the sun." She said, "I'm too

tired. And by time them trees be big enough for shade, I'll be gettin my shade from the earth I'll be under." I wanted to get mad at her for givin up, but I was livin the same kinda life and I just understood her.

MLee didn't know what all had happened to her. She said to me, "The last thing I remember sayin 'yes' to was when the preacher asked me do I take Alec to be my husband and I say, 'I do' and that was that. All else that happened, just happened, and I accepted it and did the best I could with it. Now, inside my head is the wonderment of what all has happened and why. And why ain't I got nothin to show for my life cept two gone children and this ole yellow house? I'm gettin old. I ain't loved Alec like a man in a long, long time. When he cheated on me, I just lost somethin I can't get back. If he had done all the other good things for his family, I mighta coulda fixed it in my mind, but he ain't done all them good things. And me, what have I ever done for myself? If I happen to live twenty or thirty more years, what's my life gonna be? They got plenty things in the world and I ain't got none of it, ever, cept this here rockin chair. So . . . I'm just gonna sit in it and look down this old yellow dirt road and wonder where it's goin that I didn't never get to go to.

Now, one day when she had done jumped up and run them hens back in her yard a couple of times, she wiped the sweat from her face with that rag and watched her ole sassy hen go through another hole in the fence and get out. MLee just sat there and looked at that hen. She watched it hasten up to get to the unpicked, unscratched grass, justa cluckin and tryin to find a new bug or somethin. She watched that hen move further and further out, away from that yellow house, searchin. She thought to herself, "I must can't feed her enough. I ain't got no right to make her stay in here where she done already found most all the food she can. She ain't scared; ain't got sense enough to be." The hen was just'a cluckin that satisfied sound and peckin away. "But she's eatin better already."

MLee still didn't go get the hen, just watched her a hour or so, til the hen came back all on her own. MLee thinkin, "She came back, but she fuller." The hen came through the fence, turned its head one side to the other starin at MLee, then she walked on side the house to the backyard, out of sight. When MLee went to bed that night she went to sleep thinkin bout that ole hen.

The next morning MLee covered her rockin chair with a ragged sheet cloth, patted it, said, "You wait, I'll be back I reckon." She sat at the wobbly kitchen table and wrote her daughter, Northa, a letter. Then she walked back to the barn/shed and stood lookin at Alec. He was rubbin the cow's tits, masterbatin, with his eyes closed. She let him finish, thinkin, "I don't never give him none cause I always think he got another woman. I guess she don't give him none neither."

When he was finished, he sat down on a stool and crossed his arms over his knees, layin his head down on em. She spoke into the dark misery of that dark barn. "I'm gone."

He jerked his head up, startled. "Where you goin?"

"Goin."

He stood. "When you be back?"

"Don't know."

"MLee, you my wife. I ask you a question. I wants a answer."

MLee sighed, said, "You just put your wife back in your pants."

Alec groaned. "Oohhm, Lord."

"I said I'm goin. That's all. I be back."

Alec took a step toward her. "One these days, MLee, I'm gonna kill you."

She looked at him a long silent moment. "Why not? You done killed everything else. My love for you don't live in me no more ever since . . . So, anyway . . . I'm goin."

Alec looked at her, hurt and pain in his eyes too. Then there was anger in his face. "I done tole you, I ain't never done that again." He raised his hand and took a step toward her, threatenin.

MLee stood up straight. "Careful now. I got some strength, but I need all my strength." She looked at the cow. "Rosey, you try to take care yourself. I'm gone."

Then she was gone. Walking up the long, long, dusty yellow road. With each step she took, a little bit of old weight fell off her shoulders; she almost clucked like her hen. But a little bit of new weight came on. She was thinkin, "I got a new job to do. But what job? Where?" She dropped Northa's letter off with somebody way down the road and didn't look back.

MLee reached the first town that evenin. Dusty and tired, scared and anxious, but determined. She took a little bit of her needed money and bought coffee at a little café in the black section of town. She learned the largest city was bout fifty more miles away, but there was a bus that passed through going that way. It wasn't too expensive if you took the late, late mail bus that stopped everywhere along the way. The gray-haired waitress gave MLee some friends to look up since she didn't know nobody in the city and she warned MLee, "In that city you got to have somebody you can trust cause you a woman."

When at last MLee got to the city she found the waitress' friends livin in a shack type house, almost like her own she had left. They wanted $5.00 for the night, $10 for the week. MLee had $12 left, but she took the week.

Next day, still tired and musty, cause she could only take a wash-off cause there was no bathtub in that house, she went and bought a newspaper and, slowly, read the work ads. She walked all over town, went a lot of places, but was not hired anywhere. Them shoes of hers was most wore out now. Secondhand and cheap from the beginnin. She was tired, disgusted and almost started cryin plenty times, but she didn't.

Near the end of her $10 week, the landlady, seein her lookin so hard for a job and knowin she did not have the next week's rent, said, "I knows somewhere they might maybe hire you, but it's kitchen work."

MLee's eyes gathered them little tears she been tryin to hold back. She didn't know if they was from tired, scared or joy. She said, "I don't care no more. I ain't even got money enough to get back home."

"They the cookie-makin family. Korky's Cookies. They lousy cookies. They always needin somebody cause they don't pay nothin. The potato chip family, they keep their help cause they pays more. Them cookie people way over on the other side of town though . . . and I can't lend you no carfare. Ain't got it."

"Give me the directions. I'll make it."

MLee washed and pressed her "goin to look for a job" clothes, laid em out, woke early next morning, dressed and was gone when the sun came up. She sure hadn't eaten much that week and she could feel that huge gapin hole in her stomach that made her kinda dizzy sometime. When it seemed like she had walked a million miles, the houses started getting better. She got to where the lawns was wide and spread out all over the place. Acres of it. She finally found the address and stood there lookin at the house a long minute trying to get the feel of the place. Couldn't stand too long though, less somebody think she was there to steal somethin.

She took a deep breath, then walked along the side of the house to the back (she thought of her hen havin nerve to go out the yard alone, by itself, and findin what it wanted). So she knocked on the big, ole white door. A strange-lookin lady answered. Was a big, husky, kind of kinky blond, with little, tiny, cold blue eyes. Had on a apron with a spatula in her hand. She was frownin, lookin real mean, said, "Well?" Then she looked behind and round MLee, asked, "You deliverin somethin? What you want?"

MLee's voice caught in her throat. "I'm . . . I'm . . . I do windows and wash clothes and clean up and . . ." She dropped "cook" cause she didn't want the woman to think she wanted her job. "Can I see the lady of the house? Please?"

The woman with a strange-soundin voice ask her, "Where you come from? Who sent you?"

MLee's voice sounded strained. "I just came."

The woman squinted her hard, little eyes at MLee. "Mr. Korky is still sleepin. I don't know what the Mrs. is doin, but I ain't gonna bother em."

MLee's voice came back. "I need a job. I came to work. I work hard. Please, mam, can I talk to somebody, please?"

The woman stood lookin at MLee. Hard. Said, "Well, I'm busy and they sleep. Sit down over there on that chair by the pool and wait if you want to. I got work to do! Who told you they need somebody for work?"

MLee said, "I just came." She went and sat by the swimming pool, which fascinated her because she had never even seen one before, much less been close to one. The woman closed the door.

In about ten minutes the woman opened it again, said, "You might as well be doin somethin while you wait. I got plenty in here to do." MLee jumped up and went almost runnin in. The woman continued talkin. "I got to fix these damn kids their lunch to take to school. Two of em. Why they don't eat at school, I don't know!" She slammed a loaf of bread on the counter. "Say they don't like the food over there in that school. You'll find everything you need in that cupboard or the refrigerator. I give em peanut butter and jelly or bologna and throw in a apple or somethin. I ain't got time for all that fixin stuff. You mighta just come by your own self, but I sure do need some help round here!"

MLee was kinda faint from reachin for food so close to her, but her heart turned over with a little joy. "Yes, mam."

"Here, girl, what's your name?"

"MLee."

"Emily?"

"Yes, mam."

"You can call me Mrs. Friet."

"Yes, mam, Mrs. Friet."

MLee took care with the lunch, which, you know, Mrs. Friet didn't do. Even putting in cookies. When Mrs. Friet saw her do that, she said, "Them kids hate them cookies. Take em out!" So MLee put in a few celery sticks and some cheese while Mrs. Friet wasn't payin no tention. She used meat, lettuce and tomatoes on the sandwiches, wrappin and puttin them neatly in the bright-colored lunch boxes, setting them on the counter. By that time the children, a boy, fifteen, and a girl, thirteen, were downstairs. They looked at MLee strangely and didn't speak to Mrs. Friet as they reached for a piece of toast, drank the juice sittin out and left with their lunch boxes. A driver took them to school.

Mr. Korky came downstairs next. Mrs. Friet told him, in a whining, overworked voice, "This here is Emily. She's lookin for work. You all was asleep, so I told her to help me til you came down. I got so much to do round here. So she done the children's lunch. She seem alright enough . . . but I don't need no real help. I can do it once I get caught up."

Mr. Korky looked at MLee, then round the kitchen. "Caught up with what, Wanda?"

Wanda laughed a servant's laugh. "It's just about done now, that's why you can't see nothin. I stay busy workin, Mr. Korky. It's a million little things round here I want to do, just can't get to em all!" Mrs. Wanda Friet wasn't really tryin to help MLee get a job, she was just a little lazy and wanted all the help she could get from somebody who followed orders and didn't ask no questions.

Mr. Korky decided to keep MLee on for the day since she had already started. He went on and left goin to his business. Wanda found plenty work for MLee to do that day, but MLee did it slow. Good, but slow, so it would take all day. She needed the money, she needed the job. Wanda whined to Mrs. Korky about how overworked she was and Mrs. Korky said, "We'll see what Mr. Korky says later." When the family sat down to dinner, later that evenin, the children talked bout their lunches. So neat, fresh and different. "Better than in a long time!" they said. It was different, because they were known not to have good appetites. Wanda glared at them. MLee thanked God, cause Mr. Korky later told her to stay on.

MLee walked back to her rented room that evenin, tired as a coal miner, but she was full . . . and she had a job. She slept like a big tree falls, hard. She rose fore dawn the next morning and walked back to work, ready. The cupboards were full of things to choose from. She baked a cake and a roast that mornin, packin a good lunch full of good things for the children. She thought of her children she hadn't been able to do that for, so she enjoyed doin it for these new ones. The children liked her and showed it.

It wasn't a week fore she was given a room and a permanent job. Now she could save every dime she made. No more rent to pay. No food to buy. And she didn't have to mind Wanda anymore. She was on her own. She wrote her children. She got lonely, but didn't know exactly why cause she would have been alone at home. She didn't miss Alec. She just felt lonely. Like somethin was missin. Yes, she was on her own. All the way.

When the Korkys entertained, MLee helped with the

bakin of breads, cakes and pies. She was good at it. She kept thinkin on some kind of cookin their children would like, cause she remembered that's how she got her job.

Now MLee found and liked that thick condensed milk in the can. All through the day she dip her finger in and lick it. She kept tryin to make up a cookie with that milk. She loved oranges and for the first time could have all she wanted. She loved baked yams with butter and she loved nuts, all kinds. So bout two months later, she took all them things, mixed em in a cookie batter she already knew, made the cookies and the next day put some in the lunches. Them kids LOVED them cookies. Mr. Korky had smelled the cookies when he was leavin home that morning and he waited at the dinner table that night for dessert to be served. When none came, he asked Wanda what that smell had been. She told him, "Oh, Emly tryin to make cookies for the kids. I done told her they don't like cookies, but she bought the stuff herself so if she want to waste her money . . ." Mr. Korky sent for MLee and asked for a cookie for dessert. When she brought him a few, he ate them, chewin and lookin at the door MLee had went through thoughtfully. He sat there thinking a long time.

He thought of how his children (who frowned and avoided his own cookies) talked happily about their lunches; the little pies, the "great" cookies that MLee put in them. They had even had her put extra sweets in their lunches for their friends until MLee had begun to charge ten cents a pie and ten cents for a bag of cookies. I mean, she paid for her own material, so why not? Mr. Korky had laughed indulgently, at first, but now, with the good taste

of the cookies spreadin over his tongue and fillin his mouth
and nose, he decided to take MLee's bakin more serious.

Wanda had quit about that time, sayin to Mr. Korky as
she left, "This nigga done come in here and started kissin
up to the kids and doin all that extra work round here and
now I don't get no respeck for nothin I do! And I do
plenty! You can take this job back! See how well you do
without me!" They hadn't thought of her again. MLee was
savin them $35 a week by takin over all Wanda's duties.
She got a $5.00 raise and now made $30 a week, and she
saved $28 of that. The only thing she bought was stamps
and writing paper, sugar, flour and condensed milk. Her
work was good and her cookin was good, too. And them
cookies and pies was excellent!

Of course, soon now, Mr. Korky asked her for the recipe in
a offhand way. She said, "Sure," and smiled. But when she
went to spell out the list, she realized she didn't even mea-
sure nothin, and she sometimes changed the ingredient
things she put in. She leaned back in the little rickety chair
in her little rickety room and thought about these being
Mr. Korky's walls, his house and the money, his, he paid
her with. She thought about them two big cars in his garage and that great big swimming pool she could see the
corner of from her room. Then she thought of that little
yellow house by the yellow road and how men like Mr.
Korky had never been willin to give her husband a good
job, or even any job. Or they give him the worst job and
he would be among the first to go when lay-off time came.

She crumbled the paper she was writing on and sat back. The chair didn't rock so she just sat and thought bout money and life. When next she saw Mr. Korky, he brought it up.

"You get that recipe written down for me, Emmy?" he asked over his eggs.

MLee stopped walkin back to the kitchen. "Well . . . No, sir, I ain't."

"Well, get to it, girl. I wanted to look it over this morning."

"Well . . ." she began.

He looked up at her. "Say, can you write? You know how to write?"

"A little bit, sir."

He pushed his plate aside. "Well, get me a piece of paper and a pen and tell it to me. I'll write it down for you."

MLee tilted her head, smiling. "No need to write it down for me, sir. I already know it."

He took one of them ex . . . as . . . per . . . ated breaths and said, "I mean write it down for myself. I need that potato pie recipe too."

His children, glad their father might make a cookie they would like, looked at him like, "Oh boy!"

MLee said, "Sir, I don't think I want to do that. It's . . . it's a secret recipe my mama gave me."

He made that breath again. "Emmy, there are no secret recipes anymore. The world has changed. Everybody knows everything now."

She turned to go. "Well, if they know it, then let em use it. It's okay by me."

Mr. Korky pushed his plate away. "You work for me, Emmy. That recipe belongs to me same as you do."

"No, sir, I don't see it thataway."

Mrs. Korky spoke up. "Harold, the breakfast table is not a place to take care of business."

Mr. Korky looked at his wife with suddenly hard, cold eyes. "If we were SPENDING money it would be a good time. All times are good for you to spend money. I'll take care of my business when and where I have to."

MLee was gone on in the kitchen, thinkin, "Lawd, I don't want no trouble on my job. I need this here job."

MLee had been there a year and she had saved bout $1340. The most money she had ever had at one time in her life. She still didn't want to lose the job cause she had plans to go back home and fix up her little house. Paint it, put on a roof and do somethin for her little grandchild what was on the way, if there was enough money. She wanted to work a little longer. Two years? Five years? She was always countin money in her head as she be doin her work.

She thought about Alec too. "We ain't never gonna be nothin no more. He probly done out and out got him another woman by now. Well, if he still there, he can take the barn and live out there. Poor Rosey cow, maybe he could marry her." She didn't blive he had done nothin to that cow, but he did linger feelin Rosey's tits when he milked her.

Mr. Korky thought about MLee's recipes all the time as he looked out his factory window. He thought about how he needed something new, something different! He turned away from the window with a frown, thinkin how his wife didn't help him at all. "She wasn't good for nothin but bringin some good blood from the right people. Was all she was good for!"

One evenin when he came home from work, he stopped in the kitchen to talk to MLee. But MLee had been thinkin every day too!

"Well, Emmy, you ever think you're goin to get that recipe written down? Have you got it yet?"

"No, sir, I sure don't."

"Why, Emmy? You are going to give it to me, aren't you? You know, Emmy, if my business does badly you are goin to lose your job. You know that, don't you? Do you think of that? I need new things all the time to keep people interested. Now, in this house we are one big happy family, all of us. You too. And we have to help each other. Now, I need . . . want that recipe . . . then we can all settle back for awhile and you can get paid and keep your job, and I can keep mine." He smiled, lookin like a vulture.

MLee looked down at her worn hands. "Well, sir, I know what you are sayin . . ."

"Well, good! That's more like it!"

"But . . ."

"But?" He frowned. "Emmy? I blive you are the greedy sort. Not God fearing. I blive you want some money for that recipe. Wellll, I'm sorry to know that. Greed is a terrible thing. A tool of the devil's, my mother always said. I'm a fair man, though." He heaved a big sigh. "What do you want for the recipe? How much?"

MLee looked down at her hands again. "I don't rightly

know, sir. Let me . . . Let me think about it a few days, please, sir."

Mr. Korky was impatient, "Well, give me some idea. Tell me 'about' what it would cost . . . $50? $100? Can't be no more than that because I can pick up recipes all over the place." He started to leave the kitchen. "Better tell me soon because I'm losin interest." He left in a huff, what you might say.

That night when MLee sat in her rickety chair looking out her window that faced the utility house outside, she tried to think of what to do. Strained at it, but it didn't do no good. She knew there was a chance somewhere in this for her, but couldn't figure out how to dig it up, how to handle it. She opened and stared at the order written out by the Korky children, the list they had given her for their friends. A little light went on dimly in her mind. She tried thinkin harder. She finally fell asleep with the list in her worn, water-soaked, callused hands. Her children, grand-children, the yellow house, the recipe and Mr. Korky were in her dreams.

In the mornin when Mr. Korky spoke to her about the recipe again, she told him, "I will tell you somethin this evenin, sir."

He pursed his lips. "You like your job, Emmy?"

"Yes, sir."

He turned to go. "Well, think on that." He left. He never talked like that when his children were around. They loved MLee and would never have wanted to see her go.

———

That same day MLee asked for a little time off and was going back down to her old landlady to try to get someone to help her think this thing out. On the way, she passed a real estate office and noticin it, went in and asked about houses that didn't cost much. The agents looked at her, laughin, and told her why didn't she go down to the Black agent that worked out of his house. She got the direction somehow and found her way there, askin him, Mr. Austin, the same question bout some cheap houses.

He sat her in his little beat up, but clean and polished car and showed her around.

MLee sat way in the corner of the car like she never been in one before. Maybe she hadn't, cept a bus. She answered his questions. "I want to live close as possible to that white school for rich kids." MLee had done built up quite a list of customers at that school, teachers and all.

"You talkin bout big money, Ms. MLee."

"I say close as possible. It don't have to be right up on it."

"This is close as possible. Just get you a car and drive there if that's where you work. You can get a used car cheap."

"How cheap, Mr. Austin?"

"Bout $300 at least, for one you can count on pretty good."

MLee smiled a little. "Find the house, Mr. Austin."

He showed her a little lopsided house with whitewash on it. "This one just been had a roof put on fore the widow died, so it won't leak. It's a shotgun house, it's old, but it's clean, well kept."

MLee thought of her own house. "I reckon she was a clean lady."

"She was. And her son kept the house up pretty good. Needs some work, still, but just for this little money, you can't get no better."

"What it take to get it?"

"They askin $4000. You got $500 or so dollars, I think we can swing it for $3000. You got good credit?"

"I don't know. Ain't never bought nothin."

"Well, if you ain't got bad credit, I think we can swing it."

MLee smiled. "Let's swing on it."

They signed papers that same day and he took her around until he found her a used car for $350. A little green Chevrolet coupe. MLee loved the car, but didn't know how to drive. Mr. Austin told her, "I know you know somebody can teach you that. I can't do no more right now." She had him park the car near his place and went in his office and wrote a letter to Alec. "He gonna be good for somethin! After all, I been married to him for goin on nineteen years now," she thought.

She wrote him, "Here is a ticket. Come here now on the next Sunday and teach me how to drive. I'll get you back home that day." Then she went to buy a bus ticket, mailed the letter and went back to her job.

Now she counted her money . . . $600 for all to be done bout the house . . . $350 for the car. Little less than $250 left. MLee sighed. "Money sure will get away from you. But this time, I got things I can put my hands on. It ain't gone up in thin air. I'm gonna own TWO houses.

AND I got a car! Chile, chile." She smiled to herself, but thought again, "I got a debt. Responsibility. I have to make this thing work and I don't know what I'm doin!" She sighed and went on out to fix the evening meal.

When Mr. Korky came home, first thing he did was ask MLee bout them recipes. "What have you decided? What have you done about the recipes, girl?"

MLee hated to lie, but . . . "I been feelin a little sick, Mr. Korky."

"You're not that sick you can't even write, are you?"

"I just don't feel good. I'll . . . see you bout that in a few days, sir. I'm gonna feel better soon."

"A few days?"

"Yes, sir. A few days."

Mr. Korky looked at her in silence a minute. "I don't blive you want this job, Emmy girl. Plus that, you're going to get sick on me and we need help here, not sickness."

"Yes, sir."

He slammed the door behind him.

Now the woman MLee was when she got up that mornin, worried, was not the same one who laid down that night, worried. The nighttime worry had a little glow to it. It meant a lot of work, but she was doin somethin for herself. By herself. And she de . . . ter . . . mined in her heart she was goin to make things work!

Sunday MLee waited at the bus station all morning and Alec came in the early afternoon. He told her, "Was a long walk and wait at the bus station. So . . . this where you are! Why didn't you write me before? Everybody hear from you, but me."

"I only wrote Northa." She had wrote to me, her friend, too.

"What you been doin here so long? Why you got to learn to drive?"

MLee was walkin fast, leadin Alec. She didn't bother to answer, she was wonderin if she could learn how to drive.

Alec repeated, "Why you got to learn how to drive?"

"I got a car."

He was shocked. "YOU got a car? Where you get a car from? What you doin here, MLee?" He stopped walkin, angry.

"I'm goin to pick up my car, Alec."

"Is some man done bought you a car, MLee?"

Now MLee was gettin angry. "What you care? And if one did, he could teach me how to drive, couldn't he?" She started walkin again. He followed. She was silent, he argued all the way til she pointed and he saw the car.

He rubbed it, looked under the hood, kicked the tires and looked at MLee. He did know how to drive, but he had never owned a car. He asked her how much she had paid for the car, she told him. Then they got in and drove back to the car lot. MLee was gettin mad, "I have taken care of everything! Just teach me how to drive this thing!"

Alec jumped out the car and went to talk to the car lot man. MLee tried to stop him, but as she listened, Alec sounded like he knew what he was talkin bout and the car lot man was listenin too. When Alec was through talkin, the man ended up puttin a few more things on and in the car and even gave her a spare tire that was a good one. Then they got in the car and Alec drove away lookin like the man of the house, proud. MLee smiled, glad that she could respect Alec for somethin! Then, she made up her mind to somethin else.

She had him drive to her little house and MLee opened it with her own keys. Alec thought she had rented that house. MLee said, "They left the stove and the icebox here, that's good. What can you do to help me fix this house up? I want you to check the wirin and the gas pipes . . . and get this yard straightened out. And look here." She pointed out the back door. "I got TWO trees! Ain't they pretty?"

Alec scratched his head. "Well, they ain't yours no longer'n you live here. I done planted you two at home. They ain't this big yet, but they growin good. MLee, why you got to stay here? Why'nt you come on home like you got some sense?"

MLee looked at Alec like he had lost his mind. She knew he musta lost his memory. She said, "I got some sense. And a woman got to do what a woman got to do." She started toward the front door, then asked him, "You got any money to help me do what I have to do?"

Alec shook his head no, sadly. "I'm still tryin to get a job somewhere, but don't nobody want to hire me cause I'm old, and they don't want to pay me nothin if they do hire me. I done worked some . . . but . . . not enough to do nothin with. What you have to do, MLee? What you tryin to do?"

MLee looked around her new, little house. Said, "I'm tryin to do somethin for myself. Tryin to live with a capital 'L' for a change. You promise me a lot when we got married. You didn't do it, so now I'm gonna try to do it for myself."

"MLee, I tried. Lord knows I tried. But a man gets tired . . . and disgustit, when everwhere he turns he got to take the lowest thing there is. Then, when he do get somethin good, some white man come along and want it . . . for hisself, for his son, for his friend. They make you don't feel like nothin! You got more nerve than me, cause I was scared to go out in the world and find somethin, like you done done. And I wanted to stay where you are."

MLee took one of them deep, heavy sighs. "Them ain't all the reasons, but we ain't got time now to talk. We done already had nineteen years and you didn't use it and you ain't said nothin. Now we on my time and I got things to do. Let's go."

She didn't tell him the house was hers. She had put a small mattress in for Alec to sleep on. She told him, "We gonna go get a few things you can work with for a few days. You stay here til next Sunday, and by that time maybe I can drive good enough to drive you home and myself back." They went out to the hardware store and lumber yard for a few small things. Then they went on her drivin lessons. She practiced every day when she went to the market and every evenin after the dinner things was cleared away. She was afraid of drivin, but she learned cause she had to.

Mr. Korky was angry with MLee now, but didn't fire her. He was tryin to think of a way to get the recipe. He was tryin different things at his plant, but he didn't know about the condensed milk and the sweet potato. MLee used these things and threw cans and peelins away in the bottom of big bags as soon as they were used. She knew Mr. Korky wouldn't dig in em, and Mrs. Korky either, though Mr. Korky had told his wife to. He hired another girl to "help" so she could report on MLee. But MLee got up early and the girl was lazy.

On Saturday, before the Sunday she was to take Alec home, Mr. Korky came rushin into the kitchen. He smiled. "Well, are you ready to hand over that recipe and make your mama and you famous?" He chuckled. "Heh, heh, heh."

"Sir, I can't give away my mama's secret."

"No? Not even for $200?"

"No, sir."

He rubbed his chin, "Well, I got another answer. My children, you know they just love you, and they like those cookies and pies of yours too! Suppose you come work down at the plant? We'll have another girl, in the meantime, and you can still live here, cause this is your home. And you can make the cookies yourself! I'll give you all the help you need. We'll keep it small, at first, then as you learn to trust me and know I think of you as family, so the recipe belongs to me too, in a way, Heh, heh, heh. And I'll increase your pay by . . . oh . . . $10 a week! No! No, $20 a week! I know it's a lot, but . . . well, you're worth it. Alright? You'll be going up in the world! Progress!"

MLee looked at him, startled, "You mean I could work in the office down there? But I don't know nothin bout office work."

Mr. Korky shook his head quickly, "No, no!" He knew

his office help would die if a Negro worked in such a place with them. "No, no. Just dumbbells get stuck in a office! I want you right down there, in there with the people who count!"

MLee turned back to her dishes, "Sir . . . My husband is maybe gonna move here to be with me, so I ain't gonne be here in the evenin's no more. I sure would like to keep my job, but . . . it's gonna take me a long time to make up my mind bout my recipe. Why can't you and me just forget bout them ole things anyway? I need my job, I surely do. And I like workin for you and the Mrs. I love the children and all. But I wish I didn't ever make them cookies! They just done ruined my life."

Mr. Korky wrinkled his forehead, thinkin, then he said, "Everyone wants you to stay. Don't worry . . . now. We'll talk again when you get to know we really are your family." He turned to go, "Oh, and we are giving you a $5.00 raise a week anyway. That ain't as good as $60 a week you would make at the plant makin them cookies, but, I'll . . . delay . . . drop the matter now. We'll talk again, Emmy." He left.

On Sunday, MLee took Alec home. She did the drivin.

She was surprised when she drove up to the little yellow house. The yard was clean and she saw the two trees planted on each side of the porch. Her rockin chair was still covered and sittin there, waitin for her. She shook her head in wonder, cause it seemed like that chair and everything else was years and years ago. She got out to see if there was any sign of another woman bein in her house. The house was clean. The kitchen table didn't wobble anymore. There was no sign of any other woman anywhere. She went out into the backyard. Rosey was tied to a post in the next field, eatin new grass. The fence had been repaired and the chickens was runnin around, but they couldn't get out. He hadn't spent a lot of money, but he had spent some time on things. She was shocked and in wonder at it all. Alec had been doin somethin with hisself. Not much, but somethin!

MLee moved into her own house when she got back to the city. "I got a house note now, better get to work." She worked at night doin her bakin, and delivered cookies, pies and, now, sandwich orders in the afternoons. She barely had time to cook for the Korkys. She spread out to the work places she passed goin to and from that school, and took orders for the next day. It became a good and regular thing. She was deep in it before she realized it, and she had thought of it all by herself . . . with Mr. Korky's help at askin and seekin out her secret recipe.

Now, it was a little slow at first, very slow, so MLee kept on workin for the Korkys. She was dog-tired, dog-tired. After another year or so of all this workin, MLee counted her money and she had quite a bit. She never had spent a dime less it was on her business. MLee was really doin good on her cookin. She had even hired a little help. She paid her help extra to teach her how to read and write better. That MLee was somethin! And she could drive that car on her route with her eyes closed almost. She saved every dime that didn't go in her food. She paid the house off. It was hers, for real!

One day Mr. Korky said to her, "Emmy, where you rush off to every day so much? Mrs. Korky say you always runnin off. Since you got that car you say your husband bought you, you leave outta here quick as lightning. You making them cookies somewhere? Selling em?"

"No, sir. Just got a family to tend to."

"Emmy, if I find out you are selling them cookies you wouldn't give me the recipe for, I'll put the city on you. They got laws and all, you know?"

"Yes, sir."

"Alright now."

As soon as Mr. Korky left for the plant, MLee finished the jobs she had to do that mornin, cleaned everything up, then she went to see Mrs. Korky. "Mrs. Korky, mam, I blive I'm gonna have to quit."

"Oh, Emmy!" Mrs. Korky was what they say, dis . . . mayed.

MLee went on. "My home needs me so much, and . . . and, well, I just got to go. The new girl, Sarah, can take over. She knows bout all I know now."

"Oh, Emmy. Well . . . I . . . You wait til Mr. Korky comes home."

MLee was takin her apron off. "So, I'm leavin today, now."

She was scared about the city license people and she was tired of arguin with Mr. Korky, so she quit. He like to died and so did his wife, cause MLee was clean and the best cook they had ever had. MLee stopped takin cookies and things to the school where the Korky children went. But she went every place else she could, always lookin over her shoulders for Mr. Korky. For the next three years she worked day and night, for herself. Savin, savin that money. She had other dreams now.

She went home to the country two or three times cause she now had two grandchildren by Northa. Her son was still overseas somewhere I don't remember. She was bout forty years old now, and she was tired, but she looked better than she had before she left here. And she had done put a spark under Alec, cause he was workin more steady. Tween the mill, which still gave Negroes the lowest, dirtiest work and the lowest pay, and other handyman jobs, he tried to hold in there. He finally gave up the mill, cause to keep his heavy labor job, the leaderman told him he would have to help build him a house and barn on that man's own property! Wantin him evenin's after his mill job, for no pay! Or lose his job! He started at it, paintin and carpenterin, but finally quit. "They make you feel like a nigger," Alec said.

Some other company had done bought up a lotta land round here, bout five or six miles away, and did a lot of plantin. When time came, they hired people to pick and gather the fruit and vegetables. Alec was one of em. They paid reeeall low wages, but he stuck with it. "I blongs to myself," he said.

He didn't know what else to do to get MLee to come on home. One Sunday, sittin on the porch in the heat of the sun, he looked over the front yard; seein the two trees were doin real good, he decided to plant more of em. He walked two, three miles and dug up every young tree he wanted, brought em home and planted em, front and back-yard. Trees everywhere.

When MLee had been gone for bout five years she went back to the country. Drove up in front of her old house in a real nice car. Her purse full of money (a bank account full, too), her head full of dreams. The trees made

the house look better, but MLee knew what was inside.
The fence was patched, the yard was clean, but the house
was still yellow and dry as she had left it.

Alec came out and stood on the porch lookin at her,
waitin. MLee had not come home very much, just come to
see her grandchildren and leave. She finally got out the car
and walked slowly through the little crooked gate.

"You come home to stay this time?" he asked in a low
voice.

"I don't know."

"I want you to come home."

"Why?"

"Cause. Cause I love you, MLee."

MLee didn't say nothin, just walked into the house,
noticing it had a new screen door. MLee loved her little
house. Had raised her children in it. Had loved Alec in it.
Had stopped lovin Alec in it (cause of the pain, you know).
Alec followed her around.

She asked him, "You workin anywhere, Alec?"

He sighed. "A little. Tried to go back to the turpintine
plant. Walked way over there bout a week, but them smells
make me sick. I tried, just couldn't take it."

"What about the sawmill?"

"It done closed, MLee. Put a whole lotta men outta
work. It done closed. All the colored men built all the white
boss's houses and barns . . . for free . . . then the mill
closed. I'm . . . I'm workin, plantin and pickin in the
right seasons for a new company." His voice brightened.
"MLee, sometimes I'm workin right side of white men.
Poor white men who ain't doin no better than me! That
company don't care nothin bout them either. They makes

the same money I do, some of em! They hungry some-times, too!"

MLee sat down in the kitchen. Said, "I need some of them men over here. We gonna get some work done to this house."

Alec sat down, puttin his head in his hands. "MLee, I ain't got much money. I got some I saved from cuttin logs a little for the white man who sells cords, but he gotta whole lotta men to work for him now, so he don't want to pay but $4.00 a day for a ten hour day. Sometime, only $2.00 or $3.00 when he got somebody waitin around. I been tryin to sell eggs. They good hens, but they ain't steady. I sell Rosey's milk, don't keep none for myself. Give some to Northa for them babies. I sell the calf when there is one. But I still ain't saved no money, hardly."

MLee stirred in her chair, "You need to go somewhere and learn a real trade, Alec. Learn how to do somethin with your hands that let you work for your own self."

"I'm a old man, MLee."

"You may be beat out, but you ain't old."

"Too old to be goin back to school like a boy."

"You know how to fix some things, Alec. Put up a sign say, FIX IT SHOP. Folks can't afford new things. They need to get the old things fixed."

"MLee, these folks round here ain't even got old things to have fixed in the first place."

"Then go into town to the Salvation Army or somethin and buy some and fix em and then sell em to somebody so they will have somethin for you to fix when it breaks down again."

Alec just looked at her. "With what, MLee?"

"I found a way."

"You a woman."

"I'm a people. Plenty women don't do nothin for their self. Some people do!"

"A woman have it easier."

"I'm so tired of hearin people say things like that. Ain't nobody got it easier less they born with all the money they gonna need, then they still ain't got it easier, cause HAPPY don't run that way. You! You got to work for what you think makes you happy! You got to try, anyway. I done found out."

"I'm proud of you. Proud of you, MLee. You somethin more than I figured. I don't know how you done it, but . . ."

"I tried. That's how I done it. I tried."

Alec hung his head down, said, "Well . . ." His was a sad, sad sound.

MLee took a deep breath. "I'll tell you what I want you to do, so I can come home." Alec raised his head. His little eyes moist, longin to have his wife back. She been gone more'n five years.

Wellll, MLee fixed that old house up like new and Alec helped her every step of the way. They painted it! They hired a builderman who built houses and added three rooms and made the kitchen larger and it was full of all new things. Put on a new roof, put in new wirin, new plumbin. Her favorite thing was the bathroom INSIDE the house, with a tub AND a shower. Threw that ole tin tub away. Tore the old barn down and built it further away from the house, and Alec helped build a workshop for himself to WORK in. Alec even built a brand-new chicken house and got a sister for Rosey the cow, cause Rosey was old now. Built MLee a garage for her car. Now!

Alec managed to take some lumber from the lumber MLee got for the house and he built her a good size booth a little to the side, front of the house, facing the road so she could have a cookie store. The lead builder complained bout Alec' stealin wood and buildin things. He wanted to kinda tear Alec down cause he liked MLee. She was a wide-awake, go-getter woman. But MLee knew what Alec was doin, so she told the lead man, "Don't worry bout it."

MLee drove back and forth from the city a couple times a week. She was buyin new curtains, spreads, tablecloths, drapes, sheets and just anything she wanted. Now . . . the last thing she got, she had to bring the man from the city to do. She wanted her a swimmin pool! She got it. Small, but it was a swimmin pool with a cover, and MLee used it too!

Alec liked to died cause he didn't know how much money MLee had. She told him, "I'm gettin broke. We'll both be the same. You will have to work and take care of me." He scratched his head and grinned, cause it wasn't nothin he could say. She was not sleepin with him yet. They both had their own room. She heard him walkin round in his room on the nights she stayed at home and she wanted to call him in, but she said to herself, "When I do let him in, he ain't gonna be so easy to cheat on me again." Cause, you know, she did love the father of her kids.

One of them rooms was built for her grandchildren. Northa was not happy with her life nor her husband. She was livin MLee's old life. MLee wanted to take the kids and send Northa to the city to run the business and even start college if she wanted to. "Have a new chance in life. Do somethin for herself," she said. Northa cried from sheer happiness and she started goin up to that city with her mother to learn how to do things. MLee was plannin to go up twice a week and make cookie batter til Northa learned everything. Then, too, her son would be comin home some day. It was his too, if he wanted it. Her whole life was steady changin! Touchin a lot of people. Even I start lookin up that ole dusty yellow road.

Well, when all the buildin was done, the pool filled, the dust had settled, MLee went out early one mornin on the new front porch. Alec had set her rockin chair out, still covered, and he had set another one out for himself. She uncovered her rockin chair, looked at Alec and smiled. He just grinned, glad his wife was back. He read a lot into her smile at him. Who knows? But I blive he better be more manly about everything, cause MLee done found out she can DO things by herself, for herself.

Anyway, then she sat down and started rockin. Rockin and smilin. Lookin at her trees. Lookin at her store booth. Lookin up that long, ole, dusty, yellow road. Just'a smilin. And rockin. And lookin. Thinkin. Smilin, chile.

Somebody for Everybody

Being alone, feeling alone, in a small town can be pretty hard on you, cause you don't hardly have too many people to choose from to fall in love with. Being alone and feeling alone in a big city can be worse cause there be so many people and, still, ain't none of em yours. You got a lot to choose from, but it's more to loneliness than just choosin somebody. They say it's somebody for everybody, but just prove it sometime!

Now, this story is shaped like a "V" to me. Two different stories startin at the top and meetin together at the bottom. I don't know zackly how to begin, but . . . here goes.

Kissy, born Kissella Mae, was in Chicago on this cold,

cold, wind razor-sharp, snowy night. She huddled in her bed trying to keep warm. She had worked her eight hours plus two hours overtime because the girl to relieve her was late. It was drafty in the little place where she worked as a waitress. The door openin all the time. Even though she only lived in a room with kitchenette, it was her "home" and she wanted to get back to its warmth.

Kissy was alone in this big city. Didn't have nobody. She didn't want anyone she knew and, maybe, they didn't want her either. She had tried, several times, to be together with somebody, but it just didn't work out. She was still alone.

She lay there, feeling bottomless depression in that deep, endless, loneliness. No husband, no child, no friend even, that she was close to. Just nobody, but herself. She shivered, thinkin, "No electric blanket either. Not even a small electric footpad."

Kissy's mind roamed back, reluctantly, over the twenty years since she had left her tiny, small hometown. She had gone to California to have an operation she had heard she could get to make her, you know, smaller. California cost too much to live in and she couldn't save for the operation, which also cost a lot, so she moved on to Chicago to try to see a doctor she read about and stayed twenty years tryin to save the money for the operation. And, too, twenty years of looking for somebody to live her life with. Wasn't nobody for her in her hometown. She had tried. She thought here, in a big city, she would find "the ONE." At first, she was excited and hopeful, surely expecting a lover who would turn into a husband. Someone with money, maybe. A business, maybe. No luck. Lady Luck was busy helpin somebody else who probly didn't even need her.

Then, she just wanted to meet somebody with potential. Well, that's a good thing to have. No luck. Then, just a man with a good job. All good dreams, but good fortune didn't even seem to know Kissy, much less smile on her.

Though Kissy was not a virgin, she thought of herself that way because she had never felt what it was to be a satisfied woman. Never did feel good up under a man. So to her, she WAS a virgin. And, to Kissy, masterbation was degrading. To have to make love to your own self was a sign of something she did not like for herself.

Now, the main problem was something Kissy was born with. She was a small size woman. Petite, they call it. But her personal part, the part she made love with, her whatchamacallit, was very large. Nobody fit. They tried and some of them laughed. A few got up before they were finished, which is unusual for men cause you know they'll stay no matter what a woman has to offer. Now, that hurt in Kissy's heart.

She had never, even the first time when she really was a virgin, known the pleasure of lovemaking. Or love that lasted any time. Who had stayed? Nobody. Later, those same few, who stayed for her little money or tips she made, laughed and called her "Lucy." "Juicy Lucy" the mean evil ones said. They left to find someone more fitting to them. You know what I mean?

Wasn't nothing Kissy could do, it was naturally natural. Not her fault that she was too large for the average man to know what he was into. Cause of her pain . . . and loneliness, she got desperate. Kissy wanted to be like other women. Wanted. Loved. That pushed her to try men she didn't really want, never would have tried in any other circumstance. She did not intend to be a loose woman. Once she tapped a new lover on his shoulder and said, "Please, let's stop. I can't even tell what you are doing." One time she waited for someone to make love to her and thought he took a long time with that foreplay stuff. Finally, when he got up "through," she was still waitin for him to start. Never felt a thing.

Well, now, life ain't ugly. Ain't too far sad. But it does have little twists and turns for each of us. Don't laugh. Kissy knew what it was, or was not, for her. Do you know what yours is?

One morning, not long after that winter day in Chicago, Kissy gave up and decided to go home. She was now thirty-eight years old. "Hell with it!" she cried out in her little kitchenette. "I'm tired! I been here all this time and I ain't doin nothing for myself really. Ain't findin no lover or husband. I can't help it if I am built wrong. I'm goin home to rest. And die. I got my nieces and nephews. Plenty of em. I ain't gonna think of sex and love again!" She was fussing with the air, but she lay down on her bed and cried when she was finished fussin.

Now, Kissy had been tryin to save money for that operation she wanted, and she had saved some, but something always came up and she had to use it. Lots of time she sent it home to her mother cause somebody in the family needed it. They thought cause she was up there, in the North in that big city, she must be makin big money. They were wrong, but she always sent what she had and started again.

That operation she was savin for was one she had heard about that they could cut part of your "private part" away and leave it smaller. Nicer. More normal for life. So she had a little money now somebody hadn't sent for, yet. She decided she would use it to go home and get herself settled, then look for a job.

She informed the apartment manager and her job she would be leaving. She began working on things getting ready to go home. She thought, "I'm goin home worst than I was when I came. I'm older. A failure. Still a single woman. No children. Alone."

Now, Buddy is on the other side of that "V." He had moved to a smaller town from a big city, thinking his chances to get a good wife would be better there. More reasons for a wife to be faithful cause there were less men to choose from. He had had his problems growin up because he was not all that good-lookin. He had a strange way about him, but it came from his takin time to listen to others and try to help them in some way. People aren't used to that.

Buddy was the kind of man that was just nice. There is, I believe, at least one in every town, nice to the point of bein a fool sometimes, I think. Cause all he wanted was some friends and a woman of his own but all the women did in this town was use him. Used him! Play with him. Teasin and talkin about him. I don't know the WHOLE story, cause people lie a lot, but I do know them women used him. And because he wanted somebody so bad, he would take what he could get and give all he had.

It seems it was a fact that Buddy had been too well blessed (?) with that whatchamacallit men, and some women, make such a fuss over. All the ladies in town claimed to be built too small (?) to handle his problem. They mostly talked about him at Curlee Ree's Beauty Shop, cause that's who he liked best or did the most for, Curlee Ree. She talked about him like a fool dog! The others would purse up their lips real tight when they said what a shame he couldn't find nobody to fit his size. They believed Curlee Ree was lyin when she said, "I done seen it, but never, never would I allow him to ruin my body with that . . . that. He can rub it on me, but don't shove it on me." They would just almost roll on the floor laughin at that poor man.

Bud worked two jobs. One was as a deliveryman at a bakery and one driving a cab evenins and weekends. He needed extra money cause a lady here and there, and specially Curlee Ree, always needed somethin even if they didn't give him nothin. They was always on the lookout for him to bring the garbage from the rear of their house to the front or bring firewood in, nail a shelf or fix a door or a drain. Things their own men ought to do if they had one. Bud did it all. Sometimes he would get a peep down a dress or a sight of a thigh or even a open robe showin plenty more. Sometimes he just got a piece of chicken . . . but not a piece of what he really wanted. No sir! But I know he enjoyed that chicken cause he didn't get no home-cooked food. He always ate out at them little overcooked dinner

spots, lookin sad as he chewed his food and stared at the
fly-specked walls. They all worked him that could, but they
didn't care nothin bout him cept to laugh at him. But he
even helped old women and men, so he just liked to help
people anyway.

Welll . . . Bud was gettin older . . . and sadder
. . . and lonelier. His hair was graying. He'd be clean one
day, but wear that same shirt bout three or four days. His
clothes needed mendin and nobody offered to do it for him.
Me neither, I'm guilty, but my husband would never, never
have stopped arguing bout it. Once I felt sorry for Bud and
mended some torn pants for him and I told my husband he
paid me. But I couldn't do that too much.

Once I invited him to a church social so he could get a
home-cooked meal. He ate bout five of em! Then he played
with the kids. Runnin round after the ball and things like
that. He didn't have no children of his own, just always
looked out for other people's children cause he loved them.
Just had to love SOMEBODY, I reckon.

Anyway, I don't have to tell you he was a very unhappy,
lonely man. Even with all the "friends" he did friendly
things for.

Now, I work at a little ole magazine shop near the Greyhound bus station. I was leanin on the counter, lookin out
the window the day Kissy got back in town. I had been
talkin to her mother so I knew she was expected. I was
really glad cause Kissy had been my friend when we was
growin up, in school and all. That's why I knew so much
bout her life and all.

When I saw her, I ran out off my job to hug her, wonderin had she changed much. She looked older and so small and miserable, tired and dirty. She was still open and honest-hearted though. City hadn't changed her none. Said she was gonna be lookin for a job. She didn't even wait for me to ask her why she came back home, just said slinging hash in a city like Chicago, that big and busy, wasn't easy and slingin ass gettin to work in the winter was even harder. I saw my boss was lookin out at me so I told Kissy I would see her later and went on back in to work.

She had a big fluffy wig on and her big lips (that's why they called her Kissy) were brightly painted and glistenin. I knew she had just slashed it on as the bus turned into town. With age, her legs had seemed to bow out a little more and her knees had got fat the way age hit you sometime. But she was dressed cheap and flashy, youngish like. Not in anything real short and revealin, but bright and fluffy. It was like her clothes was tryin to look happy for her.

That first day she came in town on the Greyhound bus, Bud's cab was sittin out front and she turned to it, carrying two cardboard bags, some books and a big purse. Not magazines, but real books. She bent down to ask him how far something was and how much it would be to get there. She said, "I can go on and walk if it's gonna be too much. I need to save money." He told her what she wanted to know but offered her a free ride and reached for her bags. She pulled back, cause she from the city now and knows about strangers givin you something for free. She looked at him good, askin, "Do I know you?"

He said, "No. Don't think so. If I knew you, I'd remember."

Then she said, "Well then I better walk til I find out what I'm doing!" I was tryin to wave to her through my work window that he was alright, but she didn't see me.

Bud scratched his head, watched her leaning with them suitcases as she walked on away from him and thought about how he never saw anyone in this town refuse anything free before. He jumped in his cab and followed her. Rollin down the window, he said, "Why don't you walk if you want to, but give me the bags and I'll drop them off at your house. You won't owe me nothin!"

Kissy asked, "Really?" Cause she really was tired.

Then Bud asked, "What's the matter with you? Where you from? Ain't nobody ever been friendly to you?"

Kissy started walkin again, sayin, "Some friendly cost too much."

Bud stopped the cab, got out, walked around and took the bags and the books. He smiled at her as he handled the books. "You read these?" She nodded yes. He smiled at the books, said, "This friendly won't cost you nothin. Go on and walk if you want to."

Kissy walked home. When she got home there they were, her bags. She looked at them a long minute then she hugged her family, still lookin at them bags.

By and by, we talked and she got around a little. I told my boss about her and Kissy came by about a job. We was just a small shop and there ain't no big readers round here, but I told Kissy the next job come up it was gonna be hers or I was gonna be lookin for a job myself. I also told her to go to the hairdresser and forced the money on her as a welcome home present. Well? She was my friend and she was in need!

Well, when she went to the hairdresser, Curley Ree's, you know that, they was jealous of her cause she had been off to a big city, Chi . . . ca . . . go!, and they only always talked about goin. So they commence to pickin at things to tell her, make her feel like less or somethin. They told her about what she ought not wear and how she ought to wear her hair. Told her she was too old for what she was doin. Ask her didn't she learn nothin up in Chi . . . ca . . . go? Stuff like that, you know?

Well, when she finally got mad, her hair was half done, standin all over her head and all, but she stood up, knocking them irons out her dresser's hand and said, "How you gonna tell me how I feel? How I should dress? It ain't how long your dress is that matters, it's how quick you pull it up! You may feel old, but I don't feeeeelll old. I'm young inside. I couldn't be oooold if I tried cause I don't feel it! What's old anyway? You?! (They didn't like that.) Old is when you're dead! Old and cold! That's the only too old I know! So you leave me alone and tend to your business cause you look like you need some advice help with yourself!" She started to sit back down, but turned back to the startled ladies. "Another thing. I'm back. Back to stay. I don't bother nobody. So don't cloud up over me or I will make it rain." So they let her alone and talked about her only when she was a long way from hearin.

By now, Kissy knew how most grown people felt about Buddy. Women first, then the men, on account of how the women belittled him to make themselves and their men look better and smarter. Kissy's sister, who Kissy had moved in with, was a little put-on phony herself and she was a little put off by the way Kissy dressed and talked and didn't care bout lettin people tell her how to run her business, so she was thinkin of puttin Kissy out. But Kissy found a job and told her sister she was movin out before the sister had a chance to pull her grand stand. That made the sister mad too, and she was one of those Kissy had sent money back home to and helped!

Kissy had got a nice, sweet, little job at the library! She found a nice little housekeeping room with kitchenette and private bath, chile. It was not far from where she was with her sister and she did not have much to move, but I told her "Call Bud. (See? I knew what both their troubles was.) Ask him to move you." She did and he did. He was glad to do it. He even hung around and did things like hammerin a nail where it was needed, fixin a window that wouldn't open, you know them things. He wouldn't take no money (I told him not to, to try to get a home-cooked meal). He told her, "What I would really like, Ms. Kissy, is a home-cooked meal. To eat sittin cross from a real live woman keepin me company while we eat. I ain't had that since I was a child. And maybe you can tell me what's in some of these beautiful books of yours. Yes, mam, I sure would like that best."

Now . . . don't ask me how I know so much. You know they both friends of mine. But after dinner they had talked a lot and she turned her little portable record player on and played some of her little record collection. Charlie Parker, Billie Holliday, Dinah Washington and B.B. King. And then read him some poems and stuff out of Langston Hughes and Zora Neale Hurston. Then some Black history, bout how wonderful we are and our strength and all. About our African-American men who came through and lasted (we still here) and our women who had the strength and backbone to stand up and take and take and still keep comin back, then raisin children to stand up too. (I also borrowed them books from her, cause the library didn't have em til much later.)

She told him there were other strong peoples, like pioneers or the poor of any color who went through many hardships. Good people. But the greedy and the murderers always come, giving no one else a chance, but they were not really the strong. That a gun does not make you a man or make you strong. You only become death with a weapon. God makes a man, the devil makes a weapon and pain and death. Oh, all such stuff as that til late up into the night, or early morning.

And I don't have to tell you Bud fell in love. Wasn't no way for him not to. Kissy was kind. That's all it really took. Kindness and peacefulness. Like a exchange of friendship . . . not favors.

Both these hungry people . . . hungry for touch, affection, love, didn't want to go too far, too fast. They had no practice at believin in life or love.

At the door when he was leavin, she let him hold her tight and even kiss her. Now, I'ma tell you, the stars pulled loose from whatever they were hinged on way up there in the sky and all of em, all of em, seemed to circle round Bud's head and heart. He was full. His stomach, his head and his heart. Kissy felt the world turn and thought it was her own heart foolin her. She was afraid to trust life or luck again and she was too tired to hope. But, you see, hope don't wait for nobody to call it, it just shows up, sits there somewhere, makin you happy and sad at the same time, sometime.

He started droppin by her house to see was she alright. Did she need anything? Could he fix somethin? He brought groceries, sayin, "Oh, these are not for you to cook for me, they for you. I know you be tired when you get off work and you walkin too. I just picked em up thinkin you might find some need for em." Her little icebox was full. She would smile and pull out them groceries, sayin, "I can't keep them less you stay and eat some with me." Well, you know he was always polite and stayed.

One time when he tried to hug her again, she put her arms up to ward him off. He looked confused, so she told him, "Listen. I don't know nothin bout your business and I don't know nothin bout where these hugs are takin us . . . and we better stop til I do know."

Bud smiled a big smile that lit up his face. "Kissy, you know I love you. I love to hug you. Love to kiss you. I don't want to bother you none, but I wish you'd just let me hold you, least let my skin kiss yours."

Kissy, thinking bout ole Lady Luck was teasin with her, not really gonna give her nothin this time either, she stepped back. "I like huggin you too, but I still don't know nothin bout your business. If you have any . . . you better get it all straight before we start any business of our own. Now, I think you better go, Bud."

Bud left there kind'a bent over, shoulders slumped down, scratching his head, thinking, "I ain't got no business. Ain't had no business."

Next day or two, Bud went back. He had really missed

her, so he went straight for the hug and a kiss. Kissy stopped him, again. "Get your business straight, Bud."

"What business?" he asked.

"Any business," she answered. "Listen, Bud . . . Say, what is your real name?"

"Budrow."

"Well, listen, Bud," she looked confused herself, "listen, I am a woman."

Bud smiled. "Believe me, I believe I know that."

"I am a grown woman."

Now Bud looked like he could cry. "What must I do, grown woman?" He looked like he was really tryin to figure it out. "I love you. I don't have no other woman that blongs to me. No other woman at all." He sounded like he could cry.

"Sit down, Bud, please." He sat.

Kissy thought this was all a waste of time. She did not believe this man would work out and keep loving her either. She did not want to lose him. She wanted more of him. In fact, she loved him. His kindness, his thoughtfulness, his giving of himself was all new to her. It was like . . . was like . . . havin a honest, sincere, normal, real, lovin companion. She had been happy for longer than ever before in her life. But she felt the moment they made love . . . together . . . close love, he would get up, laugh and leave. "I don't want the pain anymore," she told herself as she sat there lookin into his earnest, sincere and confused eyes. "And . . . he don't have a thing to his name but his heart. I'm too old to have too many kinds of pain in my life anymore."

She knew it had to be said, so she said it. "I live here in

a small, dinky, kitchenette room." Bud looked around the room like he was in heaven, but he nodded to satisfy her. Kissy pointed at him. "You live in a smaller, dinkier room with NO kitchenette even." He looked at her then looked away. She went on talkin. "I just got here and I have more than you to come home to in the evenins when I finish work. If you don't have no 'business' then what do you do with your money?"

Bud, in a split second, was glad to know it was about money, then was sad to know it was about money. He bent his head, lookin at the floor. He started to speak, but Kissy interrupted him, "No, no! Don't tell me. Just stop doing it. Save it. You a grown man, too. You need somethin of your own! A home maybe. Some decent clothes. If I ever sleep with you I am not crawlin between no dingy sheets next to no day-old underwear. Not me and my precious skin and perfume and nice gowns. I got two gowns and one jar of expensive cream for my skin and one bottle of one of the best perfumes there is. I saved hard for them so I could feel like a woman again, after I had worked like a dog." He took hold of her hand. She took a deep breath, angrily wiped a tear from her face and said, "And I already been hurt . . . enough. I ain't throwin my heart out there again to have it thrown back in my face. Not me . . . and my precious skin and perfume and cream. No siree."

Well, Bud look like he didn't know whether to laugh in happiness at the first real, good, personal, intimate, sensible conversation he had ever had with a personal, intimate, sensible woman, or to cry because he didn't know what to do next. So he did the next best thing; he asked Kissy, "What must I do?"

Kissy was ready. She took another deep breath and said, "If you don't have no other . . . no woman, you get your money together. Look for a better place to live. Just look, don't pick. I'll help you pick. Don't have so much time to waste on people who don't really care about you. Help the old and the helpless, but help yourself. Do something for yourself . . . and then, maybe . . . you can do something for us . . . and I can do something for us. We can do something for each other. BE something to each other!"

He, hesitantly, gently, took her in his arms, she didn't fight it. She said, "I'll tell you the truth. I'm tired. Tired of movin on and ending up alone. Being wrong bout . . . things. I . . . like you . . . a lot, and I want a home. But I don't want no fool."

Bud blinked. Either he could hardly blive it or he was bout to cry.

Well, needless to say, Bud began passin up them requests, "Hey, Bud!" hollared across a street or "Buddddddy! from a door or window. Even the door of the Curlee Ree Beauty Shop. Passin like a freight train passin by a hobo! He was tendin to his business!!! Going to the bank instead of a bar or the liquor store. I mean, he changed and it didn't make him unhappy none!

Now . . . I know what you want to know. It went like this. For a long, long time Kissy would not let him make love to her. I mean a loooong time. She thought the minute he did that, he would be gone because he would not fit and she loved that man so hard by then. She did NOT want to lose him. They kissed and hugged. They petted and rubbed. He respected her, but he wanted to be WITH her. He wanted to marry her. She didn't want a marriage that would turn out bad for him. She had resigned herself to never no real lovin, but she loved him enough to just be with him and never be satisfied in THAT way. She loved his kissin and huggin and rubbin stuff.

Finally, of course you know, she let him sleep over her house sometimes after a good dinner. She wore pajamas and him not wanting her to know the size of his problem, he wore big, loose pajamas. He had decided he loved her enough to never try to REALLY make love to her either. He could do without that all his life with her, if she would just marry him and stay his. I'm tellin you! Lady Luck may never have smiled on her, but she had something better than luck. She had a blessing!!

We all know how, in time, that kissin and rubbin just naturally goes further and further. One night they got carried away and they was already in bed. He moved over on top of her, just rubbin, that's all. She was crying a little, her body was so hungry for his love, his touch. She opened her mouth to say, "Bud, I got somethin to tell you." He opened his mouth at the same time (course, he didn't move his lips from her lips). "Baby, baby, I got somethin to tell you." Then she said in a slow, raspy, needin you whisper, "Go on, do it, do it." He said, "I want to, but I can't hurt you, I just can't." They still kissin, too. She almost screamed, but her mouth was full of his, but she did say, "Go on, do it," even though her heart was breakin cause she knew she was gettin ready to lose him. He said, "Just a little, just a little." Kissy was cryin, her last thought, as he got started, was "Well, I done lost my good man now." But he was started now. It was really the first time for both of them.

She opened her eyes and looked up into his as they

began. He opened his eyes and looked down into hers and he moved in closer. They were lost in each other's eyes and WONDER as everything fell into place. They fit!!!

Chile, them stars came unhinged again, zoomed right out of the sky and filled up that bed and that room and the hearts and minds of the two people whose love was closing in on them. I'm talkin bout love, chile, love and happiness.

They got married, soon, you know that.

Oh, the women laughed and whispered behind her back. They knew her business! they smirked. "Big business!" they said. "Lord! If she could take that!" Well, she did. And she stayed smilin and happy! Bud did too.

Then soon, Bud decided to go to school to learn plumbing cause he didn't like bein away from his little heaven so much. After the first year, he started workin at it as an apprentice. He bought his wife and his expected baby a home. Then he bought her her own car! And Bud? Kissy had him lookin good and dressin real nice, even sharp sometimes and he kept her bright and fluffy, lookin pleased and happy all the time. Her dresser was full of bottles of the best perfumes and creams. Her closet was full, in spite of the fact she tried to slow Bud down to save money because she wanted some income property so it could bring in some money and he could stay home even more.

Them people still whispered and talked about Bud and Kissy! Well, how you gonna shut people up? Even Jesus couldn't do it! But they were lower whispers and less laughter. Curlee Ree talked the hardest. Her jealousy was evident. All them jealousies were! Ain't life funny? Nobody wanted him, they said, and the women didn't want to like her, just mean and ugly and now jealousy was added just about two people being happy.

Well, I can tell you, Bud ain't never gonna leave Kissy and Kissy don't look like she ever gonna leave Bud. They both have found and made a home. A home that fits them to a "T." Like a glove, chile. They were not the mistakes other people thought they were. One man's poison is another man's dessert! There is somebody for everybody! I know that for myself!

A Will and a Way

Aberdeen, Abby, was born in the middle of a metropolitan city, straight from a hardworking, hard-living, worn-out mother, Callie. Callie, born in the South, had worked hard from the time she could walk good til the time her own mother moved to the North chasing her husband and then chasin love or companionship to the tune of seven children. The last three bein by different fathers. She had got tired of chasin the wind, then got caught up in them breezes.

Callie didn't know if that was her nickname or her real name. It's all she was ever called and all she and her family knew since her mother had died and she hadn't thought to ask her before her death. But she did know she was worn out and tired. Tired of her life, her children, her search for

love through the rubble of her life and tired of tryin. Tired
of her domestic jobs that took all they could squeeze out of
a woman who could not read or write and, still, she could
not stretch her pay to cover decent food for her children
still at home and they was mostly all still at home. Even
those who left came back regularly to eat. So she went on
welfare. It paid more than her jobs.

Callie loved her children. Wanted them all to be full
and have things. So she would sneak and do odd jobs of
work, leaving the smallest children at home, alone with
their brothers and sisters who were supposed to watch
them. They would watch them for an hour or two, then
they would leave the smaller ones alone to care for themselves. The small ones probably did as good a job as the
older ones would have.

Abby was raised about any which way. She knew her
mother loved her because mothers were supposed to love
their children. But there were so many children, so many
needs. Another baby came when Abby was one year old.
That didn't matter none, nor change much, since bein a
baby meant having a raw behind because you couldn't
change your own diaper or train yourself to use the toilet.

Food was there on the first and you went in and got out
what you could, while you could. That's why Abby learned
to walk early, cause in her house you better get up and see
bout yourself.

They lived in the ghetto, naturally, cause there wasn't
any choice about it. Only money could get you a better
place to live and who had money? It wasn't the healthiest
place to live either, and without health, there is not much
joy in life, if any. Everybody bein poor means there were,

had to be, thieves. So even though you live in the poorest place, somebody was still waiting to steal what you did have from you. Sometimes right in your own family. Poverty is a bitch.

Abby fought her way through her family. There was a pat or a hug, now and again. But after that you were on your own again.

I don't have to tell you there was colored, Black, African-American in this place, cause you don't ever need to tell nobody that. Just tell the story. Though there are some white and Hispanic and Chinese ones out there squalling in the squaler of life too.

Anyway, Abby fought her way through school. And since she wasn't much different from other children tryin to survive and have a little fun out of life sometime, Abby did all the usual things some, mostly poor, children do. She went to school sometimes, got in trouble sometimes.

But she knew when she went home there would be somewhere to sleep with a locked door between her and the world. In time, seemed like the rest of the world was in her home too, cause her sisters and brothers were now products of that world out there. They stole from you too and they might fight you about something they thought you did to them. One sister had even fought the mother, Callie.

So Abby grew up. Open to love. Needin it. And everyone talking about boyfriends and girlfriends, and young men wanting to be like the father they never had and looking at TV and movies where it seemed the point was to screw somebody or kill em. When Abby was thirteen she got a boyfriend, too, and he gave her a baby cause he didn't know how not to and really didn't care.

Callie could only look at Abby with tired, tired eyes. Everybody else in the family screamed at Abby for bein dumb. Callie had cried with the first two daughters when they got pregnant. Once, she had tried to beat a son into marrying a girl he got pregnant, but she knew that wouldn't be doing the girl nor the child any favor. In the end, she just helped her girls get birth control pills. The government would give them to you free.

She had thought Aberdeen was too young. Thirteen. She had loved Aberdeen's father and tried hard for him. She grieved when he left because her life was too big for him once he got out of her bed. This was one of her babies. Abby, whom she loved, as all her children. Who, try as she might, she never had enough time for. She was almost always dead tired from scuffling with life, then too, she had to find some love for herself, some lovemakin. She wanted to do and say nice things to her children, but mostly screams came out of her mouth. And the hope she tried to hold in her hands was always gone when she opened them for her children.

Abortion, abortion was the next thing that came from everyone's lips. Even the preacher's. But, through it all, Abby held on to her little swollen stomach and shook her head no. She didn't love its father. She didn't know nothing about love anyway. It seemed she had just needed him at the time. But, now, she would have her baby for herself. Her child. Her own human being to love. So she kept her baby. She dropped out of school in the seventh grade. Wasn't hardly there anyway.

Callie helped Abby get welfare help so she would have

prenatal care. What else did she have to give her daughter, but welfare? Callie helped Abby sign up for and get a small apartment after a long, long wait, cause it had to be in the ghetto. Wasn't enough money to get out the ghetto.

When the little dark brown baby was born it was a girl and Abby wanted to give her doll baby the best, most beautiful name in the world. She choose Uniqua, from the word "unique" she had heard a man use on the television.

Abby was a good mother. If she never did anything else, that baby, Uniqua was clean, fed and healthy. It was Abby's first and only child. She wasn't tired yet. If anything looked wrong on Uniqua, Abby went straight to the hospital and if she had to stay two, three days, she did. She packed Uniqua's clothes, food and a small ice pack to keep the milk fresh. She stayed in a doctor's face or office till Uniqua was well.

Abby hadn't done well in school, but she could sign her name, count money and things like that. All she had to do was sign her check and watch her money and her child. She baby-sat, sometimes, for other mothers for two reasons. It gave Uniqua someone to play with and she could use the extra money. Welfare wouldn't let you work and the mothers didn't want welfare to know they even needed a baby-sitter (to get away sometimes), so no one told on Abby. After a while, Abby cut it down to one or two children because, sometimes, the mothers lied and didn't pay like they were supposed to.

Uniqua grew up. Abby worshiped the child. Uniqua's view of the world was different from many other children in the ghetto. There was always something to eat or snack on and clothes in her closet. She had her own small room with shelves for the picture books she loved. Uniqua said she was going to write a book someday.

Then Uniqua started preschool. Well, let me tell you. Uniqua had grown up watching Abby take care of, and speak up for, herself. Abby was tough. Abby would fight a man if he tried to run over her and she sure would whip a woman. I know even preschool can be tough on some children, but Uniqua was tough too. She held her own.

Now, Abby was a short, plump brown-skin woman with a really attractive face, long eyelashes, pretty eyes and short hair.

Uniqua was a thin, wiry, dark brown child. Thin, but healthy. Little bump-like muscles made up the calves of her thin legs, bump-like bones made up her knees and two tight bump-like muscles made up her little butt. Her hair was . . . I can't say kinky cause there were no kinks in her well-combed hair. I can't say nappy cause she had no naps there either. It was not straight, but it was soft and fine. Abby combed her bangs and had a braid on each side of her little round face with the big, pretty eyes and straight teeth with only one slightly crooked tooth in front. She had a big beautiful smile that came from her lips, her eyes and her heart. That child, Uniqua, was sweet . . . and tough. She thought she could do whatever Abby did and she wasn't going to let anyone run over her either!

One day when tiny little Uniqua came home from school, she had been crying. She explained to her mother that some boys had grabbed her behind and they had kept doing it no matter what she told them and she couldn't

always catch them to hit them for it. The child was really
mad. Abby went to see the principal to have him stop that
kind of goings on with her daughter. Because she also did
not want them "grabs" to finally feel good or be done by
someone Uniqua might eventually like, and thereby give
Uniqua something she could not handle. But, mostly, she
did not want anybody's hands on Uniqua's behind at all.

The principal laughed and said, "Now you know, Ms.
. . . ah, you know boys will be boys. That's just as natural
as night and day." (They don't always get the best teachers
in the ghettos.)

Abby put her hand on her hip and said, "Naw it ain't.
Maybe for your daughter. Not for my daughter!"

The principal looked at Uniqua. "Do you know who
they were?" He looked back at Abby. "Honestly, Ms. . . .
ah, there is really nothing we can do. There are too many
children here as it is and we can't possibly control every one
of them every minute."

Abby shook her head, said, "That might be true, but
this here one is mine." She put her hand on Uniqua's shoulder. She hit herself on her own breast with the other hand.
"And if something like that happens to her again, I'm
comin over here and whip YOUR ass. Every time. Til she
gets out'a this here school. I want her to get a education,
not a screwin!"

The principal blanched, startled. Abby went through
his office door with her hand back on her hip and looked at
the principal's secretary who was frowning at her with dis-
taste. Abby pointed at the secretary, said, "Yours too! I'll
kick every ass in this here place down to the cook in that

shitty cafeteria! The reason these kids is actin out like they ain't got no sense is cause you all act that way." Uniqua was behind Abby, smiling and proud of her mother taking up for her.

Now there was a very religious lady lived down the hall from Abby who liked Abby because she was clean and well mannered to her, even though she did have a party now and then. The lady had a child who went to the Catholic school not too far away. "It costs a little," the lady said, "but I blive it's worth it."

Abby went to talk to the school to find out about the money. Then she went down to the welfare office for two days trying to get that money. She had to talk loud again.

The welfare lady said, "We can't do this. Suppose everybody . . ."

Abby held her hand up. "I ain't everybody. How many other mamas done asked you? I want my daughter to be safe. Go to a decent school. Like your child does, if you got one."

The welfare lady continued, "That is none of your business. Your business is why you are here. And we cannot . . ."

Abby held her hand up again. "Miss lady what-ever-your-name-is. I mean my daughter to be treated like a decent child. If you ain't gonna help me do that, then I'm gonna treat you like what you think I am. I am going to kick your ass, starting Monday, for every day my daughter has to go back to that sex fiend school."

The lady backed up, said, "You can't talk like that in here."

"If Uniqua don't get to go to a better school . . ."

The lady said, "You will get put off welfare if you . . ."

Abby put her hand on her hip. "If I get put offa welfare and can't feed my child and send her to a decent school"—she waved the other arm all around the office and had everyone's attention—"everyone of you"—she looked back to the first welfare lady—"specially you, gonna meet me outside this door or your own front door and you won't be comin in to get your check either, til your ass gets well, if I let it get well!"

"You can be put in jail . . ."

"I may go to jail, but you will be in the hospital! You can send me back to jail, but I'm gonna send you back to the hospital! I mean it! With ALL my heart! This is my chile and you gonna give me that little money for her to go to a better school and give her a chanct to grow up and get her a education without somebody pullin on her behind! Or else!"

When Uniqua started the new school a week later, Abby walked her there every school morning for a year. Then she let Uniqua go alone. Uniqua was so proud of her mother. That's one way self-esteem builds up. You know you are loved enough for somebody to fight for you. Somebody thinks you are worth it. Makes you learn how to love and fight for yourself. Uniqua did well at the new school.

Abby lived her personal life while Uniqua was at school. Most she did for a social life was play cards, drink a little too much sometimes on the weekend. Every once in a while, somebody would dance. But that was only on the weekends. Abby didn't think that little bit of livin would hurt Uniqua. Everybody knows that when you get to playin cards, you get to cussin when you get a good hand or a bad one or pull a boston on somebody. All them things was natural.

At the new school parents had to read a little more and write a little more on the report cards. Uniqua had never noticed her mother's handwritin, but when she was about nine years old, she proudly handed Abby her report card and stood beside her as Abby looked at the card.

Frowning, Abby asked, "Where do I sign?"

Smiling, Uniqua said, "Where it says parent."

"Where do it say 'Parent'?"

In a patient tone, softly, in wonder, Uniqua said, "Right there, Mama. At the bottom. Can't you read it?"

Abby gave an embarrassed laugh. "Chile, your mama didn't stay in school too long." She looked at Uniqua, with a smile beggin Uniqua to laugh. "If I had'a I wouldn't a had you! Now point to where I sign this thing."

Uniqua pointed and watched the laborious effort it took for Abby to sign her name.

Uniqua frowned slightly. "Date it, Mama."

Abby sighed as she handed the card to Uniqua. "You do it for me, baby. You my big girl, let me see if you know how to do it."

Uniqua was very comfortable with her mother's love and had no fear to speak her own mind, so she shook her head no and said, "Uh Uhh, you do it. You the mother."

"Don't make me mad, Uniqua!"

Uniqua put her hand on her mother's arm. "You can't read too good, can you, Mama?"

"No, not too good, but a little!" Abby smiled. "Enough."

The child was persistent. "No, it isn't enough, Mama." Uniqua pulled a book out of her book bag. "Here, this is a fifth grade book." She opened the book and pointed to a paragraph. "Read this."

Uniqua took the book, squinting her eyes at the words. "He . . . ran off . . . down . . . the . . . av . . . av . . . aven . . . av . . ."

"Avenue, Mama."

Abby handed the book back, shamed, trying not to get angry. "Well, you can read, Uniqua. That's good enough for me."

"You can read too, Mama. I'll teach you. You got to know how to read. You're my mama!"

Well, you know Abby let Uniqua start teachin her to read. Abby thought it would wear off, fade away with time, but every day Uniqua came home from school, she sang out, "School time!" and Abby did it because she loved her daughter.

In about eight weeks' time Abby noticed she could understand a lot more going on around her and could read a little bit of everything she picked up (which she did a lot at that time). In six months' time, Abby was going to the library with Uniqua and even got her own card. She discovered she LIKED to read and there were some things she didn't want Uniqua to read with her. One day she looked up and she was going to the library by herself! And finding what she wanted, alone! Abby said to herself, "Hot damn almighty! You doin alright, girl!"

Then, after one of those weekend card parties, Uniqua put her hands on her tiny hips and said, "Mama! Don't anyone at my school talk like you, cussin and all! I see the parents of them other children and they are not cussin even when they're sposed to be mad! You got to stop cussin less you real, real mad and can't nobody hear you but me. I don't want no cussin mama anymore." Uniqua put that hand that was usually on her hip, around her mother. "You too sweet to cuss anyway."

Abby looked at her daughter, thinkin, "Now this chile is not goin to run my life. I'M the mama, not her. Who she think she is to tell me what to do? Who puts the bread on this table? I can cuss if I want to." She said to Uniqua, "Go sit down and stop tryin to run my damn life! I'm grown. I supports us. You just keep goin to school and mind your damn manners!"

Uniqua put her head down, turning to go, said, "Only little children sposed to have manners, Mama?"

"No, everybody is sposed to have manners!"

Uniqua smiled up at Abby, "Then let's both of us stop cussin and we'll be happy again." She hugged her mother and they laughed together. Abby buried her face in her child's hair, thinking, "Lawd, what am I goin to do with this here you done give me? She just too smart."

Uniqua held her mother and spoke softly. "And, Mama, you aren't pretty when you get drunk with your friends at them card parties. Your clothes look all messed up and your hair . . ."

Abby broke loose from the embrace. "You betta leave me alone, girl!"

But Abby began to watch her mouth around Uniqua and stopped everybody else from cursing on the card-playing weekends. You know some of them stopped coming and went somewhere else to play. Abby would sometimes go there. But Abby could read real good now and sometimes she was in the middle of a book she didn't want to put down or just didn't feel like hearing all the same old things at the card games.

Now, Abby was young and she wanted love. But she had never, since Uniqua was about four years old, let any man spend the night. Uniqua had never seen her in bed with anybody, no matter how much Abby liked him. Abby remembered how she had felt around men and her mother and she didn't want Uniqua to disrespect her or feel that way about her. She wanted respect from Uniqua. So she had decided to wait until she wanted to marry someone. She did want to be married someday. Even have another child.

Then she fell in love or what felt like it. His name was Torchy Liver. Anyone might have guessed that was not his real name, but a woman in love, you know. She didn't care right then. Abby let Torchy go further than anyone else had done. She thought, "We love each other. We'll get married."

But Torchy didn't work steady . . . yet. He kept plannin to. When he did work it was only for a few days then something went wrong. "The boss is racist. The pay too low. The sun too hot. The wind too cold. The hours too long. I hurt my back."

Uniqua was used to talkin honest and openly to Abby, so one day when Torchy wasn't there yet, Uniqua asked, "Is he goin to be my other parent, Mama?"

Abby smiled. "Do you want him to be, baby?"

Uniqua stuck her finger in her sandwich. "Well . . . ah . . . well, if you do."

Abby grinned. "I love him. I want to marry him or he sure wouldn't be stayin here all night, sometimes."

Uniqua held her sandwich in the air, impaled on her finger, asked, "When he stays here . . . all night . . . in that room with you . . . do you all . . . DO something?"

Abby put her hand on both her hips. "Now, listen here! That ain't none of your business, young lady." She raised a finger to shake in Uniqua's face.

Uniqua softly interrupted her. "You my mother, aren't you?"

"You know I'm the mother. You just seem to forget you the chile!"

Uniqua held her mother's finger. "Don't that make you my business . . . Mother?"

Abby snatched her finger away from Uniqua. "Not that part!"

Uniqua sounded like she was about to cry. "We separated then?"

Abby sighed one of her real tired sighs. "Get outta here. Go . . . go look at TV, read or somethin."

Uniqua, with her head down, walked slowly to her room.

That night, after Torchy had eaten the dinner Abby had cooked and fixed so nice for him, they lay across her bed. Abby asked him about when they were goin to get married.

Torchy laughed and patted his naked stomach. "Girl, what chu talkin bout?"

She smiled and patted his stomach too. "Marriage. A family. You know."

"Girl, I got to have a job and somethin to raise a famly with. Ain't they gonna put you off welfare if you get married? I ain't got no . . . plans . . . on takin . . . no . . . extra bills and things . . ." He thought of his full stomach. "Right now."

"Don't you love me?" She smiled into his face.

"Shu, I love you. But that . . . that ain't got nothin to do with it."

Abby looked serious, but not fussy, "Well, when you goin to get a job? And keep it?"

Torchy laughed and pat her on her behind. "Only the Lord knows in whitey's world."

Abby didn't laugh. "There some black men workin. Steady."

He looked at his toothpick. "Yea, that's right. And they kissin somebody's ass."

She sat up. "Even the President kisses somebody's ass! Least they got somethin to work for. Somebody to love."

Torchy sat up. He didn't like it when women talked this way. "Well, baby, they got more'n me. I ain't got chick or chile. Just me. And I don't take no shit off nobody to get . . . or keep . . . a mutha-fuckin job."

Abby lay back on the bed, wondering where her brain had been. She said to Torchy, "I'm takin a chanct on losin my welfare money what feeds my chile, for a man who don't want to help me none with a dime. I got a chick and a chile." She didn't say it, but she thought, "My brains been between my legs. Well, let's get a whole brainful tonight cause he goin tomorrow."

And though it hurt her, cause she sure loved her some Torchy, to put him out and keep him out, she did. She told him, "When you get you a place I can come visit you, I'll give you some more lovin." He left, thinking of what new woman, or old girlfriend, he could stay with next.

Abby missed Torchy and her life became just a little lonelier. She was getting older and wondered what her life was going to be. Would she be alone? Forever? Wasn't nobody out there for her?

Then, when she looked in Uniqua's face and her bright proud eyes, she could take being without Torchy. She told Uniqua, "We gonna get us a good life and a good father one of these days." She thought to herself, "I hope."

When Uniqua got to be around thirteen years old, Abby began to worry that Uniqua might bring a baby home, like she had. But, instead, Uniqua came home with a flyer in her hand that promised if you went to school to become a Licensed Vocational Nurse or a RN you would never have to worry bout a job the rest of your life. "I got this off the counter at the library." She smiled up at her mother.

Abby took the paper, sighed, said, "Baby, Mama ain't never graduated from high school. Didn't even get there. And anyway, the welfare won't let you go to no school. This here is reachin too high, even for you. Specially for me."

Uniqua, excited, said, "They got something called a GED test for school dropouts to get to be a high school

finisher! A diploma! Mama, you can make anybody do anything you want them too! Them welfare people don't tell
you everything to do!"

Abby smiled at her daughter's pride, but she cried in
her lonely, sad bed that night cause she thought she
couldn't do it.

Well, to make a long story short, Uniqua told her
teacher what her mother had said, welfare and all. The
pretty, brown-skin teacher talked to the lady principal and
the principal called the nurse training school and they
talked back and forth, back and forth. Finally they came up
with if Abby got her GED, she could come "volunteer"
time and while she was "volunteering" she would be learning to be an LVN and studying. At the end, if she passed
the tests, she could get her license. The teacher was excited
too, and came home with Uniqua to tell Abby.

Abby was afraid and didn't want to hope or dream, or
even go to school, except she didn't mind reading now.
Uniqua and Abby studied together, everything the teacher
had told them to study. Abby took the test and . . .
passed! With a good grade!

Abby was so proud of that little piece of paper. She
hugged, kissed and cried all over her daughter. Her daughter said, "See? You was too good and smart for that ole
Torchy man anyway!" They laughed and Abby loved her
little tiny knotty kneed butt daughter more than life itself.

Just so you will know, Callie, Abby's mother, and Abby
kept up with each other. Callie was sick and couldn't work
at all now, so she was stretching the welfare check as far as
it could go, but she bought Abby a small ring on credit for
her graduation present. Callie was proud of her ONLY

daughter that was living a clean life and had graduated from high school and had a certificate!

Abby, still afraid she might not be able to do it, in a class with REAL high school grads, started school anyway, pretending to be a part-time volunteer to keep her welfare checks coming. She rode the waves of tension, fear, joy, dread and excitement to the time when it swept over her that she was performing and was not the lowest grade in her class! It took eighteen months, but the day came when she graduated from LVN school. Uniqua graduated from junior high school on her way to high school. They planned on Uniqua going on to college. Abby, feeling her muscle, said, "I might go to college someday myself!" They laughed in the warmth of their love.

Well, Abby looked into quite a few jobs and found private doctors paid more than hospitals. In two years she and Uniqua were able to move out of the ghetto. They were happy, laughing and smiling.

Uniqua said, "They say we aren't supposed to leave the ghetto and leave all our sisters and brothers here to suffer, Mama."

Abby sighed. "Well . . . we ain't stoppin them from coming with us and gettin out. We don't have to stay here til they get ready. The smart ones would want us to go and make a way somewhere else for them, maybe."

They left. Into a better neighborhood. Not the best, you know that. They weren't doing that good. But better, thought safer, certainly cleaner and more wholesome and healthy. Near a park where it was mostly quiet and they could sit and talk after a hard day's school and work, while they watched children play. Without guns.

Two more years of sacrificing and struggling, Uniqua had qualified for and applied for her college entry. There is no way to tell of the joy in Abby's heart. The first one! She was going to miss her baby, Uniqua, but it would all be for the better. Uniqua was going to have a different life. A better life. A decent husband, children and home. Abby was preparing herself to let Uniqua go now that Uniqua's life was opening up and broadening out. Abby thought, "How can I cry when I lose her? It's for the better or for her happiness."

One day around that time, in the early evening, Abby and Uniqua were sitting in that little park. The sun was shining down on the tall trees and smooth grass. Glinting off the play rings, swings and slides the children were playing on as they laughed.

They had noticed the group of unfamiliar boys that hung around the water fountain. Uniqua was becoming annoyed because the big boys were teasing and bothering the little children who came to get water. It was like a little cloud of evil had settled over the playground. You could almost feel something in the air.

A dark blue, low-cut car swung around the corner. Carrying evil and death in the hands of the young boys with the evil empty minds. They stared at the boys around the water fountain, then raised the glinting deadly guns. Four of them. With fingers that had no care or conscience. (They had never heard of God, because the only place they hung out where you might learn something good was around school, sometime, and God wasn't allowed there.) With these fingers, they smiled a dumb and vicious smile and pulled the shining triggers with the barrels pointed at the boys around the fountain teasing the little children.

Uniqua who usually saw everything around her, knew of drive-by shootings and knew the bad element of those of her age. She saw the sparkle of the gun metal, pointing, and she ran, screaming at the small children near the fountain. Trying to wave them away.

The shots were fired. Ringing out and filling the air with death. The end of hopes. Shattering dreams. Full of pain and loss. Uniqua was still running on her pretty, healthy, slim legs; still waving those long, frantic arms at the children, when she was hit. As she fell she was still reaching for a child when the blood burst through her mouth and nose.

Abby ran to her daughter, Uniqua, regardless of the bullets, which, mercifully, were leaving with the death car. She reached for and pulled her daughter, Uniqua, into her arms. She yelled at the car screeching away. "You fatha fuckers! Look! Look what chu have done! Kill each other, why don't chu?" She turned back to Uniqua, said, "I'm not cursin them, baby, that was a blessing."

She pulled Uniqua close to her again, and when Uniqua's head fell back in total, hopeless death, Abby screamed, "Oh, God, no, no, no, no, no, no, NO!" She took a deep and jagged breath. "Why? Why? Why? Why?" Her last why was buried in her dead daughter's hanging neck. Her heart begged, too late, that the singing bullets had hit her. But they had already found a mark, and their ultimate end, covered with blood.

It was in the papers and all kinds of people came to the funeral. Almost all of Abby's family had respected Abby and Uniqua, though some had not liked her because they thought she was uppity because she wasn't puffin on some pipe or sucking on some bottle, or . . . well. They dropped their pipes (for a minute), their whiskey bottles (they brought them in paper bags) and their lovers to come to the funeral. Callie was there to hold her daughter. Abby did not remember everything about the funeral. She was not really conscious. She sat, she cried, she moaned and she stared off into space. Longing, grieving for her daughter. Her only child. Her beloved child.

When it was all over, Callie was the last to leave and she had to because she wasn't really well. She had stayed so long, in pain, because she was proud, and loved Abby and Uniqua because they were strivers and she had given birth to one of them, who had given birth to the other.

Abby kept repeating, "I don't care. I give up. I don't care no more. Ain't nothin else. I give up. I just don't give a damn."

Time passed. Thank God. Everyone talked to her and finally, they let her alone because life goes on and everyone had to keep up with their own stresses.

Losing a child can be a horrible, terrible thing. Abby had to go to work, so she did. But when she came home, evenings, she began to live in the bottle again. She was near drunk every night. "So I can sleep," she said.

After a month or two, she began havin them card games again. "So I can hear life talkin," she said. Sometimes a man would stay over. Seldom the same one. "So I can try to feel life again," she said. She raised hell most of the time. Was hard to get along with, even with old friends. "I don't care," she said. When there was no card game she went out and sat in a bar. "Pain waitin for me when I go home," she said.

All that love for Uniqua was turning into hate. Hate for everything. She sank that love deep inside her somewhere and it turned bitter and ugly on its way to hate. "I don't care. Don't nothin matter," she said. How she kept that job I don't know, but the doctor she worked for was tryin to understand. She had been a good and caring worker. Only, now, she would start cryin out of the clear blue sky and have to go home. "I'm just cryin for nothin," she said, "cause ain't nothin in me but a big empty hole." Abby thought a minute, then told him, "No. That ain't true. There is somethin in my heart. I'm mad and I hate everything. Everything I had is gone." The doctor was going to have to let her go, but he held on, and she held on, for bout a year.

One day her friends ask her, "Why you cryin so much? It's been most a year now. You makin yourself sick. Why you still cryin so much. Cryin ain't gonna bring Uniqua back."

"That's why I'm cryin," she said.

Grieving and staring at Uniqua's pictures and turning her love into hate for the killers, Abby was getting sick inside. She didn't eat. Had lost weight. Was going to get really sick. She didn't know which way to go. Somehow, somewhere in that fog that stayed in her head, she remembered how Uniqua and she would read the Bible when they had a problem. Uniqua went to church more than Abby, but Abby believed in God and used to act like it.

One morning when the fog in her head was clearer than usual and Abby could see the dirty sheets and the sinkful of dirty dishes and the empty icebox, Abby was bout ready to cry again for what she had come to without her baby. She sat down to cry, but she sat near a table with the Bible on it. Abby, snifflin, picked up the Bible and before she read a word, she heard in her mind, "Don't bury it, use it. Don't keep it in, give it away. Don't turn that love in, turn that love out." She closed the book and held it to her breast as she kept repeating the last line. "Don't turn that love inside, turn that love outside." She thought about that as she finally cleaned up her neglected home. Cleaned out Uniqua's room. Packing things up to give away. It hurt again. She had to leave and shut the door to Uniqua's room. Sat down, tears coming again. She took up the Bible again. She heard the same words. "Don't turn that love in, turn that love out." She thought about those words all that week.

Another week later, Abby talked to the doctor she worked for. Then she went to a foster child agency. She applied for one child. One whose parents might not come back to get it. One that needed a real home they could stay in til they graduated from college or til they were grown. The foster service lady looked at Abby like she was crazy. She laughed about it in the lunchroom later. "Imagine thinking any of these kids will get through grammar school, much less college! Ha ha."

But another social worker, Ms. Trye, who was a realistic dreamer, later asked for the case, which the first worker was glad to get rid of since she felt overworked anyway.

Ms. Trye called on Abby, went by her job, did all the

usual things and when all the paperwork was almost completed, Abby said, "I've changed my mind, I want two of them. A little boy and a little girl. I don't care what their age is, I just want them to need me, or somebody."

In two weeks Abby had a little girl, age thirteen, named Patricia. Patricia needed a home badly, needed love greatly. Needed care all the way. Couldn't read, couldn't write and hated baths. "Just my meat!" Abby smiled and pulled the girl into her home. In another two weeks she had another one. A boy four years old, named Joey. He had been abused a great deal, even as young as he was. Abby pulled him into her arms, smothered him in her breast as she waved the social worker, Ms. Trye, away.

As she gathered her new family to her breast and her life, her love poured out. An emptiness filled up. There were three, Abby, Patricia and Joey, all feeling empty, but who were filling up the emptiness in each other. Until, now, they are full.

Sometimes, when Abby gets home from work (she has a very good baby-sitter for the days), she fixes dinner, clears up after, then takes baby Joey on her lap as she leans over to help Patricia with her homework. She puts her hand out to smooth Patricia's hair, which always needs combing, and looks over the children to Uniqua's picture. Uniqua seems to be smiling so bright, her eyes lighted up. Abby cries a little, but these times it is from joy. She couldn't hold Uniqua anymore, but she was holding love. Not burying it inside. Letting it out. Using it.

She tells the children, "It ain't always going to be easy, but we will make it! You're gonna be all right. We are a family now. We're gonna be all right . . . together. Where there is a will, there is a way. For us, we only need a way. There will always be a way." She hugged her new family. "Because we have love. There will always be a way."

About the Author

J. California Cooper is the author of the novels *Family* and *In Search of Satisfaction,* and four collections of short stories: *Homemade Love,* the winner of the 1989 American Book Award; *Some Soul to Keep; A Piece of Mine;* and *The Matter Is Life.* She is also the author of seventeen plays and has been honored as Black Playwright of the Year (1978). She received the James Baldwin Writing Award (1988) and the Literary Lion Award from the American Library Association (1988). Ms. Cooper lives in California.